PRAISE FOR

The History of S[

"This remarkable mosaic of interconnected stories, many of which were previously published, spans generations to relay the strange, somber, and deeply entwined histories of two Jewish families. In 1914, Chana, a Russian, and Sophia, a German, meet as young girls in a magical forest that somehow connects Lviv, Ukraine, and Munich. Though they promise to return, the girls are kept apart by war and family conflict. The branches of their family trees have semimystical experiences for generations to come . . . Powerful and dreamlike, this intergenerational meditation on family, mortality, and hope is far more than the sum of its parts."
—*Publishers Weekly*, **starred review**

"Intriguing stories from the world of Humperdink and Sholem Aleichem, that return us to a time when a world that is achingly familiar and wonderfully strange is coming into being among the Jewish children, beginning the imaginary journey of marvels forth and back between then and today."
—**Samuel R. Delany, Hugo and Nebula Award–winning author of** *Atlantis: Three Tales, Dhalgren,* **and the Return to Nevèrÿon series**

"If David Mitchell plotted a speculative novel-in-stories that then Alice Munro wrote, you might get something approaching the ambition and beauty of Krasnoff's *The History of Soul 2065*. Krasnoff creates a world so excessively alive, both with woe and human kindness, that history can't contain them, and thus, they leak into haunted, uncanny realms. Told in prose so unassuming you might suspect irony, what you get is here the exact opposite of irony: hard-won empathy, though hidden beneath protective layers of wit and circumspection. That's why Krasnoff's stories retell themselves in our minds long after they're finished. Like gentle ghosts that don't know they're dead and don't realize they're terrifying us, they just want to keep on having a nice chat with the reader. Forever."
—**Carlos Hernandez, author of** *Sal and Gabi Break the Universe*

"As a writer of mosaic novels—short stories that connect to tell a larger one—I admire the craft, humor, and emotional storytelling that Ms. Krasnoff brings to her work. Each of her stories, starting with two small European girls meeting in a woodsy park, has its own particular moment while connecting to the general theme."
—**Richard Bowes, World Fantasy Award–winning author of** *Minions of the Moon* **and** *Dust Devils on a Quiet Street*

"There's a lot of heart in Barbara Krasnoff's collection, *The History of Soul 2065*—the warmth of home, the lies of families, the demons that lurk in trees, myths both great and small. It tells the fantastic history of two families, their journey through time, what they kept and what they lost. Plunge into *The History of Soul 2065*, there's nothing like it."
—**Jeffrey Ford, World Fantasy and Nebula Award–winning author of** *Ahab's Return: or, The Last Voyage*

"Barbara Krasnoff's great gift is for manifesting the invisible: immigrants and outcasts, the queer, the bereaved, elderly, children, ghosts. And, ah! The ghosts! The ghosts in *The History of Soul 2065* arrive from both the past and the future to interact, and interfere, with each other and the living. Timelines tangle, bloodlines mingle, the mundane becomes magical. There is horror here, bitter droughts of hopelessness and gall, but each sip is offered with such a spirit of camaraderie and solidarity that sharing in it makes the aftertaste linger long and sweetly. The more I read this book, the more deeply I was impressed. Yes, impressed: in the sense of being indelibly *marked* by Krasnoff's stories. I've been—ever so gently—cicatrized."
—**C. S. E. Cooney, World Fantasy Award–winning author of** *Bone Swans: Stories*

"Like all good mosaic novels, *The History of Soul 2065* rewards its readers with both a beguiling narrative arc and a succession of individually riveting stories—in this case, twenty cannily uncanny tales involving ghosts, gods, demons, dybbuks, magic jewels, and time-bending birds. With its echoes of Tony Kushner's *Angels in America* and Jonathan Lethem's *Dissident Gardens*, Barbara Krasnoff's multigenerational, phantasmagoric saga kept me turning the pages at a rapid pace."
—**James Morrow, World Fantasy and Nebula Award–winning author of** *Galápagos Regained*

The History of Soul 2065

Introduction by Jane Yolen

The History of SOUL 2065

Barbara Krasnoff

Mythic Delirium
BOOKS

mythicdelirium.com

The History of Soul 2065

FIRST EDITION
June 11, 2019

ISBN-10: 1-7326440-1-2
ISBN-13: 978-1-7326440-1-4

Library of Congress Control Number: 2019901286

Published by Mythic Delirium Books
Roanoke, Virginia
mythicdelirium.com

Further copyright information begins on page 217.

Our gratitude goes out to the following who because of their generosity are from now on designated as supporters of Mythic Delirium Books: Saira Ali, Cora Anderson, Anonymous, Patricia M. Cryan, Steve Dempsey, Oz Drummond, Patrick Dugan, Matthew Farrer, C. R. Fowler, Mary J. Lewis, Paul T. Muse, Jr., Shyam Nunley, Finny Pendragon, Kenneth Schneyer, and Delia Sherman.

*Dedicated with love and thanks
to my mother Dorothy, my father Bernie, my brother Neal, and
my partner and companion Jim Freund.*

Table of Contents

The Book of Sophia's Family

Completing the Circle

Can I Tell You

Jane Yolen

C an I tell you right up front how much I love this book? Am I allowed to do that? I don't know, really know, the author, though I have met her once or twice in passing at cons. I've read a few of the stories in magazines. We're not related. But my goodness, I love this book.

First, I love it for personal reasons. It feels like the Yolen family story in places. I can hear my Uncle Lou, the oldest of the family of eight children (my father being the second youngest) saying as he once did at a family seder, while reading out of the Haggadah, "And how do I know all dis? I vas dere." *Dere* being the Ukraine, not the Levant.

The people in Krasnoff's stories are my people. The villains are the same who would have destroyed us. Think Cossacks, Hitler, Chernobyl. The Yolens came over in three groups, all settled in America by 1914. So Krasnoff's characters are my people.

Of course, you needn't be Jewish to love this book. (But it couldn't hurt.)

I also love the book for the storytelling, the depth of characters, and how I wept wet, fat, sloppy tears at some of the story moments, or sighed over the characters' situations. Even laughed a few times.

Barbara Krasnoff's mosaic novel—not a term I invented but one that was handed to me—is a new sort of creature. Not quite a novel, not necessarily just linked stories. But definitely a book about two intertwined families told in quick, quirky bursts. Yes, these are short stories, yet part of a wonderful whole novel somehow. The publisher says that more succinctly: "A mosaic novel about two Jewish immigrant families, set mostly in Brooklyn, with numerous elements that could be considered magical realism and soft sf."

If you, like me, love quirky and original fantasy stories, I advise you to dive right in. If you, like me, admire tough writing that's not afraid of the grit, dive right in. If you, like me, want to hang out a while with characters rich in their own traditions, dive right in. This is storytelling at the top of the heap. But make sure you have a bunch of tissues handy. And if you don't trust someone writing an introduction that is all about sighing and sobbing, and without any meat on its bones, don't dive in yet, read on. But remember, I'm warning you, there will be some sloppy, snotty crying in your future.

So what indeed do you have at hand in this book? A bit of time travel, ghost stories, old age homes, new babies, Death in her various guises, a coven of witches, a bit of Yiddish, a "little song, a little dance, a little seltzer in your pants." Oh, and a lot of Jews. I especially like the stogy-smoking, atheistic, Marxist rabble rousers. There were a lot of them around when I was growing up in New York. My father even said he ran guns for the Irgun. Since he never shot a gun in his life and was much more left wing than center, I doubt that story. But the Yolens were all storytellers. Best not to believe everything they said. My mother's people, the Berlins, were the intellectuals. Not sure I trust them completely either when they tell tales.

And so it is with this book. A lot of truth, a lot of magic, a lot of hand-waving, a lot of shifts in the zeitgeist. But in the end the subtler truths emerge.

(Note: See Emily Dickinson: "Tell all the truth but tell it slant..." She was a mensch before the word was invented.)

All but five of the stories here were published first in magazines/journals ranging from *Weird Tales* and *Lady Churchill's Rosebud Wristlet* to *Mythic Delirium*, as well as in anthologies, though most in slightly different versions. Some had to be rewritten a bit to become part of the growing mosaic.

You ask: which stories in *The History of Soul 2065* are my favorites? "Sabbath Wine" (the Nebula finalist) is one. It builds slowly and inevitably towards its tear-burst of a last line. "The Ladder-Back Chair," another weeper, with its nod to September 11. But it doesn't go where you expect it will, and it's the surprise that sandbags you. However, Krasnoff has played fair all along the way with both these stories. And my third choice is the title story that concludes the book, though it is a mosaic within a mosaic, being made up of different stories. It is both a revelation within the story/ stories themselves, but also reveals how tightly everything has been woven together.

Everything really does end on the final pages. And begins. Well, it's a spiritual/fantasy conclusion. And yes, you will cry again.

These stories mess with time and space in a multitude of ways, but the entire book is really about ghosting. We all have ghosts in our lives, seen or unseen, heard or unheard. Some ghosts are driven by photographs or family tittle-tattle or old letters or the remnants of distant wars. But here in Krasnoffs's novel, those ghosts from the past, present, future are clever, vivid, and real. Individual stories may rise one above another depending upon the readers' responses, but the whole—that mosaic—is an amazing sum of its parts. Perhaps not in clay, as actual mosaics, but certainly in the silver of history, the gold of story.

Chana's Family Tree

Reisl Sora Schwartz Hirsch
1881–1897

Malka Hirsch
1896–1905

Abe Hirsch
1880–1961

Chana Rivka Krasulka Hirsch
1902–1983

Sheila Mandel Hirsch
1925–2008

Carl Hirsch
1960–2028

Debra Hirsch
1956–2026

Sidney Hirsch
1924–1995

Mary Lang Hirsch
1955–2020

Abraham Hirsch
1982–2035

Jakie Feldman
1921–1996

Becky Hirsch Feldman
1921–2010

Eliot Amara
1960–2025

Marilyn Feldman
1961–2026

Annie Feldman-Amara
1990–2064

Rachel Bowman
1990–2067

Morris Feldman
1954–2001

Joan Kirshenbaum Feldman
1956–2026

Sophia's Family Tree

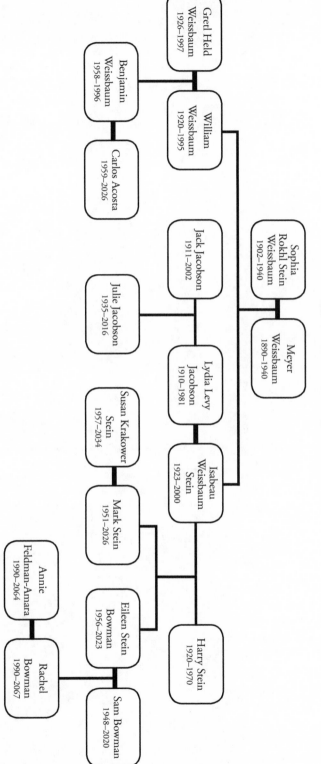

Beginnings

The Clearing in the Autumn

A story of Chana Rivka Krasulka and Sophia Stein

1914

Chana had seen a real forest once, when she was six years old. Her parents had taken her to the wedding of a relative in another town, one not all that far from Kiev. Tremendously excited, she had spent nearly the entire journey kneeling on the seat with her nose pressed against the train window as stations and farms and towns sped by. And then, at one point, they went through an endless tangle of trees—dark and thick and frightening.

It was a forest, her father told her, and forests were not only full of trees and birds and mushrooms and other delightful things, but also contained wolves and bandits. "What kind of bandits?" Chana asked, intrigued at the thought. "Like the little robber girl in *The Snow Queen?*"

At which point her mother made her sit back in her seat, and informed her that the trees also hid the spirits of dead children, who would lure little girls to come and play with them, and then steal them away from the world of the living.

Even at six years of age, Chana knew that her mother was just trying to frighten her. The rabbi's wife, who taught the young children their letters and numbers, had explained that the spirits of the dead, when they did walk the earth, were forced to stay by their graves unless a vulnerable body presented itself. That was why children weren't allowed to attend funerals—they were too new to this world to defend themselves against possible attack by a dybbuk or other wandering soul. So the dead children couldn't possibly be in the forest, unless they had been accidentally buried there.

In addition, the idea of having ghost-children to play with was an intriguing one. Chana knew her mother well enough not to say

19

so, but somewhere inside herself, she hid the hope that one day she would meet a real ghost child.

Unfortunately, there weren't many opportunities. Lviv, where Chana lived, was large and modern, and she somehow suspected that ghosts and spirits preferred forests and glens rather than noisy streets. Even the local park, where her parents and aunts and uncles took her on Sundays when it was fine, was so carefully cultivated that Chana suspected anything supernatural would avoid it like the plague.

Until one sunny afternoon. They had eaten a lovely picnic lunch in the park, and now the grown-ups were arguing about politics, and Chana's cousins, most of whom were older, were avidly examining the fashion illustrations in a magazine. Bored to distraction, Chana asked her mother if she could go for a walk.

"Don't go far," her mother warned her absent-mindedly, absorbed in her conversation. Chana called out, "I promise!" and left quickly, before her mother had any chance to change her mind.

She walked down a small gravel path, kicking at the occasional stone, and making up stories in her head about how she would become rich and famous when she was older. And then looked up, and discovered that she was at the beginning of a small pathway that led into a grove of large, well-grown trees. A forest!

Of course, it wasn't a real forest, not a full-sized, hike-for-days-and-be-lost forest. But maybe, once inside, she could pretend it was a real forest. At the very least, she'd be able to leave the manicured lawns and metal benches behind.

The late afternoon sunlight filtered through the trees, muting the sounds of the town behind her. The path was narrow, even for a young girl, and sometimes the trees pulled at her dress or caught at her hair, tugging strands away from her tight braid. Chana walked slowly, enjoying the sense of secrecy and possible danger, occasionally stopping to admire a wild flower, or to pick up a small stone so she could throw it into the trees and watch the startled birds fly off.

And then there was sunlight dappling a soft grass carpet, and space on either side. Chana looked around; she had reached a small clearing that had a canopy of branches overhead. Before her, resting on the grass and dandelions, there were three logs—the remains of a tree that had fallen ages and ages ago.

Chana grinned and spun around, taking it all in. At last she had her own secret place!

After she had examined the area thoroughly, Chana sat on the grass next to one of the logs, which had a large hole in it that was just the right size for a tiny apartment. The girl arranged stones and branches into furniture and stick dolls, occasionally looking out of the corners of her eyes just in case any ghostly children were lurking nearby. But to her disappointment, none made an appearance.

"Chana Rivka! So this is where you disappeared to!" It was her father, hot and annoyed. "Your mother has been frantic!" He gave her a swift swat on the behind, grabbed her hand and walked her back to the picnic. As she was led away, Chana gave a quick glance behind to keep the small clearing in her memory. She'd return as soon as she could.

And she did, every chance she got. As Chana got older, the clearing became more than just a quiet place to play—it was somewhere where she could escape. From the other girls at school, who teased her unmercifully because she was sent out of the room when the priest came to give the catechism lesson. From her mother, who complained that her daughter was ungrateful for all the money they spent making sure she had a good Russian education rather than being sent to the local Jewish day school. And from the world, so she could read her books uninterrupted and dream about the day when she would be old enough to travel and see wondrous things.

On the day after her 11th birthday, which happened to be a Saturday, Chana tucked one of her birthday presents into her rucksack: *The Penknife* by Sholem Aleichem, a worn but still legible book that Chaim the Litvak, who sold books and pens from a small booth in the marketplace, had given her. With that, and an early apple that she had found near one of her grandmother's trees, she was ready for at least an hour to herself.

She took the path at a run, eager to get as much reading time in as she could. She flew into the clearing—and stopped short. There was already somebody there.

For one mad moment, Chana thought that her mother had told her the truth all those years ago and that she had interrupted a wandering ghost. The girl was about the same age as Chana, but where Chana was of medium height and a little stout, the girl was tall and rather aristocratic. She wore a white lacy dress with a wide blue sash and matching stockings, pretty white shoes, and a straw hat with a blue ribbon. If she wasn't a ghost, Chana thought, maybe she was a character come alive from a storybook.

It wasn't the kind of clothing that you usually saw in Lviv.

The girl had been intently watching a butterfly that was hovering around a small bush; when Chana stepped on a twig, she turned around and stared.

"Who are you?" the girl asked. If she was a ghost, she was a very substantial one; at her movement, the butterfly darted away.

"I'm Chana," she said, acutely aware of the contrast between the girl's elegance and of her own dark green one-piece school uniform, torn black stockings and scuffed black shoes. "I live near here, and I go to the National Girl's School. I've never seen you before. Are you visiting?"

The girl's eyebrows came down, as though what Chana said didn't make any sense. "You can't live near here," she said. "I'd know it if you did. And anyway, you have a funny accent. My name is Sophia, and this is my birthday dress. My papa made it all himself; he sews dresses for rich ladies and said that I look just as pretty as any of them. Do you think it's pretty?"

Chana thought it was the most beautiful dress she had ever seen, but she didn't want to say so. Also, she thought it a bit rude to comment on her accent, especially when the girl's was so strange. But before she could make any reply, the girl—Sophia—chattered on happily.

"This forest belongs to a very rich lady, it's part of what they call an estate, and my papa said I could wear my new dress to meet her. The lady said I could explore a little, while papa measures her for a dress to wear at her daughter's wedding, and then we'll come back for the try-on and cook said that if I were a good girl and kept very quiet in a corner I could watch them make the wedding cake and might even be able to see the bride try on her dress, which would be wonderful, don't you think? Oh, don't!"

Chana, fascinated by the girl's chatter, had sat down on a nearby log. At Sophia's dismayed cry, she looked around. "Don't what?"

"Sit on that log. There are all sorts of bugs and things on that log, and you'll get your dress dirty."

Chana shrugged. "I'm always getting my dress dirty. My mama says that I'm worse than any boy, but I don't care."

"Well." The girl frowned and then her face brightened. "Well, maybe because your dress is green, and so dirt won't show so much. I couldn't sit down in this dress though, because it's white, and my papa would be angry, and I couldn't see the wedding cake. What are you going to be when you grow up?"

It took a moment for Chana to realize that she had been asked a question, and in fact, Sophia had paused expectantly. Chana thought for a moment, and said, "It's a secret. Can you keep a secret?"

"Of course!" Sophia came a couple of steps closer. "What is it?"

Chana hugged her knees and stared at Sophia. "When I'm old enough, I'm going to run away to St. Petersburg and become a doctor."

Sophia looked a little surprised, as though she hadn't expected quite so grandiose a scheme. "Girls can't become doctors."

"Oh, yes, they can now." Chana took a branch and pushed it through the leaves on the ground. "They've got a university there now that teaches girls to become doctors—my big brother read about it in the newspaper—and my science teacher says I'm one of the smartest girls in her class. I'll become a great doctor, and will come back in my own carriage and horses, and all the girls will want me to treat them, and will have to pay me lots of money before I'll do it."

She looked up triumphantly. "So there!"

She waited for the laughter or the jeering, but Sophia just nodded and said, "And do you know what I'm going to be?" She backed off a little and spread her arms theatrically.

Chana thought she could guess. "An actress?"

"Yes, or a great singer." Sophia came closer again, her eyes shining. "My papa took me to see *Hansel and Gretel* at the National Theatre. We sat all the way high up, like birds, my papa said, and he gave me a pair of real opera glasses so I could see the singers close up. It was the most beautiful thing you ever saw, and they had children on stage, although my papa said that Hansel and Gretel were actually both played by grown-up ladies, and I asked him if I could grow up to be one of them, and he said, 'Who knows?' So that's what I want to do."

"Which National Theatre?" asked Chana, as soon as Sophia stopped to take a breath.

"The one in Munich, of course," Sophia said. "We took a train. It's only a short trip."

Chana stared. "Munich, Germany?" she asked. "Because over there," she pointed, "is where my school is. We live in Lviv."

Sophia tossed her head scornfully; her hat flew off, revealing shining auburn hair cropped to her shoulders. "Where is that?" she asked, retrieving the hat and brushing dirt off it. "Because I never heard of it, and I got top scores in geography this year."

Chana, whose own brown hair was confined in a tight braid, admired the way the other girl's carefully brushed hair bounced around her face. Still, she put her hands on her hips and said, with as much authority as she could muster, "Well, I've got top marks in all my classes, including history, and I should know in which city I live."

The two girls glared at each other fiercely. "I'd fight you, but I don't want to ruin my dress," Sophia said, almost tearfully.

"I'd fight you," said Chana, "but I'd win, and I'm too old to pick on somebody weaker than me."

"You wouldn't," said Sophia.

"Would so!" said Chana.

As if to join the argument, a small grey pigeon suddenly dropped down to the ground between them. It shook itself, looked around, and then took a tentative, limping step forward.

"Look!" Sophia said, her anger forgotten. "It's hurt!" One of the pigeon's wings was slightly outstretched, and as it tried to walk, it made a small, unhappy sound.

The two children knelt down and examined the bird. "Maybe we should put the wing in a splint," said Sophia. "My cousin broke his arm, and the doctor put it in a splint until it healed. He cried, although he lied later and said he didn't," she added with some satisfaction.

Chana looked doubtful. "I'm not sure we could do it properly," she said. "We might hurt it more. We need to take it to a grownup who knows how to fix animals."

She carefully reached out and put her hands around the soft, feathered body. "Oh, be careful!" Sophia said, alarmed. "It might peck you!" But although the pigeon shivered at Chana's touch, it didn't otherwise react. She stood, her hands wrapped protectively around the bird.

"Do you know a doctor?" asked Sophia, also standing. She reached over and stroked the pigeon carefully. "There's the doctor who fixed my cousin's arm, but he probably doesn't do animals."

"I'll take it to my grandmother," Chana said decisively. "She cured the cat when its tail got run over by a cart; I'll bet she can fix the bird. If I take it home right now, it might be all right."

The two stared at each other for a moment.

"But can we both go home?" asked Sophia tentatively. "I mean— if I'm visiting the Rosenschloss and you're in Lviv, then one of us is in the wrong place. Isn't that right?"

Chana thought a moment. "Maybe it's this place. Maybe it's magic, and when we leave, we'll go back to where we belong."

Sophia brightened. "So maybe we could both come back! Next week, this same time? That way, you could tell me what happened to the pigeon." She paused and thought. "That is, if I can come. I can ask my father if I can visit."

Chana nodded. "I don't know if I can come either. My brother told me that there was political trouble, and that meant that we had to be extra careful, and that maybe I'll have to stay home from school a few days." Her expression cleared. "But even if they keep me in, I can always sneak out."

"We have to swear, though, or it won't be any good." Sophia straightened and recited formally, "I swear that I will never reveal to anyone about our secret place or anything we say here. May the Evil Eye find me otherwise."

"And I swear," proclaimed Chana.

"And that we will meet again no matter what evil angels try to drive us apart." Sophia held up two fingers and spit through them three times.

"And I swear," Chana repeated. She shifted the pigeon awkwardly to her right arm, brought her left hand to her mouth and copied Sophia's actions.

The two girls stared at each other solemnly, and then broke out into giggles. The pigeon squawked and they immediately sobered again. "I'm sorry, pigeon," Sophia said guiltily. Chana carefully took the bird back into both her hands.

Around them, the clearing was starting to darken as the sun dipped below the tops of the trees. The breeze died down for a moment, and in the stillness, there was a low rumble of thunder.

"Well, I guess we'd better go," Sophia said, brushing some leaves off her dress. "I'll see you this time next week, or the week after, if we're punished. If you come and I'm not there, leave me a note under that rock," she pointed at a medium-sized rock that sat under a downed branch, "and let me know what happened to the pigeon."

"All right," said Chana. She watched as her new best friend turned and ran into the woods, the white dress quickly lost amid the darkening trees. In her arms, the pigeon shivered again.

1920

"We're leaving," Chana said to the trees. "We're going to America."

Summer was almost over. Autumn was just a golden edge to the leaves and a hint of chill in the air. It was just the kind of crisp, clear day that Chana loved when she was a little girl. But she wasn't a little girl anymore.

The clearing looked almost the same as it had the day she and Sophia met for the first—and only—time. Chana sat crossed legged on the ground and picked up a sturdy twig. "Did you ever get back here after we met, Sophia?" she asked, scratching a small stick figure of a girl in the dirt. "Did you come, and I wasn't here? I'm sorry if you did. I tried to come back, I really did, but was never able to. When I got home, my parents told me that there was going to be a war, and that I was no longer allowed to leave the house alone. Even when I got work at the hospital, I had to promise to be escorted either way. And then later, we had to hide."

She took a breath.

"I don't know what it was like where you are," Chana continued, using the twig to push through a few dead leaves that scattered the ground, "but the war was bad here. And then there was the pogrom last November. Papa was smart; at the beginning of the war, he made arrangements with Mrs. Solakov, a nice old woman who lived nearby and who my mother was good friends with. So when we heard that the Jewish militia had been disbanded we all ran and hid in her barn."

She had cleared a small spot and now used the twig to dig into the loosely-packed dirt. "After three days, Mrs. Solakov said she'd heard it was safe for us to go home. My brother Jakob went to check and came back and said it was true, but that there wasn't much to go home to."

Her lower lip trembled, but she mastered it and dug harder. "People had broken the doors and windows of our house, and took all our things, except for some of the furniture, which was all broken. All my mama's clothes were torn up, and my books . . . " she paused. "Although we were lucky. Jakob's wife Gitl—he got married last year—her family didn't hide in time and her father was hurt and her sister . . . Well, I'm not supposed to say about her sister."

The tears started to flow despite her best efforts. "So now we're going to go to America. I begged papa to let me stay, and go to St. Petersburg to the women's doctor's university, because now that there's been a revolution and everybody is going to be equal, there's no reason I shouldn't go. I met a young man last year, a musician, who had left the army to join the revolution, and he said that there were a lot of young people there and that there would be housing for women students. He even gave me a red kerchief to remember him by, and said I should look for him when I came to St. Petersburg. But papa says that it's not safe, especially for a girl of 16, and that the family needs to stay together. It's not fair!"

She took a breath and wiped her eyes and nose on her sleeve. "I guess you're not here," she said.

She then stood and turned around slowly, trying to impress the scene in her mind for the rest of her life: the small grassy clearing, the tall, strong trees just beyond and the clouds streaming overhead. Although there were a few leaves on the ground, enough remained on the trees so that the branches that stretched out over the clearing blocked out the late afternoon sun. There was a chill in the air.

It was time to leave. Chana took a breath and began to walk toward the path when, amid the green and brown and gold of the foliage around her, she spied a flash of blue. She walked slowly toward it, afraid that it was an illusion; a reflection from a drop of water, or a shadow.

But no—it was a limp piece of ribbon, faded to a pale blue-gray by the elements, tied with a series of knots to a tree root that pushed out of the ground. Chana knelt and felt the smooth piece of material as though it could tell her something.

Next to the root was a large gray stone. Chana wrapped her hands around it and pushed at it; it took a bit of effort, but she was able to move it aside.

Underneath the stone was what looked like the top of a tightly stoppered jam jar, buried in the soil. Chana reached for a nearby branch and dug at the dirt around the jar until she could pull it from the ground.

It contained a single piece of paper, folded several times. Chana opened the jar with some difficulty (moisture and dirt made the lid resistant to her grip), pulled the paper out, and carefully unfolded it. In precisely lettered but badly spelled Yiddish, it read:

Dear Chana—

I hope you are well and not dead. My uncle Kurt died in the war and my mother is very ill, so we're going to Berlin to stay with my grandmama and find a doctor who can make my mother well. So I may not be able to come back to the forest in the estate for a while, and I left you this so you'll know I didn't forget. Did the pigeon get better?

Most sincerely yours,

Sophia Stein

Chana sat on the ground and read the letter twice. Then she reached into her backpack, pulled out her pen, turned the letter over and put it on her backpack so that she could use it as a writing surface. And paused.

She thought about all the other things that she had wanted to tell Sophia: About her second cousin who had run away to America in order to stay out of the army and who promised to find them someplace to live. About the musician, who had bright blue eyes and the most beautiful smile she'd ever seen, and who'd gently kissed her on the lips before he left for the city. About what it was like to hide beneath a pile of hay, the smell of horse manure and fresh grass around her, her mouth dry with fear, listening to the shouts of drunken men outside and praying that they wouldn't decide to investigate the barn.

But what little light there was in the clearing was starting to fade, and there wasn't time to write it all down.

Chana wet the tip of her pen with her tongue, thought for a moment, and wrote.

Dear Sophia—

The pigeon recovered and flew away. We're going to New York City in America. If you can, come to America as well and find me.

Very sincerely,

Chana Rivka Krasulka

She folded the paper, put it back in the jar and placed the jar in its hole. After burying it, she stopped, sat back on her heels and stared at the small mound for a moment. She untied the faded blue ribbon and put it into her pocket. Then she reached into her back-pack, took out the red kerchief, and tied it firmly to the root.

"We will meet again," she told the kerchief. "I swear." She stood, and left the clearing.

The
Book of
Chana's Family

Sabbath Wine

A story of Abe Hirsch, Chana's husband-to-be

1920

"**M**y name's Malka Hirsch," the girl said. "I'm nine."

"I'm David Richards," the boy said. "I'm almost thirteen."

The two kids were sitting on the bottom step of a run-down brownstone at the edge of the Brooklyn neighborhood of Brownsville. It was late on a hot summer afternoon, and people were just starting to drift home from work, lingering on stoops and fire escapes to catch any hint of a breeze before going up to their stifling flats.

Malka and David had been sitting there companionably for a while, listening to a chorus of gospel singers practicing in the first floor front apartment at the top of the stairs. Occasionally, the music paused as a male voice offered instructions and encouragement; it was during one of those pauses that the kids introduced themselves to each other.

Malka looked up at her new friend doubtfully. "You don't mind talking to me?" she asked. "Most big boys don't like talking to girls my age. My cousin Shlomo, he only wanted to talk to the older girl who lived down the street and who wore short skirts and a scarf around her neck."

"I don't mind," said David. "I like kids. And anyway, I'm dead, so I guess that makes a difference."

Above them, the enthusiastic chorus started again. As a soprano wailed a high lament, she shivered in delight. "I wish I could sing like that."

"It's called 'Ride Up in the Chariot,'" said David. "When I was little, my mama used to sing it when she washed the white folks' laundry. She told me my great-grandma sang it when she stole away from slavery."

"It's nice," Malka said. She had short, dark brown hair that just reached her shoulders and straight bangs that touched her eyebrows. She had pulled her rather dirty knees up and was resting her chin on them, her arms wrapped around her legs. "I've heard that one before, but I didn't know what it was called. They practice every Thursday, and I come here to listen."

"Why don't you go in?" asked David. He was just at that stage of adolescence where the body seemed to be growing too fast; his long legs stretched out in front of him while he leaned back on his elbows. He had a thin, cheerful face set off by bright, intelligent eyes and hair cropped so close to his skull that it looked almost painted on. "I'm sure they wouldn't mind, and you could hear better."

Malka grinned and pointed to the sign just above the front-door bell that read CORNERSTONE BAPTIST CHURCH. "My papa would mind," she said. "He'd mind plenty. He'd think I was going to get converted or something."

"No wonder I never seen you before," said the boy. "I usually just come on Sundays. Other days, I . . . " He paused. "Well, I usually just come on Sundays."

The music continued against a background of voices from the people around them. A couple of floors above, a baby cried, and two men argued in sharp, dangerous tones; down on the ground, a gang of boys ran past, laughing, ignoring the two kids sitting outside the brownstone. A man sat on a cart laden with what looked like a family's possessions. Obviously in no hurry, he let the horse take its time as it proceeded down the cobblestone street.

The song ended, and a sudden clatter of chairs and conversation indicated that the rehearsal was over. The two kids stood and moved to a nearby streetlamp so they wouldn't get in the way of the congregation leaving the brownstone in twos and threes.

Malka looked at David. "Wait a minute," she said. "Did you say you were dead?"

"Uh-huh," he said. "Well, at least, that's what my daddy told me."

She frowned. "You ain't," she said and then, when he didn't say anything, "Really?"

He nodded affably. She reached out and poked him in the arm. "You ain't," she repeated. "If you were a ghost or something, I couldn't touch you."

He shrugged and stared down at the street. Unwilling to lose her new friend, Malka quickly added, "It don't matter. If you wanna be dead, that's okay with me."

"I don't *want* to be dead," said David. "I don't even know if I really am. It's just what Daddy told me."

"Okay," Malka said.

She swung slowly around the pole, holding on with one hand, while David stood patiently, his hands in the pockets of his worn pants.

Something caught his attention and he grinned. "Bet I know what he's got under his coat," he said, and pointed at a tall man hurrying down the street, his jacket carefully covering a package.

"It's a bottle!" said Malka scornfully. "That's obvious."

"It's moonshine," said David, laughing.

"How do you know?" asked Malka, peering at the man.

"My daddy sells the stuff," said David. "Out of a candy store over on Dumont Street."

Malka was impressed. "Is he a gangster? I saw a movie about a gangster once."

David grinned again. "Naw," he said. "Just a low-rent bootlegger. If my mama ever heard about it, she'd come back here and make him stop in a hurry, you bet."

"My mama's dead," Malka said. "Where is yours?"

David shrugged. "Don't know," he said. "She left one day and never came back." He paused, then asked curiously, "You all don't go to church, right?"

"Nope."

"Well, what do you do?"

Malka smiled and tossed her hair back. "I'll show you," she said. "Would you like to come to a Sabbath dinner?"

M alka and her father lived in the top floor of a modern five-story apartment building about six blocks from the brownstone church. Somewhere between there and home, David had gone his own way, Malka didn't quite remember when. It didn't matter much, she decided. She had a plan, and she could tell David about it later.

She stood in the main room that acted as parlor, dining room, and kitchen. It was sparsely but comfortably furnished: besides a small wooden table that sat by the open window, there was a coal oven, a sink with cold running water, a cupboard over against one wall, and an overloaded bookcase against another. A faded flower-print rug covered the floor; it had obviously seen several tenants come and go.

Malka's father sat at the table reading a newspaper by the slowly waning light, his elbow on the windowsill, his head leaning on his hand. A small plate with the remains of his supper sat nearby. He hadn't shaved for a while; a short, dark beard covered his face.

"Papa," said Malka.

Her father winced as though something hurt him, but he didn't take his eyes from the newspaper. "Yes, Malka?" he asked.

"Papa, today is Thursday, isn't it?"

He raised his head and looked at her. Perhaps it was the beard, or because he worked so hard at the furrier's where he spent his days curing animal pelts, but his face seemed more worn and sad than ever.

"Yes, daughter," he said quietly. "Today is Thursday."

She sat opposite him and folded her hands neatly in front of her. "Which means that tomorrow is Friday. And tomorrow night is the Sabbath."

He smiled. "Now, Malka, when was the last time you saw your papa in a synagogue, rocking and mumbling useless prayers with the old men? This isn't how I brought you up. You know I won't partici-pate in any—"

"—bourgeois religious ceremonies," she finished with him. "Yes, I know. But I was thinking, Papa, that I would like to have a real Sabbath. The kind that you used to have with Mama. Just once. As . . . " Her face brightened. "As an educational experience."

Her father sighed and put down his paper. "An educational ex-perience, hah?" he asked. "I see. How about this: If you want, on Saturday, we can go to Prospect Park. We'll sit by the lake and feed the swans. Would you like that?"

"That would be nice," said Malka. "But it's not the same thing, is it?"

He shrugged. "No, Malka. You're right. It isn't."

Across the alley, a clothesline squeaked as somebody pulled on it, an infant cried, and somebody cursed in a loud combination of Russian and Yiddish.

"And what brought on this sudden religious fervor?" her father asked. "You're not going to start demanding I grow my beard to my knees and read nothing but holy books, are you?"

"Oh, Papa," Malka said, exasperated. "Nothing like that. I made friends with this boy today, named David. He's older than I am—over twelve—and his father also doesn't approve of religion, but his mama used to sing the same songs they sing in the church down the street. We listened to them today, and I thought maybe I could invite him here and show him what we do . . . " Her voice trailed off as she saw her father's face.

"You were at a church?" her father asked, a little tensely. "And you went in and listened?"

"No, of course not. We sat outside. It's the church on the first floor of that house on Remsen Avenue. The one where they sing all those wonderful songs."

"Ah!" her father said, enlightened, and shook his head. "Well, and I shouldn't be pigheaded about this. Your mama always said I could be very pigheaded about my political convictions. You are a separate individual, and deserve to make up your own mind."

"And it's really for educating David," said Malka eagerly.

Her father smiled. "Would that make you happy, Malka?" he asked. "To have a Sabbath dinner for you and your friend? Just this once?"

"Yes, just this once," she said, bouncing on her toes. "With everything that goes with it."

"Of course," her father said. "I did a little overtime this week. I can ask Sarah who works over at the delicatessen for a couple pieces chicken, a loaf of bread, and maybe some soup and noodles, and I know we have some candles put by."

"And you have Grandpa's old prayer book," she encouraged.

"Yes, I have that."

"So all we need is the wine!" Malka said triumphantly.

Her father's face fell. "So all we need is the wine." He thought for a moment, then nodded. "Moshe will know. He knows everybody in the neighborhood; if anyone has any wine to sell, he'll know about it."

"It's going to get dark soon," said Malka. "Is it too late to ask?"

Her father smiled and stood. "Not too late at all. He's probably in the park."

* * *

"So, Abe," Moshe said to Malka's father, frowning, "you are going to betray your ideals and kowtow to the religious authorities? You, who were nearly sent to Siberia for writing articles linking religion to the consistent poverty of the masses? You, who were carried bodily out of your father's synagogue for refusing to wear a hat at your brother's wedding?"

Abe had immediately spotted Moshe, an older, slightly overweight man with thinning hair, on the well-worn bench where he habitually spent each summer evening. But after trying to explain what he needed only to be interrupted by Moshe's irritable rant, Abe finally shrugged and walked a few steps away. Malka followed.

"There are some boys playing baseball over there," he told her. "Why don't you go enjoy the game and let me talk to Moshe by myself?"

"Okay, Papa," Malka said, and ran off. Abe watched her for a moment, and then looked around. The small city park was full of people driven out of their apartments by the heat. Kids ran through screaming, taking advantage of the fact that their mothers were still cleaning up after dinner and therefore not looking out for misbehavior. Occasionally, one of the men who occupied the benches near the small plot of brown grass would stand and yell, "Sammy! Stop fighting with that boy!" Then, content to have done his duty by his offspring, he would sit down, and the kids would proceed as though nothing had happened.

Abe walked back to the bench and sat next to his friend, who now sat disconsolately batting a newspaper against his knee. "Moshe, just listen for a minute—"

But before he could finish, Moshe handed him his newspaper, climbed onto the bench, and pointed an accusing finger at a thin man who had just lit a cigarette two benches over.

"You!" Moshe yelled. "Harry! I have a bone to pick with you! What the hell were you doing writing that drek about the Pennsylvania steel strike? How dare you use racialism to try to cover up the crimes of the AFL in subverting the strike!"

"They were scabs!" the little man yelled back, gesturing with his cigarette. "The fact that they were Negroes is not an excuse!"

"They were workers who were trying to feed their families in the face of overwhelming oppression!" Moshe called back. "If the AFL had any respect for the people they were trying to organize, they could have brought all the workers into the union, and the bosses wouldn't have been able to break the strike!"

"You ignore the social and cultural problems!" yelled Harry.

"You ignore the fact that you're a schmuck!" roared Moshe.

"Will you get down and act like a human being for a minute?" asked Abe, hitting his friend with the newspaper. "I have a problem!"

Moshe shrugged and climbed down. At the other bench, Harry made an obscene gesture and went back to dourly sucking on his cigarette.

"Okay, I'm down," said Moshe. "So tell me, what's your problem?"

"Like I was saying," said Abe, "I'm going to have a Sabbath meal."

Moshe squinted at him. "Nu?" he asked. "You've got yourself a girlfriend finally?"

Abe shook his head irritably. "No, I don't have a girlfriend."

"Too bad," his friend said, crossing his legs and surveying the park around him. "You can only mourn so long, you know. A young man like you, he shouldn't be alone like some alter kocker like me."

Abe smiled despite himself. "No, I just . . . " He looked for a moment to where Malka stood with a boy just a little taller than her, both watching the baseball game. That must be her new friend, he thought, probably from the next neighborhood over. His clothes seemed a bit too small for his growing frame; Abe wondered whether he had parents and, if so, whether they couldn't afford to dress their child properly.

"It's just this once," he finally said. "A gift for a child."

"Okay," said Moshe. "So what do you want from me? Absolution for abrogating your political ideals?"

"I want wine."

"Ah." Moshe turned and looked at Abe. "I see. You've got the prayer book, you've got the candles, you've got the challah. But the alcohol, that's another thing. You couldn't have come up with this idea last year, before the geniuses in Washington gave us the gift of Prohibition?"

"I want to do it right," said Abe. "No grape juice and nothing made in somebody's bathtub. And nothing illegal—I don't want to make the gangsters any richer than they are."

"Well . . . " Moshe shrugged. "If you're going to make this an ethical issue, then I can't help."

"Oh, come on," Abe said impatiently. "It's only been a few months since Prohibition went into effect. I'm sure somebody's got to have a few bottles of wine stashed away."

"I'm sure they do," Moshe said. "But they're not going to give them to you. And don't look at me," he added quickly. "What I got stashed away isn't what you drink at the Sabbath table."

"Hell." Abe stood and shook his head. "I made a promise. You got a cigarette?"

Moshe handed him one and then, as Abe lit a match, said, "Hey, why don't you go find a rabbi?"

Abe blew out some smoke. "I said I wanted to make one Sabbath meal. I didn't say I wanted to attend services."

Moshe laughed. "No, I mean for your wine. When Congress passed Prohibition, the rabbis and priests and other religious big shots, they put up a fuss, so now they get to buy a certain amount for their congregations. You want some booze? Go to a rabbi."

Abe stared at him. "You're joking, right?"

Moshe continued to grin. "Truth. I heard it from a Chassidic friend of mine. We get together, play a little chess, argue. He told me that he had to go with his reb to the authorities because the old man can't speak English, so they could sign the papers and prove he was a real rabbi. Now he's got the right to buy a few cases a year so the families can say the blessing on the Sabbath and get drunk on Passover."

Abe nodded, amused. "Figures." He thought for a moment. "There's a shul over on Livonia Avenue where my friend's son had his bar mitzvah. Maybe I should try there."

"If you've got a friend who goes there," Moshe suggested, "why not simply get the wine from him?"

Abe took a long drag on his cigarette and shook his head. "No, I don't want to get him in trouble with his rabbi. I'll go ask myself. Thanks, Moshe."

"Think nothing of it." Suddenly Moshe's eyes narrowed, and he jumped up onto the bench again, yelling to a man entering the park, "Joe, you capitalist sonovabitch! I saw that letter you wrote in the *Daily Forward* ... "

Abe walked over to his daughter. "You heard?" he asked quietly. "We'll go over to the synagogue right now and see what the rabbi can do for us."

"Yes, Papa," Malka said, and added, "This is David. He's my new friend that I told you about. David, this is my father."

"How do you do, Mr. Hirsch?" asked David politely.

"How do you do, David?" replied Abe. "It's nice to meet you. I'm glad Malka has made a new friend."

"Mr. Hirsch," said David, "you don't have to go to that rabbi if you don't want to. I heard my father say that he and his business partners got some Jewish wine that he bought from a rabbi who didn't need it all, and I'm sure he could sell you a bottle."

Abe smiled. "Thank you, David. But as I told my friend, I'd rather not get involved in something illegal. You understand," he added, "I do not mean to insult your father."

"That's okay," David said. He turned and whispered to Malka, "You go ahead with your daddy. I'll go find mine; you come get me if you need me for anything. He's usually at the candy store on the corner of Dumont and Saratoga."

"Okay," Malka whispered back. "And if we do get wine, I'll come get you, and you can come to our Sabbath dinner."

Abe stared at the two children for a moment, then pulled the cigarette out of his mouth, tossed it away, and began walking. Malka waved at David and followed her father out of the park.

The synagogue was located in a small storefront; the large glass windows had been papered over for privacy. CONGREGATION ANSHE EMET was painted in careful Hebrew lettering on the front door. Evening services were obviously over; two elderly men were hobbling out of the store, arguing loudly in Yiddish. Abe waited until they had passed, took a deep breath, and walked in, followed by Malka.

The whitewashed room was taken up by several rows of folding chairs, some wooden bookcases at the back, and a large cabinet covered by a beautifully embroidered cloth. A powerfully built man with a long, white-streaked black beard was collecting books from some of the chairs.

While Malka went to the front to admire the embroidery, Abe walked over the man. "Rabbi," he said tentatively.

The rabbi turned and straightened. He stared at Abe doubtfully. "Do I know you?"

"I was here for Jacob Bernstein's son Maxie's bar mitzvah two months ago," said Abe. "You probably don't remember me."

The rabbi examined him for a minute or two more, then nodded. "No, I do remember you. You sat in a corner with your arms folded and glowered like the Angel of Death when the boy sang his Torah portion."

Abe shrugged. "I promised his father I'd attend. I didn't promise I'd participate."

"So," said the rabbi, "you are one of those new radicals. The ones who are too smart to believe in the Almighty."

"I simply believe that we have to save ourselves rather than wait for the Almighty to do it for us," Abe rejoined.

"And so," said the rabbi, "since you obviously have no respect for the beliefs of your fathers, why are you here?"

Abe bit his lip, ready to turn and leave.

A small voice next to him asked, "Papa? Is it safe here?"

He looked down. Malka was standing next to him, looking troubled and a little frightened. "One moment," he said to the rabbi and walked to the door, which was open to let the little available air in.

"Of course it's safe, daughter," he said quietly. "Why wouldn't it be?"

"Well," she began, "it's just . . . there isn't a good place to hide. I thought synagogues had to have good hiding places."

His hand went out to touch her hair, to reassure her, but then stopped. "Malkele," he whispered, "you run outside and play. You let your papa take care of this. Don't worry about anything—it will all turn out fine."

Her face cleared, as though whatever evil thoughts had troubled her had completely disappeared. "Okay, Papa!" she said, and left.

Abe took a breath and went back into the room, where the rabbi was waiting. "This is the story," he said. "My little girl is . . . Well, she wants a Sabbath meal."

The rabbi cocked his head. "So, nu? Your child has more sense than you do. So have the Sabbath meal."

"For a Sabbath meal," said Abe. "I need wine." He paused and added. "I would be . . . grateful if you would help me with this."

"I see." The rabbi smiled ironically. "In other words, you want to make a party, maybe, for a few of your radical friends, and you thought, 'The rabbi is allowed to get wine for his congregation for the Sabbath and for the Holy Days, and if I tell him I want it for my little girl . . . '"

Abe took a step forward, furious.

"You have the gall to call me a liar?" he growled. "You religious fanatics are all alike. I come to you with a simple request, a little wine so that I can make a Friday night blessing for my little girl, and what do you do? You spit in my face!"

"You spit on your people and your religion," said the rabbi, his voice rising as well. "You come here because you can't get drunk legally anymore, so you think you'll maybe come and take advantage of the stupid, unworldly rabbi?" He also took a step forward, so that he was almost nose-to-nose with Abe. "You think I am some kind of idiot?"

Abe didn't retreat. "I know you get more wine than you need," he shouted. "I know how this goes. The authorities give you so much per person, so maybe you exaggerate the size of your congregation just a bit, hah? And sell the rest?"

The rabbi shrugged. "And what if I do?" he said. "Does this look like the shul of a rich bootlegger? I have greenhorns fresh off the boat who are trying to support large families, men who are trying to get their wives and children here, boys whose families can't afford to buy them a prayer book for their bar mitzvah. And you, the radical, somebody who makes speeches about the rights of poor people, you would criticize me for selling a few extra bottles of wine?"

"And so if you're willing to sell wine," yelled Abe, "why not sell it to me, a fellow Jew, rather than some goyishe bootlegger?"

There was a pause, and both men stared at each other, breathing hard. "Because he doesn't know any better," the rabbi finally said. "You should. Now get out of my shul."

Abe strode out, muttering, and headed down the block. After about five blocks, he had walked off his anger, and he slowed down, finally sitting heavily on the steps of a nearby stoop. "I'm sorry, Malka," he said. "Maybe I can go find the people that the rabbi sells to . . . "

"But David said his father could get us the wine," said Malka, sitting next to him. "David said that his father and his friends, they have a drugstore where they sell hooch to people who want them. Lots of hooch," she repeated the word, seeming pleased at its grown-up sound.

Abe grinned. "Malka, my sweet little girl," he said, "do you know what your mother would have done to me had she known that her baby was dealing in illegal alcohol? And by the way, I like your friend David. Very polite child."

"He's not a child," Malka objected. "He's almost thirteen!"

"Ah. Practically a man," said Abe, stroking his chin. "So. And his father, the bootlegger—he would sell to someone not of his race?"

"Well, of course," said Malka, a little unsure herself. The question hadn't occurred to her. "David said that they were looking for somebody to buy the kosher wine, and who else to sell it to but somebody who can really use it?"

E ven from the outside, the candy store didn't look promising—or even open. The windows were pasted over with ads, some of which were peeling off; when Malka and her father looked through the glass, shading their eyes with one hand, it was too dark inside to see much.

"You stay out here," her father finally said. "This is not a place for little girls." He took a breath and pushed the door open. A tiny bell tinkled as he stepped through; Malka, too curious to obey, quietly went in after him and stood by the door, trying to make herself as small as possible.

The store looked as unfriendly inside as it did out. A long counter, which had obviously once been used to serve sodas and ice cream, ran along the right wall of the store; it was empty and streaked with dust, and the shelves behind it were bare except for a few glasses. At the back of the store, there was a display case in which a few cans and dry-looking cakes sat.

The rest of the small space was taken up by several round tables. Only one was occupied, and it was partially obscured by a haze of cigarette smoke. Malka squinted: Three men sat there, playing cards. One was short and fat, with the darkest skin Malka had ever seen; he scowled at the cards while a cigarette hung from the corner of his mouth. A second, much younger and slimmer, was carefully dressed in a brown suit with a red tie; he had a thin mustache, and his hair was slicked back so that it looked, Malka thought, like it was always wet.

The third man, she decided, must be David's father. He had David's long, thin face and slight build, but the humor that was always dancing in David's wide eyes had long ago disappeared from his. A long, pale scar ran from his left eye to the corner of his mouth, intensifying his look of a man who wasn't to be trifled with. As she watched, he reached into his pocket and pulled out a small flask. He took a pull and replaced it without taking his eyes off his cards.

Malka's father waited for a minute or two, and then cleared his throat.

None of the three looked up. "I think you're in the wrong store, white man," the fat man said.

Malka's father put his hands in his pockets. "I was told that I could purchase a bottle or two of wine here."

"You a Fed?" asked the man with slicked-back hair. "Only a Fed would be stupid enough to walk in here by himself."

"Ain't no Fed," the fat man said. "Listen to him. He's a Jew. Ain't no Fed Jews."

"There's Izzy Einstein," said the man with the hair. "He arrested three guys in Coney just yesterday. I read it in the paper."

"Too skinny to be Izzy Einstein," said the fat man. "Nah, he's just your everyday, ordinary white man who's looking for some cheap booze."

"I was told I could buy wine here," repeated Malka's father calmly, although Malka could see that his hands, which he kept in his pockets, were trembling. "I was told you had kosher wine."

The man with the scar stood and came over as the other two watched. Now Malka could see that his suit was worn and not as clean as it could be; he walked slowly, carefully, as though he knew he wasn't sober and didn't want to give it away. When he reached Malka's father, he stopped and waited. He didn't acknowledge the boy who followed him solicitously, as though ready to catch his father should he fall.

Malka grinned and waved. "Hi, David," she said, and then, aware that she might be calling attention to herself, whispered, "I didn't see you before."

David put his finger to his lips and shook his head.

"So?" Malka's father asked. "You have wine for sale?"

"My landlord is a Jew," said David's father, challenging.

"So's mine. And I'll bet they're both sons of bitches."

There was a moment of silence. Malka held her breath. And then one corner of the man's mouth twitched. "Okay," he said. "Maybe we can do business." His two colleagues relaxed; the man with the hair swept up the cards and began shuffling them. "Where did you hear about me?"

"Your son David, here," said Malka's father. "He suggested I contact you."

"My son David told you," the man repeated, his eyes narrowing.

"Yes," Malka's father said, sounding puzzled. "Earlier today. Is there a problem?"

There was a pause, and then the man shook his head. "No, no problem. Yeah, I've got some of that kosher wine you were talking about. I can give you two bottles for three dollars each."

Malka's father took a breath. "That's expensive."

"Those are the prices." The man shrugged. "Hard to get specialized product these days."

David stood on his toes and whispered up at his father. The man didn't look down at the boy, but bit his lip, then said, "Okay. I can give you the two bottles for five dollars. And that's because you come with a—a family recommendation."

"Done," said Malka's father. He put out a hand. "Abe Hirsch."

David's father took his hand. "Sam Richards," he said. "You want to pick your merchandise up in the morning?"

Abe shook his head. "I've got to work early," he said. "Can I pick it up after work?"

"Done," Sam said.

Malka's father turned and walked toward the door, then turned back. "I apologize," he said, shaking his head. "I am an idiot. David, your son, has been invited to my house for dinner tomorrow night, and I have not asked his father's permission. And of course, you are also invited as well."

Sam stared at him. "You invited my son to your house for dinner?"

Abe shrugged.

"Hey, Sam," called the well-dressed man, "you can't go nowhere tomorrow night. We've got some business to take care of uptown at the Sugar Cane."

Sam ignored his friend and looked at Malka, who stood next to her father, scratching an itch on her leg and grinning at the success of her plan. "This your little girl?"

It was Abe's turn to stare. He looked down at Malka, who was nodding wildly, delighted at the idea of another guest at their Sabbath meal. He then looked back at Sam.

"Okay," said Sam. "What time?"

"Around five P.M.," Abe said, and gave the address.

"We don't have to be uptown until nine," Sam said to his friend. "Plenty of time."

He turned back to Malka's father. "Okay. I'll bring the wine with me. But you make sure you have the money. Just because you're feeding me—us—dinner don't mean the drinks come free."

"Of course," said Abe.

A t five P.M. the next evening, everything was ready. The table had been pulled away from the window and decorated with a white tablecloth (from the same woman who'd sold Abe a boiled chicken and a carrot tsimmes), settings for four, two extra chairs (borrowed from the carpenter who lived across the hall), two candles, and, at Abe's place, his father's old prayer book.

Abe, wearing his good jacket despite the heat, and with a borrowed yarmulke perched on his head, surveyed the scene. "Well, Malka?" he asked. "How does that look?"

"It's perfect!" said Malka, running from one end of the room to the other to admire the table from different perspectives.

Almost on cue, somebody knocked on the door. "It's David!" Malka yelled. "David, just a minute!"

"I'm sure he heard you," said Abe, smiling. "The super in the basement probably heard you." He walked over and opened the door.

Sam stood there, a small suitcase in his hand. He had obviously made some efforts toward improving his personal appearance: he was freshly shaven, wore a clean shirt, and had a spit-polish on his shoes.

David dashed out from behind his father. "You see!" he told Malka. "Everything worked out. My daddy brought the wine like he said, and I made him dress up, because I said it was going to be religious, and Mama wouldn't have let him come to church all messed up. Right, Daddy?"

"You sure did, David," said Sam, smiling. "Even made me wash behind my ears." He then raised his eyes and looked hard at Abe, as if waiting to be challenged.

But Abe only nodded.

"Please sit down," he said. "Be comfortable. Malka, stop dancing around like that; you're making me dizzy."

Malka obediently stopped twirling, but she still bounced a bit in place. "David, guess what? There's a lady who lives across the alley from us who, when it's hot, walks around all day in a man's T-shirt and shorts. You can see her when she's in the kitchen. It's really funny. You want to come out on the fire escape and watch?"

David suddenly looked troubled and stared up at his father. "Is it okay, Daddy?" he asked. His lower lip trembled. "I don't want to get anyone mad at me."

Sam took a breath and, with an obvious effort, smiled at his son. "It's okay," he said. "I'll be right here, keeping an eye on you. Nothing bad will happen."

David's face brightened, and he turned to Malka. "Let's go," he said. The two children ran to the window and clambered noisily onto the fire escape.

Sam put the suitcase on one of the chairs, opened it, and took out two bottles of wine. "Here they are," he said. "Certified kosher, according to the man I got it from. You got the five bucks?"

Abe handed Sam five crumpled dollars. "Here you are," he said, "as promised. You want a drink before we start?"

Sam nodded.

Abe picked up one of the bottles, looked at it for a moment, and then shook his head, exasperated. "Look at me, the genius," he said. "I never thought about a corkscrew."

Sam shrugged, took a small pocketknife out of his pocket, cut off the top of the cork, and pushed the rest into the bottle with his thumb. Abe took the bottle and poured generous helpings for both of them.

They each took a drink and looked outside, where Malka and David sat on the edge of the fire escape, her legs dangling over the side, his legs folded. A dirty pigeon fluttered down onto the railing and stared at the children, obviously hoping for a stray crumb. When none came, it started to clean itself.

David pointed to a window. "No, that's not her," said Malka. "That's the man who lives next door to her. He has two dogs, and he's not supposed to have any pets, so he's always yelling at the dogs to stop barking, or he'll get kicked out." The children laughed. Startled, the bird flew away.

"So," said Abe.

"Yeah," said Sam.

"What happened?"

Sam took a breath, drained his glass, and poured another. "He had gone out to shoot rabbits," he said slowly. "I had just got home from the trenches. We were living with my wife's family in Alabama, and we were making plans to move up north to Chicago, where I could get work and David could get schooled better. He was sitting on the porch reading, and I got mad and told him not to be so lazy, get out there and shoot us some meat for dinner. When he wasn't home by supper, I figured he got himself lost—he was always going off exploring and forgetting about what he was supposed to do."

He looked off into the distance. "After dark, the preacher from my wife's church came by and said that there had been trouble. A white woman over in the next county had complained that somebody had looked in her window when she was undressed. A lynch mob went out, and David saw them, got scared and ran. He wasn't doing anything wrong, but he was a Negro boy with a gun, and they caught him and . . . "

He choked for a moment, then reached for his glass and swallowed the entire thing at a gulp. Wordlessly, Abe refilled it.

"My wife and her sister and the other women, they went and took him down and brought him home. He was . . . They had cut him and burned him and . . . My boy. My baby."

A single tear slowly made its way down Sam's cheek, tracing the path of the scar.

"My wife and I—we didn't get along so good after that. After a while I cut and run, came up here. And David, he came with me."

For a moment, they just sat.

"We lived in Odessa," said Abe, and, when Sam looked confused, added, "That's a city in the Ukraine, near Russia. I moved there with the baby after my wife died. It was 1905, and there was a lot of unrest. Strikes, riots, people being shot down in the streets. Many people were angry. And when people get angry, they blame the Jews."

He smiled sourly. "I and my friends, we were young and strong and rebellious. We were different from the generations before us. We weren't going to sit around like the old men and wait to be slaughtered. I sent Malka to the synagogue with other children. There were hiding places there; they would be safe. And I went to help defend our homes."

"At least you had that," Sam said bitterly.

Abe shook his head. "We were idiots. We had no idea how many there would be, how organized. Hundreds were hurt and killed, my neighbors, my friends. Somebody hit me, I don't know who or with what. I don't remember what happened after that. I . . . "

He paused. "I do remember screaming and shouting all around me, houses burning, but it didn't seem real, didn't seem possible. I ran to the synagogue. I was going to get Malka, and we would leave this madness, go to America where people were sane, and children were safe."

"Safe," repeated Sam softly. The two men looked at each other with tired recognition.

"But when I got there, they wouldn't let me in. The rabbi had hidden the children behind the bima, the place where the Torah was kept, but . . . They said I shouldn't see what had been done to her, that she had been . . . She was only nine years old." Abe's voice trailed away.

The children out on the fire escape had become bored with the neighbors. "Do you know how to play Rock, Paper, Scissors?" David asked. "Here, we have to face each other. Now there are three ways you can hold your hand . . . "

"Does she know?" asked Sam.

"No," said Abe. "And I don't have the heart to tell her."

"David knows," said Sam. "At least, I told him. I thought maybe if he knew, he'd be at rest. But I don't think he believed me. And—well, I'm sort of glad. Because it means . . . "

"He is still here. With you."

"Yes," Sam whispered.

The two men sat and drank while they watched their murdered children play in the fading sunlight.

Lost Connections

A story of Marilyn Feldman, Chana's granddaughter

1985 | 1928

G randpa Abe is angry.

Marilyn watches as he nearly knocks over the portrait of Emma Goldman that sits on the large radio, overlooking a comfortably chaotic living room. The apartment is not a large one, and every corner that isn't taken up with furniture seems awash in books, magazines, and pamphlets written in both English and Yiddish.

As he strides into the room, she steps back involuntarily. He doesn't see her, of course. She is merely an artifact of his future, a ghost of potential tomorrows. "Did you hear, Chana?" he demands of the empty room. "It never changes. No matter what country you are in, it never changes." Short, dark hair curls up, radiating electricity ("You got your hair from your grandfather," Marilyn's mother always told her). His hands, heavily stained with the chemicals he uses as a textile worker, sweep the air as he speaks.

He prowls the room, unable to keep still, a vibrant presence that astounds Marilyn, who just knows him as a flat, black-and-white presence in old photos. A moment later, a stout, pretty woman comes in from the kitchen, drying her hands on a towel. "Shah—stop yelling," she cautions. "The little one is napping." Her long dark hair, uncovered in defiance of her religious upbringing, is pinned precariously up behind her head. The skin on her face is firm, with only a few small lines around the eyes and mouth. Marilyn stares, amazed at her youth.

"So, what happened?" asks her grandmother Chana patiently.

"What do you expect?" Abe answers. "Moshe just came back from Kentucky. He said that the bosses sent out the police, some heads got bashed, some good men put in jail. Enough scabs showed

51

up so that the strike is broken. Just the same as every time. What should be different?"

"At least this time nobody was killed," her grandmother says firmly. "Not like last year, remember? Mrs. Shapiro's boy Noah, who is recruiting down South? He told her that five were shot, right there in front of him." She drapes the towel lightly over her shoulder and settles herself in a chair, staring at him with the air of a woman ready for a long, familiar discussion.

"Noah is a liar," her grandfather tells her. "And a lousy one at that. Nobody else seems to see the horrors he has. And somehow, he always escapes injury by the skin of his teeth. A real Superman, that one."

Chana shakes her head. "How can you say that? You remember, his wife Martha called me to take a look at him the last time he came home. I myself saw the scars."

"Scars? More like bruises from Martha's tongue. And while he plays at revolution down South, the real battle is right here . . ." And the argument goes on.

Don't waste your time, Marilyn tells them. In another decade a war will come, and after that prosperity. The factory workers will win their raises, and they will buy cars and homes, while their shop stewards become friends of the companies and everyone forgets why the unions were formed.

They ignore her, while she presses on: Listen to me, Grandpa. Leave the union and the job before your health is ruined by chemicals and long hours. Grandma, stop fighting the owners, and the politicians, and your own children, and find yourself something of your own, something for yourself. Before it's too late.

Marilyn is interrupted by a girl, about seven years old: torn dress, smudged face, knees raw and bleeding. "Papa," she yells, her dark eyes triumphant. "Papa, Jakie said that his father said that we were dirty Reds. I beat 'em up good, Papa!"

Chana stands, resigned. "Another fight," she sighs. "I'll get the peroxide. Abe . . . " She pauses. Abe is staring at the girl as though he has just now recognized her. "Abe!" she repeats, louder. He shakes his head and turns to her. "Stop woolgathering and talk to your daughter."

"I'm sorry," he says. "But for a moment . . . She is very like Malka."

His wife kisses the top of his head. "I know," she says. "But this is not Malka. This is Becky, and right now she needs her father to explain why she shouldn't attack the boy next door."

She leaves, while my grandfather pulls the girl over to him gently. "Becky," he says, smoothing her hair, "Becky, it's good to defend your ideals. But remember, Jakie is also a member of the proletariat, and it is better to persuade him to join you in the fight against the landlords and the factory owners than beat him up. We have to all stick together. You understand?"

The girl thinks for a moment, scraping her foot against the carpet. Marilyn knows that carpet; a small square of it served as a welcome mat the day her grandmother died. "I guess," Becky says reluctantly, then she looks up and grins. "Okay. I won't beat 'im up next time. But this time, I did it good!"

"Becky!" comes a cry from the bathroom, and the girl kisses her father and marches triumphantly off. Marilyn wants to rush after her, but she can't move. Come back, mom! she tries to yell at the child. Don't listen to your father. Keep your mouth closed and your opinions to yourself, or you'll waste your adulthood running from McCarthy's blacklist, and your money on lawyers to keep you out of jail, and your health in disappointment at the betrayal of your dreams.

But the girl is gone. Marilyn takes a breath, puts a hand in her pocket and presses her thumb into the small control she had been given.

A different place. A large plush room. No trinkets, no photographs—only spotless wooden furniture and overstuffed green chairs. Two boys, one with a swollen cheekbone, sprawl on the rug listening to the radio while a large-jawed man sits in a chair and shakes his head over a newspaper. "Lazy," he mutters in heavily accented English. "All lazy. There's work if you look for it."

Marilyn stares at him. I know who you are, she says. You bastard. You will rot in hell, she tells him, hoping it to be true.

A crash from the next room. "Quiet, Millie!" he calls impatiently. "I can't hear the announcer."

His wife comes in, a tall thin woman with narrow, patient eyes. Her hair is hidden by a plain kerchief; she clutches a dust rag in her hands. "Sorry," she says. "Nothing broken. A book knocked over, that's all."

The man grunts, and turns back to his newspaper. She waits for a moment, and then retreats into the bedroom.

No, Marilyn whispers, don't let him grind you down. He'll do it if you let him, do it slowly and totally. Until you are too frightened to move or talk without permission. Until all your frustration and anger and fear roll themselves into a tight ball and lodge themselves in your stomach to fester and kill you before you see any of your grandchildren born.

She looks at the two children on the rug. The older boy, perhaps 14, scratches patiently at some arithmetic homework, his lower lip caught between his teeth. He pauses, reads it over, and then hands his assignment over to his father. The man scans it carefully. The boy waits.

Don't worry, Melvin, Marilyn soothes, you'll do fine. You'll get good marks, and go to college, and make your way in the world. True, you'll abandon your first wife and daughter, and you'll turn your second wife into a bitter and disappointed woman. But you will have your own house and your own business, and you will live with your father's approval, if not his love.

The father hands the paper back with a satisfied nod. The boy beams.

His wife emerges again, heading for the kitchen on the other side of the room. On her way, she pauses to gently touch the hair of the younger boy, who is lost in the world of the radio, of courageous spacemen rescuing grateful young women from ravenous alien monsters. This is my child, the gesture says.

"Jakie, the face, it still hurts?" she asks.

The father looks up. "Don't baby him, Millie," he says sharply. "He let a girl get the better of him. At this rate, he'll amount to nothing."

All Marilyn's restraint goes, and she cries to the child, Be careful! Be careful of your father, who cannot love you; be careful of the coming war, which will scar you; be careful of your job, which will stifle you; be careful of your children, who will disappoint you. And be careful of your cigarettes, which will kill you. Be careful. Please. Please!

The boy turns his head. Can he hear? Marilyn reaches out to him, and with that movement he shimmers, and disappears.

"So," asks the technician, detaching the leads. "How did it go?"

For a moment, Marilyn can't breathe. The tech hands her a box of tissues and continues to disconnect her from the system.

She wipes her nose, regaining control. "Was it real?" she finally whispers.

He shrugs. "We don't really know," he says. "The technology is really new, more alpha than beta. In fact, we have no idea whether we're going to be able to go public with it. The developers say they're pulling from genetic memory, but I'll tell you the truth, some of us are starting to believe it's just wishful thinking, built from the stories we're told as children. Depends on who you talk to."

He stores the last component in its place and helps her up. "You should go home," he advises. "Lie down. It's a pretty intense experience, and there can be physical aftereffects. Some dizziness, maybe, some nausea. You should be fine by tomorrow, though." He pauses. "And remember, you signed a non-disclosure. You can't tell anyone about this until it goes commercial. If it ever does."

Marilyn nods, and thanks him, and walks out of the room, through the lobby, and out into the late day sun. It's the end of a work day; around her, people talk, laugh and argue as they make their way home. She keeps pace with the crowds as she heads toward the train station; a flock of pigeons soars overhead.

The spirit of her unborn daughter follows and cries out to her, unheard.

Hearts and Minds

Abe's story continues

I t's late in the afternoon, and I'm sitting around playing Hearts with Abe, Ruth, and Paolo on a rickety card table in front of an old-fashioned drug store, the type with a soda fountain that I used to see in old black-and-white films from the 1930s and '40s.

Abe is dealing out the cards while Paolo watches him with narrowed eyes. Paolo is sure that Abe cheats, but hasn't caught him at it yet. Ruth told me that she thinks Abe fakes cheating to drive Paolo crazy.

"So, Ben—what the fuck is a nice, middle-class boy like you doing here, anyway?" asks Abe, dealing me an ace of spades. "I mean, you're welcome here, but we're not the type of people an active young man like yourself usually knocks around with."

He's a balding, slightly paunchy guy who looks as if he should be smoking on a big cigar and screaming at his downtrodden sweatshop workers. Actually, according to his daughter Malka (a sweet little kid who once stopped by to pay her old man a visit), he headed up a major cell in the American Communist Party and got beaten up regularly for unionizing fur workers during the Depression. Go figure.

I look at him. "Well, Abe, I guess I got tired of dancing around with the other queers," I tell him. "You can only hang out in fabulous bars just so long before you get incredibly bored."

"Bullshit," says Ruth. She swings out of the drug store with a couple of bottles of Coke in one hand and a pack of cigarettes in the other, letting the screen door slam behind her. Today she is wearing a big-shouldered 1940s dress that makes her look like Lena Horne on a really good day. I've got to admit, that woman has style. "You never hung out at bars. Sugar, you probably had a monogamous relationship with a nice Jewish doctor and adopted 2.5 kids."

"No kids. Two cats," I tell her. "And the nice Jewish doctor was actually a nice Cubano graphics designer."

"So," she says, lighting a cigarette thoughtfully, "why do you stick around? Not that we don't enjoy your company, but it's not like we have a lot in common."

"More than you'd think," I tell her. "I did my time in the protest wars. A smashed head is a smashed head, whether you get it in Harlan County or at the Stonewall riots."

"Not true," says Abe, always ready for an argument. Excuse me—debate. "At Stonewall, they at least had reasonable access to media coverage, not to mention a lawyer. However, during the labor movement of the 1930s . . . "

"Shut up and play," Paolo grumbles. The guy couldn't have gotten much to eat when he was a kid; he's small, thin, and wiry. But mean. Really mean. Ruth once told me that he fought in several wars, in several countries. I've never had the nerve to ask him for any details.

Sunlight spills along the sidewalk and onto the brownstones across the street. I hear kids playing somewhere, so maybe it's after three p.m., but I don't know for sure. A couple of pigeons search under the table for stray crumbs. From inside the store, somebody puts the radio on and a clarinet starts to warble. Benny Goodman, I think. I'm normally not much for jazz—I like opera, and used to play *La Boheme* until Carlos, my otherwise patient Significant Other, threatened to break the CD player. But I've got to admit, the music does add to the laid-back atmosphere.

And that's why I'm here. I don't remember how or when I found this small cadre of slightly crazy lefties, but when I did, I knew I was home. Nothing fancy, nobody famous—just friends hanging out, drinking soda, playing cards and arguing politics.

We trade cards across the table. Paolo throws out the two of clubs and stares accusingly at Abe, who smiles and tosses out an ace. The rest of us throw in our clubs, and the game begins.

After a couple of rounds, Abe grins and starts discarding spades. Ruth sucks on her cigarette calmly, unimpressed, while Paolo studies his hand with painful intensity. I play almost by instinct, not really caring if I win or lose. It's more fun to watch the others.

On the radio, Benny finishes his set, and Cab Calloway takes over with a slow, sensual riff on Minnie the Moocher. Ruth stubs out her cigarette. "I'm bored," she announces, and stands, grabbing my hand. "Come on, Ben, dance with me."

Paolo looks up from his hand. "In the middle of a game?"

She smiles at him. "The game can wait. Come on, honey, I need to move." And she does. I never liked to dance with Carlos—he had been a disco king in his youth, and I couldn't keep up—but with Ruth, all you have to do is shuffle your feet and sway your hips, and she does the rest.

Abe sits back and opens a Coke, while Paolo reaches under his chair for the Italian paper that he always keeps there and buries himself in it. Around the second verse, Ruth starts to sing in a deep, almost tuneless voice. "She had a dream 'bout the king of Sweden. He gave her things that she was needin' . . . "

"You never dance with me like that," Abe complains, eyes firmly on her swaying rear.

"You want to dance like this?" Ruth asks. "Lose a few pounds."

Cab stops wailing, and Ruth gives me a firm kiss on the forehead. "Not bad," she tells me, and I happily take her hand for the next number when a voice says, "Excuse me?"

Somebody shuts off the radio with a click. We all turn and look. A young man is standing a few feet away, clutching a piece of paper in both hands and looking somewhat embarrassed, as though he just walked in on a bedroom scene. He's a kid, really, no more than 18 or 19. Neat blue suit, perfectly knotted tie, white shirt. Shoes so bright you could see up a nun's skirts. Short blond hair, a round, clean-shaven face—assuming he needs to shave—and a pair of shoulders that makes me want to grab him and run.

"Hi, gorgeous," I say. "New in town?"

The kid reddens, and hastily looks down at the piece of paper. "Ex—um—excuse me," he stammers. "I'm looking for, uh . . . "

"Spit it out," says Abe, amused. "We won't bite."

The kid takes a breath. "My name is Joseph Beckman," he says. "I have, right here . . . " and he fishes in his jacket pocket until he produces a small business card, which he hands across the table to Ruth.

"Joseph Beckman," she reads. "Assistant Shepherd, Church of Good News."

"Religious crap," Paolo mutters. The kid pulls himself up indignantly and starts to say something, but Ruth shakes her head at him.

"Ignore him," she advises. "He's just being obnoxious. Why don't you just tell us what you want?"

"I'm looking," says Joseph, "for a Mr. Abraham Hirsch."

Everyone looks at Abe, who shrugs. "That's me. Nu?"

Joseph puts out a hand. "I'm very glad to meet you, Mr. Hirsch. I have a wonderful gift for you. You have been baptized by proxy into the Church of Good News so that you may enter into the glory of His love."

Abe ignores the outstretched arm and bares his teeth at the kid in something that resembles a smile as interpreted by a shark. "Excuse me?" he asks softly.

"It's true," Joseph continues, pulling back his hand and ignoring—or not recognizing—the implicit threat. "In order to ensure that all souls have the chance to enter the Heavenly Kingdom, including those who may have not have accepted the Word, we enable them to be baptized by proxy. In this case, your son . . . "

"My son?" Abe shakes his head firmly. "You mean Sidney? The last I knew, the little weasel was married and living in Queens. And had stopped talking to his older sister Becky, for which I'm sure she's grateful."

Joseph looks a bit taken aback by this show of fatherly disaffection, but plows on gamely. "Well, about two years ago, your son remarried and moved to Provo, Utah. He became a prosperous business owner . . . "

Abe's face is starting to get red. "A business owner, huh? I always knew he'd end up no good. Probably pays minimum wage, the little shit."

" . . . a member of good standing of his church . . . "

Suddenly Paolo slams down his paper, stands, and points one finger firmly at Joseph. "Boy, you do not understand. The purveyors of false spirituality have brainwashed this man's son into adopting a sugar-coated hierarchical belief system and have persuaded him to kidnap his wife and children and move them to the heart of the fascist religious oligarchy. Thus, instead of carrying on the fight against the anti-democratic forces in the American government, he will be wearing the uniforms of the capitalist forces and press his innocent offspring into the mold of American McCarthyism. He has betrayed his family and his class."

There is a moment of respectful silence.

"Nicely put," says Ruth.

"A real ball-buster," approves Abe. "You ever speak in Union Square?"

"What they said," I tell him. "But you forgot to include the assumption of heterosexual privilege."

I look at Ruth, and add, "White male heterosexual privilege." She grins at me.

Paolo shrugs. "Next time," he says, sits, and picks up his paper again.

The boy clears his throat. "Yes. Well, since your son has, through the good offices of the church, enabled you to join us . . . "

Abe's eyes narrow. "Kid, does it look as if, on my worst day, I'd want to join your Church of whatever?"

"The Church of Good News," the boy says patiently. "And if you just beheld the beauty . . . "

Abe pushes himself up from the table and takes a step toward the kid, who prudently retreats. "Listen to me, you miserable gonif, you stealer of souls," he growls. "If my son, may his name be wiped from the face of the earth, chooses to join your miserable institution and spend the rest of his life kissing the feet of a murderous god and breaking his mother's heart, I can't do anything about it. But I will not—I repeat, will not—accept any responsibility for his actions. Nor will I have anything to do with you, or him, now or in the future. Do you understand me?"

Joseph, who has more backbone than I gave him credit for, stands his ground. "Please reconsider. You don't know how joyous it is to spend eternity with the saved."

I take a step forward, meaning to get between Abe and this maniac, but Ruth puts a hand on my arm. "Don't worry," she whispers. "It's okay."

In fact, Abe has gone quiet. From where I stand, dangerously quiet. "Son," he says, almost gently. "Don't you think you'd better leave before somebody gets hurt?"

The kid looks at him, baffled. "But, don't you know? I mean . . . You can't hurt me. I'm . . . you're . . . we're . . . dead."

Silence. Abe stares back at the kid for a moment. Then he takes a deep breath, sits down, and grabs his cards. "Well," he says to the rest, "Are we playing Hearts, or not?"

Paolo throws down his paper and picks up his hand. "About time," he says. "Ruth, Ben, you in or out?"

Ruth shrugs, and lights another cigarette. The radio goes on again, and Woody Guthrie starts to sing about a union maid who never was afraid. Joseph is still standing there, looking totally confused, so I put a fatherly arm over his shoulders, and walk him away from the table. "They won't talk to you anymore," I tell him. "You see, you shouldn't have mentioned the 'D' word. They're a bit sensitive on the subject."

The boy shakes his head. "I don't understand," he says. "Why wouldn't they want to enter the Heavenly Kingdom rather than languishing here in this urban Purgatory deprived of the grace of Our Lord?"

I smile. "I'm sure it's very nice where you are," I tell him. "But the thing is—they're atheists. They don't believe in an afterlife." I shake his hand and go back to the card game.

Cancer God

A story of Jakie Feldman, Chana's son-in-law

1996

It must have been about three in the morning when the cancer god paid Jakie a visit.

He was lying awake, staring at the ceiling and listening to the nasal snores of his roommate, another old fart whose wife came in for an hour every day to sniffle into a box-load of tissues. As usual, Jakie was bored out of his skull. The nurses who now ruled his life didn't let him turn on the TV after 11 p.m., he'd already read the latest issue of *Women's Wear Daily* three times from cover to cover, and the one guy he got along with—name of Ben, a kid of about 35 or so—hadn't been around for a week now.

Ben pretty much saved Jakie's sanity the week after he arrived. Jakie's wife Becky—with whom he had been happily in love ever since she clobbered him for badmouthing her father back when they were kids—had made sure he had a working TV set and plenty of books, but it wasn't baseball season and he didn't have the patience to read. His daughter Marilyn had suggested he record his memories and had even given him a little tape recorder, but he didn't see the point. What was he supposed to talk about? How to sell a suit? How to drag your carcass through the mud of a destroyed town in Poland? He briefly thought about that girl he had met there from the concentration camp, what was her name again? Gretl, that was it—a lovely *maidele* despite the shit she had lived through. But he didn't really want to talk about the war, even to a machine.

He was starting to think that he would go completely crazy from nothing to do, when one of the nurses mentioned that a patient down the hall was trying to auction off some old record albums on something called eBay. Well, Jakie wasn't much in the computer line, but he could sell reading glasses to a blind man, so he got her to help him into a wheelchair and push him down to the lounge, where this thin guy with fading red hair was cursing at his laptop and coughing between epithets.

Jakie took one look at what was on the kid's screen—he was trying to sell an album with a photo of an old guy painting a pigeon on it—and knew he was dealing with an amateur. "Slightly worn condition?" he yelled. The kid looked at him with his mouth hanging open. Okay, at least he was listening. "Who the hell would want to buy anything in 'slightly worn condition'? You want to be fancy, you type 'well-preserved,' you want to be personal, you type 'much-loved.' Either way, you want to sell your records, you better change your pitch."

Well, once Ben realized that Jakie wasn't some insane old nutcase, but actually knew what he was talking about, they formed a partnership: Ben's computer know-how and Jakie's salesmanship. They got along great. Jakie took 25 percent of everything they made. In the evenings, Ben would come to Jakie's room, they'd strategize, play a little poker—and Jakie would win the other 75 percent. He was a good kid, Jakie thought, but a lousy card player. Sometimes Ben's friend Carlos, a quiet guy who was obviously trying not to show how worried he was, would visit and they'd do a threesome. Carlos, Jakie suspected, could play cards better than he let on, but since Jakie still kept winning, he didn't see any reason to complain.

Last time he and Ben played cards, though, Ben wasn't looking so hot. He had to take a drag from the oxygen tank next to him every few minutes, and when he did say something, his voice was so quiet Jakie could hardly hear him. He tried to keep up the kid's spirits by telling a few tall tales about the big Broadway stars he sold suits to back in the old days, but Ben didn't seem interested.

Finally, Ben dropped his cards, stared at Jakie for a minute, and whispered, "Any strange visitors lately?"

"No stranger than usual," Jakie told him. "My son Morris came by—he's looking tired, I gotta get him to take a rest—and there's that new nurse who shaves his head so you can read in it like a mirror, but . . . "

Ben shook his head. He looked pretty upset and tried hard to say something more, but the coughing got so bad that Jakie yelled for the nurses, who came, took one look, and hustled Ben away.

After that, when Jakie asked about the kid, he got looks that told him that he didn't want to know. After a couple of days, he stopped asking.

So here he was, listening to the night crew wash the hallway floors and trying to distract himself from the pain. It had already begun to return across his shoulders and down his arms; only a vague shadow right now, but he could predict to the minute when it would start to throb, and then burn, and then become so unbearable that he'd start crying for his pain meds like a baby screams for its mama's tit.

He reached for the button that would bring the nurse. But instead of the evil-tempered old yente who usually did the night shift, this good-looking clean-cut young guy strolled in. Nice haircut, close shave, dark gray suit. Sixty-odd years in the rag trade made Jakie a pretty good judge of material, and he could tell that this was a quality piece of clothing. Definitely not off the rack. Good worsted wool, nice cut, tailor-made.

At first, Jakie figured that this guy was a high-priced specialist looking to pad his bank account with an extra consulting fee. But no doctor was going to be wearing his best suit where it could come in contact with a leaking catheter. So, maybe a rich kid looking for grandpa.

The man stood right inside the door for a moment. Then he whipped out one of those new little computer toys that all the yuppies were carrying around and started poking at the thing.

"Can I help you?" Jakie asked. He wasn't normally this polite, but these days he'd do anything for a chance to talk to somebody.

The man peered at his toy, walked over, grabbed Jakie's hand, and shook it like they were long-lost cousins. "You're Jakie Feldman, right? Jakie, it's good to meet you face to face. I'm sorry it took me so long to get around to a visit."

Jakie might have been drugged to the gills, but he knew who all his relatives were, even the ones whose parents he hadn't talked to for 20 years, and this wasn't one of them. They were the ones who stared around the room because they couldn't look straight at a hospital patient and tried to make conversation. "See you soon!" "Don't forget you're coming to my birthday party next month!" "I expect you on the golf course next summer!" Yeah, right. All to someone who is grateful if he can go to the fucking bathroom by himself.

So odds were that Charlie here was a con man who managed to get past the hospital's security in order to prey on patients. For a moment, Jake was ready to call a cop. Just for a moment. What the hell, he told himself. It's a change, anyway.

"That's me," Jakie told him. "What are you going to try to sell me? Insurance?"

The man grinned. "Good one," he said. "I'll have to remember that. No," and he checked his gadget again, "I'm here on a courtesy call."

And damned if the guy didn't drop the rails on the side of Jakie's bed and plant his backside on the mattress like he belonged there. "Jakie," he said, "I know you haven't the vaguest idea who I am. That's okay—I'm not offended. But there are rules even I must follow, and one of them is that every human whom I'm overseeing gets at least one visit. So here I am." And he smiled like he'd just handed over some kind of wonderful gift.

"That's nice," Jakie told him, starting to get a little nervous. Maybe this wasn't a con man—maybe it was a well-off loon who just escaped from the psych ward. "So who are you?"

He made a little bow. "Allow me to introduce myself. Cancer, at your service."

"Uh-huh. You're my cancer, sitting on my bed, talking to me?" Damn, Jakie thought, he had to get his meds changed. He was in more trouble than he thought.

The man shook his head. "No, sir. I am the god of cancer."

"The god of cancer. Right."

The man grinned. "You don't believe in me. That's okay. I don't take it personally. I'm a new guy on the block as gods go. No heroic songs, no epics—not even a lousy TV series. And then, so many people these days are sold on the whole monotheistic line. So when I introduce myself to those who have—inadvertently—joined my group of followers, I almost always meet with some initial skepticism. It's hard on me—I don't have a lot of time to spare, and I get tired of these long explanations—but it's part of the job."

Fine. Jakie knew when to play along. "Okay. Let's say, just for the sake of argument, you are the god of cancer. You're telling me that you're visiting to say thanks for catching your disease and living with it for five years. Is that it?"

The man looked pleased. "Yes. That's exactly it."

"So what took you so long to get here? I mean, if you had shown up five years ago, I would have explained that I want nothing to do with you. I could have gone back to my retirement, you would have had one less appointment to make, and we would have both been happier."

The guy crossed his legs, careful of the crease in his trousers. "Sorry, but it doesn't work that way. I generally wait to visit until you're ready to be handed off. That way, it's less likely that you'll try to tell anybody else about me. Which is best for you, really, because they'll think you're hallucinating and start with the brain scans—and you know how much fun those are."

Yeah. Jakie knew exactly what he was talking about.

"So what do I get in return for all this, uh, inadvertent worship?"

"Well, tell me: How do you feel?"

Jakie suddenly realized that he was no longer reaching for the call button. In fact, he felt pretty good.

"It's only a temporary respite," the man told Jakie, "but everyone can use a break. And there's also the advantage of belonging to one of the most well publicized disease groups in known history, if you don't count the Black Plague. Of course," he leaned forward and lowered his voice, "the AIDS god has been ahead for a while. That guy knows how to get headlines, doesn't he? But between you and me, there's a new cocktail about to hit that will have most of the rich white folks lasting into their 80s. Soon as that happens, I'll be pretty well back on top."

Jakie was only halfway listening to him. He was too busy stretching out his arms and flexing his fingers for the first time in a couple of months. He was even starting to think that he could get out of the pale green polyester shmata that they made patients wear here and get into some decent silk pajamas when something occurred to him. "That AIDS god didn't by any chance visit my friend Ben down the hall recently?"

The carefully plucked eyebrows draw down. This guy must spend a fortune in stylists, Jakie thought. "Let me see . . . "

He checked the toy again and saw Jakie craning his neck. "Neat, isn't it? One of those new PDAs—I was talking to a woman at Sloan Kettering last week, a programmer with breast cancer and an attitude, and we spent a couple of hours going over the latest tech. Told me what to buy."

"Did it do her any good? Helping you, I mean?"

"Not really." The man went back to his toy. "Here he is. Yup, AIDS just came to see your friend recently. Nice god, if a bit flamboyant, and still pretty busy. But I'm sure he got to your friend in time."

Jakie pushed himself up on his pillows. "In time for what?"

The man shrugged. "I told you—in time to be handed off to the next department." He waited for a moment. Then, realizing that Jakie still didn't get it, "You know. Death. In fact," he glanced at his computer, "your appointment is later this evening."

"Wait a minute!" This wasn't what Jakie was expecting. "What do you mean, 'handed off to Death'? My doctor told me that there were at least three more treatments to try and that . . . "

The man smiled. "Let's face it, Jakie. Those treatments wouldn't do you any good. You're not young anymore, and you've been taking a lot of strong medications lately, all of which can do nasty things to your system. Also, you've got a lot of tiny metastases floating around. In other words, you're due for a stroke in an hour or two."

Oh, hell, Jakie thought.

"Don't worry." The man stood, brushed some imaginary dirt off his jacket, and pulled the railings back up, "Death's not a bad sort. No skeletons or dark robes or that kind of depressing crap—she's more the organic cotton type. You'll like her."

"There must be something I can do." Death's wardrobe choices notwithstanding, Jakie had no desire to meet her any time soon— he'd seen enough of her work when he was a soldier in Europe, thank you very much—and he was certainly not looking forward to dealing with a stroke. "I mean, don't I get to play chess with her or something?"

The cancer god started to look annoyed. "What is it with you old guys? You've had your innings—why can't you just accept it?" He looked over at the man in the next bed. "I visited Jacobs here about a week ago, and he was worse than you. Began screaming all sorts of obscenities at me. I swear, the elderly give me more trouble than the kids."

Okay, Jakie, he told himself, get hold of yourself. As soon this putz is out the door, you are in deep, deep trouble. "Sorry," Jakie said slowly, stalling for time. "It must be hard. A lot of people probably try to appeal to you because they've got wives, or kids, or grandchildren."

"You've got no idea," said the god. "Just think of all the people out there who are losing a lot more than you are. You want to break your heart, you try to tell a ten-year-old that he's about to be separated from his mom."

Jakie shook his head sympathetically. "How do you do it?"

He shrugged. "Actually, I don't do children myself. They need special treatment, so I got permission to hire somebody. Young man—was a clown before I dropped a load of leukemia on him. Has a real gift for talking to kids."

"So why haven't you got somebody for the old guys?"

"Excuse me?"

Jakie pointed a finger at him. "Let me ask you—as human to god—how old are you?"

"Well, when you take into consideration the last Ice Age . . . "

"No. I mean, how old are you *supposed* to be? Twenty-eight? Thirty at most, right?"

"About there."

"So how the hell do you expect to convince people to pass along quietly when you look like some snot-nosed 20-something executive who doesn't give a damn about anything except his own bank account?"

The man stiffened. "No need to get insulting."

Jakie pulled himself up in bed, ignoring the drips and wires. "I'm just being honest here. I mean, tell me: How many of my generation have you really been able to convince? Or do you end up walking out of here like you were just going to with me, leaving them panicked and scared and—let's face it—hating your guts?"

The man stared. "You're trying to convince me to hire you, right? Sorry, but with all the downsizing that's going on in today's economy, we've got to pick up staff from other departments."

"I'll work on commission."

"Good try. But I told you, I'm not hiring."

Jakie knew that he had to keep the man there as long as possible. "Look, I'm just pointing something out that you must have noticed a long time ago. If you enjoy scaring the hell out of a bunch of retirees and dragging them screaming into that good night, you're doing a great job. However, if the idea is to persuade them that this is good news, and that they're going to be out of pain, and not have to deal anymore with hysterical families and doctors who only care about their wallets, then you're going to have to get somebody who can talk to them. In their language."

The man's eyebrows met. He was obviously thinking about it.

"Take a chance," Jakie urged. "Look at it this way. You can fit a man for a new suit by pushing him into uncomfortable positions, sticking him with pins, and making him feel like a total shmuck. On the other hand, you can treat him like a prince, tell him how fine he's going to look, and measure him so fast and smooth that he's finished before he knows it. You're trying to fit your . . . worshippers . . . into a brand new suit. Isn't it better for everyone if they think they want to wear it?"

The man started to nod to himself slightly, the way somebody does who has become convinced of something. Jakie knew that look. He was already congratulating himself on a new job when the god-damn PDA played a little tune, totally breaking the mood. The man glanced at it and then looked up.

"Sorry, Jakie," he said. "Got to go. Got at least ten more to deal with tonight. Death should be around in about an hour." He waved his free hand, turned, and was out the door before he could say another word.

Jakie yelled after him, "The hell with you, you son of a bitch! If you think I'm going to let you take me down without a fight, you got another think coming!" He tried to get out of bed, chase him down, but as soon as he shifted the first muscle the pain was there and he was flat on his back, trying to breathe past it and pressing the button like a maniac.

After what seemed like an eternity but was probably more like ten minutes, the nurse came in, glanced at the chart, and injected something into the tubing. Another minute, and the pain ebbed enough for Jakie to be able to do some thinking.

The god of cancer.

Right.

It was the meds. Or the disease. Or both. Hell, the guy in the next bed didn't even recognize his wife. Should Jakie be surprised that he was seeing gods with designer-label suits?

Although Ben said he had a visitor last week.

So if he wasn't imagining this. If it was true . . .

When the kids were small and didn't want to wear their boots, Becky used to tell them, "It's better to have and not need than need and not have." It may have been a little cute, but it was good advice. And if he wasn't crazy or hallucinating, then his best chance was to put together a really good sales pitch, something that'd reel Death in, that'd make her want his product so bad that she'd beg him to sell it to her.

You can do it, Jakie told himself. After a lifetime of dealing with bosses, unions, buyers, and Immigration, he'd learned how to handle difficult customers. All he had to do was prepare his pitch. Because if it didn't work, he was soon going to be staring up at six feet of dirt.

An hour later, a nice-looking young woman walked in wearing a cotton poplin number that was supposed to look hand-loomed (and, Jakie knew immediately, wasn't), and sipping from a bottle of soy milk.

Jakie was ready.

"I'm glad to meet you," he told her, smiling like somebody's sweet old grandpa. "Have a seat. A nice girl like you shouldn't look so stressed. Let's see if I can help."

In the Loop

A story of Morris Feldman, Chana's grandson

1997

*H*i, said the voice.

In fact, the voice had been saying *Hi* for at least 20 minutes, or so it seemed to Morris as he guided his Honda Civic home. The traffic on Brooklyn's Belt Parkway was lighter than usual that evening, for which Morris was grateful. If he hit rush hour, the 45-minute trip to his apartment in Bay Ridge from his parents' house in Long Island—no, strike that, it was now only his mother's house—could take almost two hours.

On his left, Canarsie Bay swung into view, looking cleaner and bluer than any Brooklyn water had the right to be. On his right, several heavy-duty vehicles lumbered across former junkyards that were now cleared in preparation for a new mall. Morris had been under the impression that malls were going out of fashion, but apparently somebody had decided Brooklyn needed another one.

Shouldn't they have started construction already? It was hard to remember. Since over a year ago, when his father first got the cancer diagnosis, and then got worse, and then died, he had been making this trip on a weekly, then daily, basis—a trip which, before then, he had made maybe once a month. But now, he could drive this route blindfolded. He certainly no longer needed to pay much attention to the road, short of keeping an eye out for crazed drivers or heavy traffic. So he'd just sit back, blast the radio, and sing along at the top of his lungs, whether he knew the words or not. Better than thinking.

But the trip didn't usually take this long. He peered through the windshield. He was only just past JFK Airport, and—wait a minute, didn't he just pass Canarsie? That came after JFK Airport, assuming that he was driving from his parents' house, rather than to . . . That

71

was it. Or was it? He glanced to his right, where several seagulls flew off the bay, and tried to remember whether he was going straight to his parents' house, which was a right turn off the Hillside exit, or to the hospital, which meant that he took the highway up to where it intersected with the Long Island Expressway.

Hi, said the voice again.

Morris tried to ignore the voice as he continued . . . West? East? On his way to the hospital? To his mom's house? Home to Bay Ridge?

Perhaps it was something on the radio, some weird subliminal message under the music that he hadn't noticed before. He shut the radio off and tried to just concentrate on the highway before him. Damn. He hated driving into Manhattan, but his father was meeting a new doctor, and his parents wanted him to be there . . .

No, wait a minute. He was going west, but not into Manhattan. His father wasn't seeing a doctor to find out whether the cancer was progressing, he was dead, and Morris' sister Marilyn was calling relatives, and Morris was driving home to pick up his wife Joan.

Was he driving home? Then why was the bay on his right instead of his left?

Excuse me? asked the voice politely.

This time the radio wasn't on and the windows were closed. Morris looked out at the car in the next lane, to see if somebody was trying to flag him, but the driver was staring straight ahead, ignoring him.

And anyway, now that he thought about it, the voice seemed to come from his passenger seat.

He looked to his right, and there was a man. No, a woman. Sitting. Bald. With red hair.

Morris wondered whether he'd better watch the road before he had an accident, and then realized that he was parked at a rest stop, in a littered parking lot that led to an equally littered beach. Because it was winter, there were just a couple of other cars there, while a lone old man collected shells on the sand and a few pigeons huddled miserably on a bench.

Hello, said the man/woman, flickering like a broken neon sign. *You are still Morris? Male offspring of Jakie and Becky? Hello, Morris.*

"Hello," Morris replied. He was not surprised that there was an hallucination sitting next to him in his Honda Civic on the side of the Belt Parkway, although perhaps he should have been.

Maybe it's just exhaustion, he thought. Weeks of spending hours at his father's bedside, arguing with doctors and looking for nurses and helping with bedpans and calling for painkillers, and probably long overdue for a day or two off. Although he hadn't been to the hospital for a while, and he remembered asking his sister to call relatives about the funeral, and wasn't he driving home to pick up his wife?

When are we, Morris? asked the figure, switching from svelte to obese. Morris tried to focus on it, to make it stop changing, and then gave up.

"You mean where are we," he said. "We're on the Belt Parkway. In Brooklyn."

Are we? asked the figure, its eyebrows rising and its dark/light/striped (striped?) hand reaching up to scratch its head.

"On my way home," Morris said. "Or to my mother's. Or the hospital. I'm not sure. I think I'm having trouble thinking. It must be exhaustion. Or dehydration." His father had suffered from dehydration for a short time, and they thought that might be causing his loss of awareness, until they diagnosed a stroke. Whatever the cause, nothing ever brought him back again.

The man/woman nodded. *Is it fun?*

"Fun? Are you out of your mind?" Morris snorted, no longer caring how strange things were or who his passenger/s might be. "Who could possibly consider this fun?"

The adult/child cocked his/her head. A small gold/silver/jeweled pin glistened in its nostril/ear/eyebrow. *Not fun? So? Leave.*

"Leave? Yeah, sure," Morris sighed, but then thought, why not leave? Start the car and drive past his parents' house, past the hospital, abandoning the loop that he'd been on since the day Marilyn had called him, sobbing, telling him about the tumor that had been found nestling in his father's spine, having grown there quietly for years until it decided to touch a nexus of nerves and scream out its presence. Back and forth, from one house to the other, detouring for hospital visits and doctor visits and then back home to stare at his computer and look for answers and hope for rescue. He could drive past all of that, east to Montauk and the ocean, or west past Manhattan to New Jersey and the rest of the United States. He could. He couldn't.

You can leave, the figure repeated. *You are not here.*

Not here? It could be true, Morris thought. If he were really here, he'd be alarmed at the multicolored multigendered multiclad multipeople flickering at him from his passenger seat. He thought of friends who had experimented with the interesting and available hallucinogens that were floating around campus when he was a student. Maybe he should look them up, ask them about the experience. Hey, remember when you put that tiny piece of paper on your tongue? Did you meet people who were many people at once, who refused to stay still and become one person so you could understand what the fuck was going on?

What the fuck is going on, the person said. *Is we are trying to rescue you. Us. From now.*

Traffic on the Belt was slow, in deference to the late hour and the early darkness. Morris took a breath, and remembered his visitors' original question.

"Okay. Let's start from the beginning. When am I?" he asked.

Good question. The creature was obviously delighted, and crossed one/two legs over the other/s. *You are now.*

Morris raised his eyes to the heavens, or, in this case, to the roof of his car. "This is bullshit," he said. "I didn't take philosophy in college, and I'm in no mood to play Mensa games."

The creature looked dismayed and vanished. There was a short pause, and Morris was about to start the motor when it returned—or, rather, she returned. This time, although the colors of her hair, eyes, skin, clothing kept flickering into familiar and unfamiliar groupings, her height, weight, and gender seemed to be reasonably consistent.

This is now for you, the woman said, as if the conversation had not been interrupted. *You decide the now. We have joined you here because you are losing this now, and have forgotten how to reach ours.*

"Ours as in yours?" Morris asked.

Ours as in yours, the woman told him.

Children screamed happily as they chased seagulls across the beach. "I can't go anywhere," he said. "My father needs me. He's ill."

Morris thought for a moment. "He's dead."

In a manner of speaking, said the woman. *As are you. As are we. In a manner of speaking.*

Morris decided he wanted to get out of the car. He wanted to walk around, to do something to prove to this crazy hallucination that he was alive, that he was real, that he really needed to drive to the hospital, to drive to his parents' house, to drive home and hug his wife. But when he put his left hand on the handle of the door, it felt slippery, insubstantial, somehow wrong.

"A manner of speaking?" he asked, frustrated and angry. "What manner is that? What the fuck does that mean, anyway?"

The creature reached forward and touched the back of Morris' hand. It felt cool, warm, rough, smooth at the same time, although Morris wasn't sure how he managed to process all those sensations simultaneously. *This is/is not you*, it said. *This is not your when. Your when is with us, but you chose to sample this one. And stay. Why did you stay?*

Stay? Morris realized that his hand was shimmering slightly, and that the sensation was a pain/pleasure/numbness that was creeping slowly up his arm. He tried to look out the window of the car, to straighten out his head, make things sane again, but snow had gathered on the vehicle and all he saw was a coating of white.

You are a visitor, the woman told him. *You were bored, numb, uninterested, and needed to be angry, upset, and here. You can leave. But you. Forgot.*

"Forgot?" asked Morris. "Forgot what?"

This now is past, she continued. *Your now is later. Much later. But you need to remember the will-be so that it can become your now.*

Morris took a breath. He stared at the blue sky outside his window and thought about the exhaustion, the terror, the grief of his trips to the house, to the hospital, to the cemetery.

This is your past, she said. *Our past, since we are part of you. You reached through the eons and chose this.*

"Chose this?" Morris flicked his hand around in a gesture indicating the car, the highway, the drive, and his life. The feeling had now crept up to his shoulder, his neck, his head, and it was making him irritable. "Why the hell would I choose this?"

This now seems unpleasant to this you, said the creature. *But it seemed fascinating to the will-be you.* She paused. *Wait*, she said. *I've learned more. I can be clearer now.*

Morris flinched. There was a brief, bright click in his head, as though somebody had finally found the right radio station, and the woman stabilized into his next-door neighbor, a thin, elderly lady with short graying hair and piercing black eyes.

"Okay," she announced in a no-nonsense Bay Ridge accent. "Here's the deal. You are, and you are not, Morris Feldman. You are the drifting remains of his genetic memory that became curious about its antecedents and went back to try to experience touch, taste, sorrow, and all those other things. However, you inadvertently took on the limited memory capacity of your ancestor. So when it was time to leave, you couldn't remember how, and as a result you've created a loop, one that has begun to contract. I'm here to remind you. To get you the hell out of here before you're permanently stuck."

Morris listened, and understood. And smiled. *Who are you, really?* he asked, already knowing.

The woman grinned back at him. "I'm your alarm clock," she told him.

Well, why didn't you say so in the first place? It was certainly time to go, well past time. Without any further hesitation, will-be Morris peeled then-Morris away and arranged him carefully on the seat of the Civic, discarding with him the car trips and the disease, the anxieties and depression and death. It reincorporated the alarm clock, checked to make sure everything was neat and clean and without paradox, and left for home. *That was interesting*, it thought, in the last few milliseconds when words were still possible. *But uncomfortable.*

The remains of what was Morris blinked, looked around, and shrugged. "Must have dozed off," he said to the empty car. He checked the traffic and pulled back onto the parkway. It was time to go home.

The Ladder-Back Chair

A story of Joan Feldman, Chana's granddaughter-in-law

2001

M orris died on September 11, 2001. At home.

It happened while Joan was sitting in the study that they had turned into a hospital room, watching the coverage of the World Trade Towers collapse on the small TV that they had put in her husband's room.

Most days, after all her morning tasks were completed, Joan would take out a knitting project and find an old movie—preferably one that she hadn't seen for a long time—and sit and work and watch, stopping when it was time to administer medication, try to get Morris to take a few spoonfuls of warm soup, or change the sheets or his diapers. She'd stopped talking to him much—the combination of the cancer and the pain medications had burned something out in Morris' brain, and he no longer responded to much anymore. However, as she watched the towers burn and then fall, she couldn't bear not to talk about it to someone, so she pretended that he was still there, watching with her, concerned about things outside the sickroom.

"My god, all those people," Joan said, her eyes on the screen. "I hope most of them got out. Doesn't Olivia's son Steve work at the World Trade Center? You know—her older boy, the one who came over last week and took the air conditioner out of the window? Perhaps I should call her. Or no, she probably doesn't want to tie up the phone. Maybe I'll wait until the aide gets here and then walk across the street, see if everything is all right. Oh, dear, it's time for your meds again."

She got up and went to the dining room table, where she kept the battalions of pill bottles that she fed him, together with a notebook where she carefully tracked what he took when. As she reached for a pen, Joan paused and pressed her lips together, remembering. It was Morris who had taught her how to deal with medications and doctors and hospice when he was helping to take care of Jakie, his father—was it only five years ago? After Jakie died, she asked Morris to have himself scanned for hidden cancers. Not that they had anything to worry about. Just in case. And then the results came in.

Screw it, she didn't have time for this. Joan shook herself, checked her records, poured three pills into her hand, noted down which ones, and went back to the study.

And saw that Morris wasn't breathing. Hadn't been breathing for a while.

Luckily, the people at hospice were willing to step away from their TV sets and take care of things. The ambulance came to take away Morris' remains—remains, Joan thought, being a good word, since the person she had loved and lived with for 30-odd years hadn't been in residence for some months now—and an hour or two later, the folks from whom she had rented the hospital bed and the oxygen tank and other equipment took that away as well.

Joan made a couple of calls to friends who promised that they would call other friends. She called the funeral home that had been recommended to her last month, told them exactly what she wanted, found out exactly how much it would cost for a small service and cremation, and gave them her credit card number. She sent an email out to a list of her friends and relatives telling them that Morris had died, and that there would be a small service two days from then, and which charity to send donations to.

She felt like she was working on automatic; as though she had programmed herself to get through the next few days for the last six months. Her focus had narrowed to the house and the funeral; occasionally she'd turn on the TV and be surprised by the grim-faced news reporters and politicians—oh, right, something terrible had happened out in the world.

She spent the next day cleaning the house. Baskets of fruit and flowers began arriving; she called the local deli and ordered some cold cuts and sides, since it looked as though very few practical supplies were going to be offered. She drove to the supermarket and got several bottles of soda, some paper plates and cups and plastic cutlery.

The funeral was the next day. Five people had volunteered to speak. Her brother, her only living relative, was working as a reporter somewhere in the Middle East and emailed his love along with a short remembrance that somebody else read for him. Morris' sister Marilyn came with her daughter Annie; she kissed Joan, smiled sadly and then sat in the front row and stared at something in the distance only she could see while Annie held her hand.

Joan hugged a few people and exchanged a few words with the others but wasn't able to listen all that closely to what they were saying. It was okay—she knew that they would excuse almost any behavior from her, as long as she wasn't too demonstrative.

Afterwards, several people came back to the house, where they ate, and talked, and told stories. Several of her friends hugged her again, and sniffed, and told her that they would call her in a couple of days; Morris' friends just looked around uncomfortably, as though they expected him to come through the door and wondered why he didn't.

Joan's best friend Gail was last to leave; she had to check up on her elderly mother. "I'm going to send some flowers to the funeral home tomorrow," she said. "Olivia is going to have a memorial service for her son; half the neighborhood will probably be there."

"Oh, god," said Joan, crestfallen. "I totally forgot about Steve. I didn't even know whether he had made it out . . . And I haven't visited or called her or anything."

"It's all right," said Gail quickly, putting a hand on Joan's arm. "Nobody expected you to, under the circumstances. In fact, I visited Olivia yesterday and she said she felt bad that she couldn't attend Morris' funeral. Poor thing, she's completely in shock."

"I should send something," Joan said, looking around as though an appropriate gift would be immediately at hand.

"I'll tell you what," Gail said. "I'll send some flowers in your name. Don't worry about it."

She paused. "Would you like me to come back?" she asked. "I can. You don't have to sleep alone tonight."

Joan shook her head. "No, really. I think I need to be alone for a day or two." Then, seeing Gail's unhappy face, she said, "Really. Call me in two days."

Then they were all gone. Joan waited for the reaction to set in, for the crying and the screaming and the cursing at God—whom she didn't much believe in anyway. She wandered around the house, stopping at the study, which they had originally planned as a room for the children who never came. It looked simultaneously familiar and strange with all its old furniture back, and Morris' hospital bed missing.

This was, she understood, supposed to be the next portion of her life. Some of her friends had already lost their partners—to death or divorce or apathy—and they told her that, after the first few months had passed, she would find a new life, either with friends or even (they said carefully and gently) with a new partner.

She looked blankly around at the old desk with the laptop sitting on it (Morris had used the study as an office when he retired), the overloaded bookcase, the boxes with the old paperbacks that she always meant to take to the used bookstore and never did, and the pile of unidentified detritus that needed to be "gone through."

Then she sat on the worn fake-Oriental carpet and thought for a few minutes. She knew she must be grieving—she had read the books and talked to the social workers at the hospital. And she had loved Morris dearly; apart from the occasional blowup over the usual minor issues, they had lived affectionately and closely. But instead of sorrow or even anger, right now all she was feeling was a sense of disconnection, as if everything that was happening now—in fact, everything that had happened over the past year—wasn't real. Had never been real.

She hugged her knees close, rested her chin on them, and stared at the old desk. The chair in front of it was the only thing new in the room; when Morris had first developed what they assumed was a simple back problem (until the MRI and the doctor's call), they had invested in an expensive desk chair with 12 different ways of being adjusted to allow Morris to sit comfortably. It didn't go with the room at all; previously, they had used an old-fashioned ladder-back with a straw seat that suited the desk much better.

Joan squinted her eyes at the new, high-tech chair and let it blur in her eyes. She thought about the old chair, which they had originally bought at an auction when they first got married. When they got the new one, Morris had wanted to keep the old ladder-back, but they really didn't have the room for it—nor the need—so they gave to Marilyn. She remembered the two pieces of straw that stuck out near the rear of the chair's seat and would catch you unawares if you sat too far back; the scrape on one of the legs where Annie had experimentally banged a metal ashtray when she was four years old; the worn places on the dark wood where a couple of generations of hands had pulled it back and forth, towards and away from the desk.

She could almost see it. If she didn't let her vision sharpen, if she kept her mind on the details, on the feel of that hard but comforting straw as she sat, the straight, unyielding wood against her spine, the smoothness of the top of the back as she stood behind Morris, one hand holding the chair, the other rubbing his neck . . .

She bent forward, then a little more, and reached out, almost blindly. And touched the cold reality of the metal-and-plastic modern chair.

"Fuck!" Joan pushed at the chair, sending it crashing into the desk—which, not being very sturdy, shook on its legs, toppling a small cheap lamp which, in turn, sent a half-filled mug (How long has that been sitting there? Joan thought dazedly) crashing to the floor. Rancid drops of what once was milky tea splashed over the carpet; the mug, a souvenir from a summer trip to Cape Cod, exploded into dozens of small sharp pieces.

Joan sat and surveyed the disaster: the broken lamp, the shattered mug and the ruined carpet—and then, suddenly and much to her surprise, started to laugh. "God, Morris," she said to the air around her, "I never could get you to put your dishes in the goddamn sink. Now look what you've done!"

She pushed herself up and went into the kitchen to get some paper towels, a brush and a dustpan. It didn't take very long to clean up the mug and the tea; she looked at the lamp and decided to worry about it later, and laid some paper towels down on the rug to soak up any remaining moisture.

The next day, she told Gail about it. "I almost thought that, if I concentrated hard enough, I could touch that old chair," she said. "Of course, it didn't happen, but you'd almost think that, if I tried enough—if I believed enough . . . "

Gail shook her head. "Have you contacted that grief counselor I gave you the number of?" she asked. "They have groups where you can talk about stuff like this. I don't think you should be alone in the house."

She brightened. "Why don't we take a weekend and go off somewhere? Splurge on a really nice hotel that we can't afford? You'd be doing me a favor; our office is going to be dealing with an avalanche of insurance claims from downtown businesses and this is probably the last chance I'll have to take time off for months." Her forced enthusiasm drew a smile from Joan, who shook her head.

"I'm sorry, Gail, but I have a lot to do," she said. "I want Morris' stuff to be useful, so I'm going to go through his clothes and things, and figure out what I want to keep and what can be given to charity. I want to do it as soon as possible, and . . . " she put up a hand as Gail opened her mouth, "I want to do it on my own."

It really wasn't as much of a chore as Joan expected. She and Morris had kept separate closets, and Morris was almost obsessively neat, so none of his clothing was in bad condition. She simply dropped his suits, shirts, and pants—all clean, and unused for several months—into a large trash bag to be deposited at the local Good Will. She used another trash bag for underwear, socks, pajamas, and all the sheets, towels and slippers Morris had used in his final illness. They would go straight into the garbage.

She went through his dresser drawers carefully. She put most the souvenirs aside for herself and her sister, and picked a few to give to her neighbors' kids. She saved the photos—she found several that had to be a couple of generations old—and some cufflinks for later inspection. Everything else went into the garbage.

She then went into the bathroom with a garbage bag and got rid of Morris' shaving cream and razor, his toothbrush and comb, the shampoo that he loved and she loathed, the shaving lotion that Annie had given him when she was ten and that he had never used. All the medications were already gone.

And that was it. The rest of the house belonged to them both. The kitchen, the living room, the garden—everything else had been owned and enjoyed by the two of them. And now, was hers alone.

He was still there, of course. Now that the gaunt, vacant, suffering creature who had replaced Morris was gone, the real Morris— her quiet, funny, infuriatingly competent husband—was still in the house, always just around the corner or in another room. She knew, in her head, that he was dead, gone, but the house didn't seem to know it, and she acquiesced in its illusions.

So when she came home from shopping, she'd wait that couple of seconds after opening the door so that Morris could rush to help her carry the groceries to the kitchen, even if she didn't need him to. She woke up to his favorite news station because she didn't want to change the settings (even though she shut it off immediately, because she couldn't bear to listen to the announcers' lists of lost relatives, security fears and upcoming wars). And she set the air conditioner in the bedroom just a bit higher than she liked, because after years of battling over how cold the room should be, that was the temperature they had compromised on.

And every evening, just after supper, she would bring her partly-finished glass of wine into the study, sit on the carpet, and stare at the desk chair, allowing her eyes to glaze over and imagining the details, the feel and smell and look of the old ladder-back chair.

About a month after Morris died, her sister-in-law took her out to dinner. Afterwards, over coffee and a shared dessert, Marilyn leaned over and said, in a concerned tone, "Joan, Gail called me and said you were obsessing over that old chair that used to be in your study."

"Oh, I'm not obsessing," said Joan. "At least, that's not what I'd call it. It's more like a—a sort of visualizing exercise."

"Well, if you really liked that chair," said Marilyn, "I wish you'd have told me. You could have kept it."

"I would have asked for it back, but you told me that Annie . . . that it got broken," said Joan gently. Marilyn looked guilty.

"She stood on it to reach something," she said, "like kids will. She didn't consider that she was probably too heavy for such an old chair; the seat tore, and the whole thing just fell apart. Maybe I should have gotten it fixed but . . . "

Joan smiled at her. "Don't worry about it," she said. "It was an old chair. And anyway, the actual chair isn't really the point."

And it wasn't.

After a while, Joan began to experiment, attempting to visualize the chair more fully. She tried it after a full glass of wine, with two glasses, and with a couple of shots of bourbon. But rather than just relaxing her, the alcohol made her too sleepy to really concentrate. She then tried pot, but it was nearly impossible; every time she tried to picture the chair, she broke into giggles.

She thought about hallucinogens, but she had never used them as a student, and thought it was probably too late to start now.

She tried fasting, but all she could do was picture ice cream; after too little sleep (but all she did was nod off); and after running hard in place until she was gasping for oxygen.

She researched manifestations, wish fulfillment, and other reali-
ties. She looked into neo-paganism and witchcraft, and tried lighting
candles and reciting spells.

But she finally decided that the best thing to do was simply com-
pose herself, sit, and think about the chair.

Visualizing the chair wasn't all she did, of course. She knew
that her friends were watching her carefully—and besides, she did
have a life to lead. She called the company where she had worked
before Morris got sick and, while her previous position was no longer available, they found her a slightly lesser position elsewhere
in the company, which was fine with her. She read the news and
watched debates on TV about what should be put in the space left
by the World Trade Towers. She went to the movies and an occasional lecture at a nearby university. She even went for a couple of
weekend trips with Gail—a strain, since she had to feign enthusiasm for museums and historic sites that bored her silly, but it was
relaxing, and it made Gail happy.

It was all fine. Joan was in no hurry.

It finally happened on a snowy day in February, almost five
months to the day after Morris died. A storm had hit late the previous night, and while it had let up around noon, the wind continued
and the clouds refused to disappear. On TV, happily alarmist news
people broke into the programs every ten minutes to report on another car stuck on the highway or a kitten rescued from a frozen lake.
Joan finally turned it off and walked quietly through the house; a
feeling of perpetual twilight, born of the weak light pushing through
the icy windows, made it seem almost as if she, as well as her husband, no longer inhabited it.

She sat crossed-legged on the carpet in the study and stared at the
new chair as it sat, still incongruous, next to the worn, tired wooden
desk, with its web of small scratches and dents (one made by that
damned lamp, which she had finally thrown out). For a moment,
out of the corner of her eye, she thought she saw Morris sitting there,
tapping on his computer, leaning forward because he hated wearing
his reading glasses. (His bad posture, she had told him, meant that
they had spent all that money for the stupid fancy chair for nothing.
Before the MRI and the doctor's call.)

No. She rubbed her eyes, closed them for a moment, then
opened them slowly and let the world go hazy.

Wood and straw. Wood painted dark brown, the original stria-
tions of the wood starting to show through where the color had worn
down. The warmth of the surface, its finish almost velvety against her
fingertips. The rough straw seat, curving toward where the strands
met at the center, hard and spiky, dangerous little pieces popping up
to prick your fingers and thighs when least expected.

Joan reached out. And felt it. The smooth, round wooden rung.
The chair. Their life.

She grasped it tightly and held on, not moving. And then, "You
left me," she whispered. "You went away, bit by bit, and left me."

"I know," said Morris. "I'm sorry. I didn't want to."

"No," Joan said. "I'm the one who should apologize. You went
away so gradually. Just a little of you at a time. The pain was so bad,
the medications so strong, that you lost reality, lost my name, lost
yourself. But I was so centered on stopping the pain, on keeping you
alive, that I didn't pay enough attention. And then I realized you
were no longer there, not really, and I never said goodbye. I'm sorry."

"I know," Morris said. "I'm not even sure how much of me is
here now. But I'm glad that you told me. It's something that I wondered about, and I'm very glad you told me."

"So am I," Joan said, and shut her eyes. She heard the creak of
the wood and the straw as he stood up and then felt his hand fondle
her hair. She reached up, her eyes still closed, and pulled the hand
close to her cheek. She felt the roughness of it, and smelled Dial soap
and cinnamon. "You've been cooking again," she said.

"A new type of apple pie," said Morris. "An experiment. As usual, I won't know whether it's come out until you taste it. Do you want
to come with me? You can tell me if you like it and we can have it
with coffee."

Joan kissed his hand, and let it go. "No," she said. "No, you'd
better go."

She felt his lips against the top of her head. "Okay," Morris said.

"Say hi to Steve from across the street if you see him," she said.
"Tell him thanks again for helping with the air conditioner."

"I will. See you around, honey." And he was gone.

Joan sat there for a moment more, unwilling to let the moment
pass. She finally took a long breath and opened her eyes. And smiled.

He had left her the ladder-back chair.

The Sad Old Lady

A story of Sheila Hirsch, Chana's daughter-in-law

1929

When she was four years old, Sheila Mandel found out that something awful was going to happen. She knew because, just that night, she had a dream about an ugly old lady with white, flyaway hair and raggedy clothes who cried inconsolably, the same way Sheila had cried when she lost her favorite doll.

Somehow, in the dream she knew that the old lady was 54 years old, an unimaginable age, way older than even her parents. She thought that the old lady might be her grandma, who was older than anyone else in the world, and lived in a small apartment in a building in another part of the city. Sometimes, Sheila's parents would take her to visit, and leave her there with her grandma while they went to do whatever it was adults did on their own.

It made Sheila sad to think that her grandma might be that lonely old woman. So one day, when she was having her afternoon milk and cookies at her grandma's small kitchen table with the bright flowery plastic tablecloth, she looked up and asked, "Grandma, do you cry sometimes?"

Her grandma, who had been listening to *The Goldbergs* on the radio, looked up and said, "Darling, everyone cries sometimes."

"But I never see you cry."

Her grandma smiled. "Grown-ups try not to cry in front of children," she said. "They don't want to frighten them, so when they cry, they do it when the children aren't there."

This sounded reasonable, and explained why the old lady was crying by herself. But Sheila persisted. "Grandma, when will you be 54?"

This made her Grandma laugh, for some strange reason. "Kindele, I was 54 a long time ago. But what a lovely thing to say."

Sheila didn't understand this remark at all, so she put it down to the weirdness of grownups. However, it also convinced her that her grandma wasn't the sad old lady. She decided to keep a look out, so that if the old lady did show herself, Sheila could run away as fast as possible.

Sheila's first period came when she was 12, and had just gotten home from summer camp. She had read all the books and had The Talk with her mom, so when she found the dark spots on her underwear, she knew what to do. And, quite frankly, it was something of a relief, since she had started to worry that she'd never menstruate, and that she'd have a baby's body for the rest of her life, and never grow breasts and be as beautiful as the actresses in the movies.

She was sitting on her bed, looking at an article in one of her movie magazines, which had photos of some old-time silent film stars and what they looked like now. Some of them still looked okay, but most of them looked old and awful. And then, suddenly, as she glanced from the photos of the young, beautiful people to their later selves, Sheila realized who the old lady in her long-ago dream was.

It was her. She had dreamed about her own future.

For one awful moment, Sheila couldn't breathe. All she could do was listen to the blood thumping in her head. It was inevitable, as inevitable as her own death. One day, it would happen. She had no power over it. One day, she would be that ugly crying old woman.

She was terrified. It was as if a witch had cursed her, and there was no good fairy or handsome prince who could remove the spell. There was no way to change it or escape it.

Or perhaps there was. Sheila tried to calm down and think. She had time ahead of her—enough time to make sure that she got married, and had lots of children. And she had Carl, her older brother, who would also get married, and have lots of children. Carl could be a pain at times and didn't like her to bother him when he was with his friends, but he was okay (as brothers went). And if they both had children, then there'd always be people around, and there would be no reason to cry like that. Even if she had to become old and ugly one day (although that was incomprehensible), at least she wouldn't be sad.

She pulled out one of her school notebooks, grabbed a pen, and wrote firmly in large letters:

How To Not Become Old, Ugly, and Sad
1. Be nice to Carl so that he'll help you when you need it.
2. Get married to a really nice guy.
3. Have at least three children, maybe four.
4. Make lots of friends
5. Create a different life.

That seemed to be at least the beginning of a plan. She pulled the paper from her notebook, folded it up, and put it in the tin candy box that her Aunt Esther had brought from Germany. She kept some old childhood treasures in there—bird's feathers that she had hoped would be magic, the leather collar of her pet cat who died the year before, and a tiny china poodle—and now she put the paper in there, sure that it would prove a valuable talisman.

"**H**oney, it's Carl."

It was Aunt Esther who called. Sheila had gone up to the Catskills with some college friends for a winter weekend; she had been saving a part of her salary (she worked weekends at her uncle's drug store) for weeks in order to afford it. So when the woman who owned the hotel knocked on her door to tell her there was a phone call, she knew that it had to be something serious.

The telegram had come a few minutes before. Carl had been somewhere in the Pacific, they didn't know where, exactly. The wording, though, was unambiguous: "...killed in action in performance of his duty..."

On the bus going home, all Sheila could think was that, somehow, it was her fault. She was heading toward that lonely, crying old woman and her brother had been killed to make that possible. If she hadn't been born, her brother wouldn't have died.

Her parents hugged her hard and frequently, but otherwise didn't say much. They sat on wooden boxes, the mirrors covered, while neighbors bustled in with food and sympathy. Sheila, unable to keep still, chatted with some of her cousins or sat in her bedroom, trying to study and pretend, for a few hours at least, that it wasn't true, that a mistake had been made, that a soldier would show up at the door with another telegram saying that her brother had actually been taken prisoner, or found floating on a life raft.

But nothing of the sort happened. The next day, they went to the synagogue. Sheila sat in the women's section, still pretending that everything was normal—and then her father stood to say kaddish. At that moment, she suddenly felt her throat constrict until she could hardly breathe; her face grew hot and her eyes wet. For the first time, she truly realized that the kid who had always been there when she was growing up, who had taken her to the playground and taught her how to cut a worm in half and told her which teachers to avoid, was gone forever. A step in her life had been taken, and there was no going back.

When she got home, she found the tin box, which she had hidden at the bottom of her closet, and got out the list. Almost ceremoniously, she drew a line through the first entry.

H er parents insisted on a large wedding, although Sheila thought that the money would be better stashed in their savings account than spent on a large hall and caterers. But when she suggested something more modest, her mother nearly burst into tears. "Never," she declared. "You deserve a nice wedding. It's seldom enough that we get to celebrate something, we should do it up proud."

Sheila felt she had chosen well. Sidney was a stocky but athletic young man, with the assurance of somebody who didn't care what others thought of him. Having spent the war years designing airplane parts, he found work after the war as the head of a manufacturing concern, and was ready to settle down. And he had a close-knit family made up of two parents and a married sister, all of whom welcomed Sheila with open arms.

Sidney seemed happy to go along with the elaborate preparations, although Sheila had always thought that grooms hated large weddings. "You don't understand," Becky, Sidney's sister, confided to her one day, as they were sorting out invitations. "In this family, if anyone doesn't get invited to a wedding or a funeral, it can result in generations of yelling over the dinner table. This way," she grinned, "everyone comes, eats your food, says 'Mazel tov,' and goes back to arguing about politics like usual."

Happy to accede to their wishes, Sheila allowed the two sets of parents to plan her wedding—and her future. Which was, she thought happily, bound to be rich, busy, and unburdened by the ghosts of ugly old ladies.

* * *

Their first child was a large, healthy and squalling girl named Debra after Sidney's maternal grandmother. Debra inherited her father's healthy physique and love of sports rather than her mother's introspection. Sheila was ecstatic; not only was she the mother of a lovely, thriving child, but her campaign seemed to be working. Sidney was moving up in his firm, they were on good terms with the rest of his family, and life was proceeding well.

The second child was a boy, much to the delight of Sidney, who, though he loved his daughter, was hoping for a son. They named the baby Carl after her brother.

The children grew with all the minor emergencies, small rebellions, and occasional bumps that follow the progress of reasonably well-adjusted kids. There were the two terrifying days when Debra ran away from home at the age of 14, and the night that Sheila screamed at Carl when she found a pint of vodka in the glove compartment of their car. But on the whole, things were going well.

Until Carl's senior year in high school, when his grades plummeted. At first, Sheila was convinced that he was just slacking off because he'd already made it into a couple of decent colleges. But it was more than that. Carl started spending more and more time lying on his bed, staring at the TV. She asked Debra, who had always been close to her younger brother, to intervene, but Debra said that when she asked him what was the matter, he just shrugged.

When he started digging a hole in the back garden because the voices told him to, his frantic parents took him to the hospital. After months of testing and visiting doctors, Carl was finally diagnosed with schizophrenia.

The breakup, when it finally came, wasn't a surprise to anyone. The arguments about Carl's illness had become long and nasty. Sheila sought refuge in hours of research on experimental treatments, while Sidney converted to a Christian sect called the Church of Good News and put his faith in prayer.

Eventually they were divorced. Sidney remarried less than a year later and moved to the Midwest, leaving Sheila with Carl, the house and a large portion of their savings in lieu of alimony. Debra, who had finished college and was embarking on a career as a magazine editor, refused several jobs so she could live nearby and help care for her brother.

Sheila found work transcribing recordings of financial meetings—it was tedious, but regular and paid reasonably well. The rest of the time, she took care of her son and continued to search for some kind of answer to his illness. Every once in a while, she brought out the tin box and stared at the list, her hands trembling slightly.

A year after the divorce, one of Carl's doctors found a medication that seemed to work. Carl stopped hearing the voices, got his long-deferred high school diploma, and took classes at a local two-year college. He was so improved that when Debra was offered a promising new job in San Francisco, Sheila encouraged her to take it. Debra thrived there, and brought a boyfriend with her when she visited for Thanksgiving. The sad old lady began to recede once again. Escape still seemed possible.

Then one night, Carl woke Sheila about 2 a.m. and earnestly asked her to lock her door, because his voices were angry with her and were starting to insist on unpleasant measures. Sheila knew better than to ask him to ignore the voices; instead, she told him to ask them why they were angry, and whether there was something they needed. Meanwhile, she locked away all the kitchen knives and called the local police, who knew about her son's condition.

About ten minutes later, just about the time Carl began looking frantically for his father's tool kit (because the voices told him that he needed a hammer), a police officer and a social worker came to the door. They managed to persuade Carl to come with them by telling him they would see if they could find a hardware store on the way. Sheila followed in her car, weeping.

Sidney flew in from Utah and helped her find a comfortable private facility that they felt they could afford. Debra called the day after they checked her brother in. She said she had talked to Carl and he denied having threatened anybody. She said that Sheila should have paid more attention to whether he was taking his medications, and that she had gotten Carl locked up only for her own convenience. Debra ended by declaring that she'd never speak to her mother again.

That night, Sheila got completely, thoroughly soused for the first time since she was in college. She put on the TV—weirdly, "It's a Wonderful Life" was playing—and, sick with fear, poured herself several juice-glasses of bourbon. She was terrified to look in the mirror lest she'd see the old lady staring back at her.

No, she thought, not yet. The kitchen didn't look quite right—although her memory of the dream wasn't all that clear anymore—and her hair was still a rich brown, although an occasional strand of silver could be found if she searched for it.

She took out the list and stared at it, dry-eyed.

"The hell with you, old lady," she finally told the TV set, as Jimmy Stewart went running through the town, looking for his now not-wife. "If I can't do anything to keep you away, in the meantime, I'm doing what I want to do."

Six months later, Sheila moved to a small town in upstate New York, where a couple of college friends had settled. She rented the top floor of a rambling old Civil War-era house and spent the rest of the money that was left from the sale of her home to lease a tiny store just off the main shopping avenue.

It started as a used bookstore (stocked from the boxes of science fiction and history books that Carl had bought almost obsessively), but after she was approached by a few of the locals at a party her friends gave, she started also stocking sweaters, painted teacups, and other crafts. Soon customers started asking for more gifts, so Sheila solicited a few professional craftspeople to let her sell their wares. Eventually, the remaining used books were moved to a small area at the back of the store, along with a coffee machine and some chairs.

She started holding book readings and hosting local musicians, and much to her surprise, found that the store was paying for itself within a couple of years, and was even pulling a small profit.

Sheila drove down to visit Carl every weekend—and when that became too arduous, every other weekend. At first she considered moving him to a facility closer to her, but he seemed so comfortable where he was that she decided to leave him alone. She wrote her daughter an email to that effect, and suggested that if Debra disliked how her brother was being treated, she was free to take over his care.

She lived quietly. She spent as little as possible, eating modestly but well, dressing in jeans and sweatshirts, and putting away as much money as she could against her eventual retirement. She found a neat little adult community nearby, and kept in touch with them in the hope that she could afford it when/if she needed to. She met with friends, babysat their grandchildren, joined one or two local civic associations, and accepted her role in the community as the somewhat weird but respectable woman from downstate.

She was, if not happy, then content.

One morning, Sheila was brushing her teeth when she looked in the mirror, stopped, and stared. It had been a busy week, and she had cancelled two appointments to have her hair trimmed and colored. Now, it shone silver in the artificial light.

She rinsed her mouth out and examined the image in the mirror critically. It didn't, she decided, look all that bad. If she cut her hair a little shorter, and dressed a little neater, she'd actually look distinguished. The idea made her smile.

With a start, Sheila remembered the small tin box that she had saved from her childhood, and that sat at the back of the linen closet where she had put it when she moved upstate. She went to the closet, reached in and pulled it out.

Wanting a cup of tea, she took the box into the kitchen and put it on the counter. She set some water to boil, and while she waited, opened the box. Amid several feathers, a small china poodle and a strip of rotting leather, she found the list.

She pulled it out and read it slowly, carefully, as though it were something written by a stranger. And then, helplessly, without meaning to, she began to cry—not for herself, but for the frightened young girl who had, with all the faith of adolescence, drawn up a plan for her life.

That's when the child appeared.

A small girl about four years old. Dressed in soft yellow pajamas decorated with tiny figures of Mickey Mouse and stained with what was probably chocolate ice cream. Sitting in the center of the kitchen table, thumb firmly in her mouth, staring at Sheila with an expression of dawning horror.

Sheila gaped at the little girl, wondering for a moment if she had gone completely insane. The small face screwed up into a grimace of fear, and began to wail.

Then she knew.

The child continued to weep, a despairing sound that rammed itself into Sheila's soul. She wiped her eyes, ran over and picked the little girl up, holding the child against her shoulder and bouncing her gently.

"There, there," Sheila murmured, stroking the silky hair, thinking of the hard tomorrows that would be faced by that fragile little being. "It will be all right. It isn't as bad as it looks. I promise."

The Red Dybbuk

Marilyn's story continues

2008

Marilyn wanders among the tombstones. The Long Island cemetery, a place for the Jewish dead for generations, is crowded with graves; appropriate, she thinks, for those who lived their lives crowded in the cities.

The grounds are so vast that guests come with maps in hand. Most drive to a specific section, park halfway on the grass (trying not to violate one of the graves), and make their obligatory visit, leaving small stones as markers of their presence. But Marilyn doesn't need a map—after losing both grandparents, her father and her brother, she usually parks at the cemetery's main gates and strolls to the section where her family lies.

It's hard to miss. Marilyn knows she's come to the right place when she spots, high against the early afternoon clouds, a statue of a woman in coveralls, fist thrust to the sky. She continues slowly, unhurried, careful to avoid a small funeral some yards away, where about 15 people stand and chant Kaddish. Otherwise, on this weekday afternoon, she is alone.

She walks through the small, rusty gate that marks the beginning of the section. Other areas were sponsored by synagogues or organizations based around whatever Eastern European town the family escaped from (one of the first tasks on any immigrant Jew's list was to make sure they had somewhere respectable to bury their dead). But this piece of land was bought by a union of fur workers. The union was eventually purged of its radicalism during the 1950s when union officials began to court respectability—and needed to avoid the taint of being Communist fellow-travelers. But the graves, and the memories they evoke, remain.

She runs her hands along faded carvings of Jewish stars, upraised hands, and hammers and sickles, and haltingly reads Yiddish poems by long-dead writers foretelling the triumph of the working class. Finally, she stops by a modest black stone that has no verse or statue, but just two names, two dates, and two small, oval black-and-white photos. A round-faced young woman and a stocky, balding man stare solemnly out at a long-dead photographer.

"Grandma," she says to the woman, and then, in halting Yiddish, "Bubbe, what have you done to our baby?"

"I know you're not going to like this, but I'm leaving college."

Marilyn stopped chopping celery and stared at her daughter. Keep calm, she told herself. You knew that something was coming. She's 18, she's the age at which she's going to make you insane.

"May I ask why?" Marilyn said, trying to keep her tone even.

Annie, her baby, her only child from a marriage that faded long ago, was still not fully grown in Marilyn's eyes, but all long legs and arms and flyaway hair. The girl reached out and took a piece of celery in an obvious attempt to be casual, but Marilyn could see her hand was trembling slightly. "Well, last weekend I went to great-grandma's grave—you remember, you told me that I should go there to see some family history? And I saw all the graves of the people who spent their lives fighting for what they believed in, and I became ashamed of how I was wasting my life. I'm going to live here for a while, take some courses in Somali and French, maybe in farming or first aid. Refugees are starving while we play student and teacher; I can't sit by while that happens."

"I see." Marilyn put down the knife, not only so she could give her daughter her full attention, but because she suspected that it was not the best time to have a knife in her hand. "What brought this on?"

Annie shrugged. "I just realized that I was wasting my life sitting around in classrooms listening to a bunch of overpaid bourgeois tutors tell me how to spend my life as a willing victim of American consumerism."

Since Annie had, until recently, been a very willing consumer of media players, computer games, expensive shoes and the occasional tattoo, Marilyn was a bit worried. Also, since when was her daughter using words like "bourgeois"?

She placed a solicitous hand against the girl's forehead. "Are you feeling well?" she asked. "Are you running a temperature?"

Annie pulled away irritably. "I'm fine," she said. "Really, mom!" and she flounced off, taking a loud bite out of the celery stalk.

"**S**he's going through a phase," said Marilyn's sister-in-law Joan when they met at the Ginger Cafe the next Sunday. "Don't you remember what you were like at that age? You can't do anything by degrees—you have to immediately jump in the deep end. It's like that vampire TV show that she and her friend Rachel are so nuts about and can't stop discussing. Now Annie's added politics to the mix." She stirred her coffee thoughtfully. "It could be worse. She could have found religion and ended up sleeping with some middle-aged guru out in Oklahoma like Sarah's daughter."

"Bite your tongue," Marilyn said, shocked and appalled. "My baby wouldn't do something like that."

"Your baby is a human American girl, and so is going to do at least one or two crazy things before she settles down and becomes a boring adult," said Joan, smiling. "If all she does is get a social conscience and perform a few good deeds, all to the better."

Marilyn, whose mother had lost her teaching job during the McCarthy era and who, as a result, could never rid herself of a sneaking fear of doing anything that might place her name in a file somewhere, just nodded and mentally crossed her fingers. Hopefully, the phase was indeed a phase, and would be over before Annie could get herself in trouble. Or actually leave college.

Marilyn sits cross-legged in the narrow grassy lane in front of the grave, slips off her backpack, reaches in, and pulls out an old, perilously yellowing album. She places it on her lap and opens it to the first photo. Three children stand stiffly in uncomfortable poses, carefully groomed for what must have been a special occasion for turn-of-the-20th-century youngsters.

"You want a prayer?"

She looks up. An elderly man in a worn faded suit, a small yarmulke askew on his balding head, stares at her disapprovingly. "You want a Kaddish?"

Of course, she thinks. As a woman, she can't say Kaddish; for a small fee, this man will say it for her. She is tempted for a moment—

what could it hurt?—but thinks then of what her grandmother would say. "No, thank you," she replies, putting a slight edge in her voice to warn him not to press his case. He shrugs eloquently and moves on.

Marilyn looks back at the photo. A ten-year-old boy in short pants and cap holds the hand of his sister, eight years old and already showing the stubborn press of lips that, Marilyn remembers, lasted into old age. The girl, in turn, clutches the hand of her younger brother, a toddler with long curls and a sweet smile.

All gone now. They, and most of their children.

Marilyn puts out a finger and lightly touches the head of the little girl. "I wanted to bring you the blue ribbon that your friend gave you," she says. "But I couldn't find it. I'm sorry."

The girl glares back defiantly.

The police station was a lot less frightening than Marilyn had imagined it to be, although it was just as seedy. The lawyer hired by the organization for which Annie had been demonstrating seemed to be a nice young man; Marilyn took his card and made a mental note to call her own lawyer when she got home.

It only took about 15 or 20 minutes for Annie, pale but determined, to emerge from a far door and walk over to her mother. A bored sergeant gave Marilyn a receipt for her bail. "Make sure she shows up for the hearing," he said, staring with tired disapproval at his pen, which seemed to be misbehaving, "And don't worry about it—the judge will most likely just throw a fine at them and lecture them for a few minutes, depending on how busy he is. Here's your receipt. Next."

It wasn't until they were in the car and at least a mile from the police station that Marilyn felt secure enough to say, "For God's sake, whatever possessed you to confront those protesters?"

Annie stared ahead stubbornly, with a new set to her shoulders that Marilyn found weirdly familiar. "Prejudice against any group is prejudice against us all. Those small-minded bigots claim to be against terrorism, but they are using a tragedy as an excuse to terrorize those in our society who don't conform to their narrow definition of what is American."

"Why didn't you just start a Facebook group, or send some emails to your representatives, or do something digital?" asked

Marilyn, wearily. "Why did you have to start tearing up their signs? Didn't you think that somebody might try to stop you? Like, say, the police?"

Her daughter shrugged and continued to look out at the road in front of them. There was a haunted look in her eyes that make Marilyn's stomach clench.

"Honey," she said, trying to keep her voice even. "Are you all right? Did anything happen in jail that you need to tell me about?"

"I'm fine," Annie said. "Just fine. Everybody was very polite. Except for one miserable son of a bitch who felt it necessary to push one of our group so she fell and skinned her knee. Of course, he chose the woman of color to pick on, the goddamn racist schmuck, a feier zol im trefen."

Marilyn swerved the car into the other lane and almost clipped an SUV, whose driver cursed her silently behind his windows. She took a breath, kept her eyes on the road, and said steadily, "Honey, where did you learn that phrase?"

"What phrase?"

"The one you just used. 'A feier zol im trefen.' It means 'A fire should burn him.' Where did you learn that?"

Annie closed her eyes. "I don't know what you're talking about. I'm tired, Mom. I'm going to take a nap, if you don't mind. We can do the whole mother-daughter you're-in-trouble-thing later, okay?"

That evening, Marilyn sat on her front porch and stared out into the yard, where a few of the first fireflies of the season were trying out their neon. The sound of her very American daughter cursing out the police in Yiddish kept running through her brain. Then something occurred to her. "I suppose it's possible," she told the insects. She pulled out her mobile phone. "Hey, mom," she said when it was picked up on the other end. "Can I ask you something?"

There was a pause. "What's wrong?"

"Nothing's wrong, mom. I just wanted to ask you. When you were babysitting Annie, when she was small, how much Yiddish did you use with her?"

"What's wrong with Annie? Is she all right?"

"She's fine. I'm fine. We're all fine. But she used a Yiddish expression today that I'd never heard her use, and I was wondering—did you ever use the expression 'a feier zol im trefen' in front of her?"

There was a short offended silence. "Of course not! You know I'd
never curse in front of a child. Your grandmother Chana, may she
rest in peace, used that expression a lot, especially when she was talking about her enemies. And she had a lot of enemies. But she died
before Annie was born, didn't she?" A pause—her mother's memory
wasn't what it used to be these days. "Of course, she did. Annie was
named after her—how could I forget something like that? Although
why you Americanized her name to Annie, I'll never understand.
And she has your grandmother's eyes."

The next album has photos of Marilyn's mother, in calf-length
dresses and high heels, dark lips that would have been bright
red if the photos had been in color, grinning at long-dead young
men in jaunty WW II uniforms. Marilyn turns to the last page: her
mother's mother, now middle-aged, hands thrust into the pockets of
a long fur coat as if to keep them still. There is a look of grim satisfaction on her face—she is obviously determined to enjoy the moment
if it kills her.

"You loved that fur coat, didn't you, bubbe?" Marilyn says out
loud. "You always said that Grandpa had ruined his hands curing
furs for rich women to wear, and you were determined that at least
one of those coats would end up on the back of somebody who actually deserved one. And then you gave it to me, your beloved granddaughter, and I refused to wear it because it was seal, and they were
clubbing seals in the Antarctic. Cause versus cause, and who wins in
the end?"

Living and dead smile at one another.

Marilyn had finally gotten around to reading that week's NY
Times Magazine section, one eye on the umpteenth rerun of
Casablanca on cable, when the front door opened. "Annie, is that you?"
she called out. "Did you remember to pick up the milk I asked you to
get?" There was no answer, just some footsteps in the direction of the
bathroom. Marilyn stood. "You forgot, didn't you? Was it that hard
to just write down . . . " and she stopped short at the bathroom door.

Annie was sitting on the closed toilet seat, a bloody washcloth
pressed to her temple. There was dried blood under her nose and
around her mouth, a cut on the bridge of her nose, and scrapes all
along the side of her face and left arm. She was a mess.

"Oh, my god." Marilyn ran over and pulled the washcloth from her daughter's head. The cut was long and ugly looking, but didn't look very deep. Marilyn opened the bathroom closet, grabbed a roll of gauze, dampened a piece and began to carefully clean off her daughter's face. "Honey, what happened? Are you dizzy? Are you feeling sick? I think we'd better get you to the hospital–"

"I'm fine, mom," said Annie wearily. "Really. I just . . . We were just trying to keep some squatters from being evicted from an abandoned building, and we thought the man who owned it would at most call the cops, but instead these three thugs, these shtarkers, came and threw us out, and I fell down the stairs . . . ." She started to cry quietly.

Marilyn didn't bother with any more details. She got her pocketbook and her coat, guided her daughter to the car (there was no resistance) and took her to the emergency room. She told the receptionist and the doctors that Annie had been in the city, and tripped at the top of some steps, and was brought home by friends (all of which was true, in a sense). Annie needed a couple of stitches in her head, and there was a chance her nose might be broken. ("Let the swelling go down," the doctor said, not all that interested in what to him was a minor case, "and then go see your regular doctor.") But that was all.

They got back around 1 a.m. The entire time—sitting in the waiting room, in the examination room, in x-ray—Marilyn just talked about everyday things: Calling Annie's friends to tell them she'd be staying home for the next couple of days, whether Annie could still go on a march that she had planned to attend in D.C. that weekend, Marilyn's plans to visit a cousin the following month . . .

Only once, when they were driving back from the hospital, did Marilyn venture a question. "Baby," she asked, "why did you go there? Didn't you realize what kind of people you were dealing with?"

Annie took a deep breath, and for the first time that evening, there was a tremor in her voice. "I don't know, mom," she said. "I just. . . . I don't know. It's just that . . . well, it's just that I have to help, I have to do these things. I just . . . "

Then suddenly she lifted her head and looked directly at her mother. "Somebody has to relieve the miseries that are inflicted by the ruling classes," she said, clearly and steadily. "If your generation chooses to ignore these ills, then it is up to mine. If your values don't include working for change and for the betterment of humanity, then mine do."

Marilyn stared back at her daughter. The girl's voice had acquired the Russian Jewish lilt that Marilyn remembered from her childhood, the same intonations that her grandmother had used all her life.

The last album is Marilyn's, from her childhood and young adulthood. She pages through well-remembered photos. Her father sits in their living room playing Woody Guthrie tunes on an acoustic guitar to a crowd of fascinated children. A tiny version of her brother Morris (now dead of the same cancer that killed their father, dammit) stares in solemn fascination at an electric train. Long-haired college kids dance enthusiastically in Washington Square Park. And a stocky woman in her 60s with white hair stands in a queue of older folks and students and grins sardonically at the camera.

"That was the afternoon I took you to see that Yiddish film," Marilyn tells her grandmother. "*The Dybbuk*. From the Ansky play? I'm sure you must remember it. About the poor yeshiva bochur, the scholar, who is not permitted to marry the girl he is promised to because of the greed of her parents, and who dies and then inhabits the body of his beloved. It is a fable, you said, of how money corrupts the older generation, and how only the dedication and passion of the younger generation can overcome their greed."

She drops the folder, kneels, and puts her hand against the stone. "But, bubbe, when the scholar Channon inhabits the body of Leah, it is with her consent, and it is two young people coming together after they have been told they can't marry. You are of another generation, another world, and you can't know what it's like for the children of Annie's generation."

There is a brief flutter as a nearby pigeon is startled away. Leaves crunch behind her and Marilyn looks up, embarrassed to be caught by some stranger. But it's Annie, standing tall and angry amid the tombstones and the dead.

Marilyn quickly stands. "Honey, I told you to pick me up around 5 p.m. It can't be that late yet."

"Is the fight all that different, even today?" Annie asks in quick, unaccented Yiddish. "Or has it simply been twisted by men in power who have used their money and influence to make socialism a curse word, to make cooperation and consensus a thing of the past, to make each worker a pawn in every government's fight to stay in power? Look around you. Are people not losing their jobs? Not being driven from their homes? How many people around the world have become statistics, irrelevant except as weapons in the wars of those who consider themselves better?"

Marilyn answers in English, in the language she knows best. She needs to be fluent. She is fighting for her daughter. "No, of course not," she says. "Things are as bad as they were—if not worse. But do you really know what is important in this world? In your day it was the bosses and the birth of the unions. In my mother's, it was civil rights and red-baiting. In mine, it was Vietnam. And what is it in Annie's? Global warming? The Middle East? Gay rights? Or are you going to drag her into causes that she wouldn't have followed herself, just because they are your causes?"

Marilyn finds herself starting to cry, and bangs her fist on her thigh, trying to keep her composure. "Bubbe, you had your life. You fought the good fight, you joined with your comrades to keep the bosses and the police and the politicians at bay. You kept the unions going, you pulled your family through the Depression, you helped women get birth control. But your fight isn't her fight."

"It is all the same fight!"

"Is it? And even if some of the battles are the same, is she ready for it? Before you appeared, my daughter was in college studying, preparing herself for whatever her life will be. Who knows what she may be able to do years from now? Maybe she'll become a doctor or a lawyer or an activist. Maybe she'll create websites or work with technologies that we can't even imagine. Or maybe she'll choose to work quietly and raise children and have a happy, safe life. Why would you deny her that? Is she worth less than any of the people you fought for?"

Silence.

"Leave her. Now."

"I can't." Annie/Chana—both and one—cries out in pain and sorrow. "I need to work! Your grandfather Abe sits with his friends and plays cards, but I can't just rest and let the world go on the way it does. It is a sort of hell, and when my great-granddaughter, the darling, the jewel, came one day to visit me and talk to me, what else could I do? She welcomed me, and I came. What else could I do?"

Marilyn takes another step, until she is close enough to reach out and touch her daughter's—her grandmother's—cheek. "Leave her, bubbe. Let her make her own life."

She pauses for a moment. "Take mine."

Annie steps back. "Mirele, what are you saying? Are you sure?"

"Yes. I am." Marilyn turns and looks out over the cemetery. "When I grew up, I knew what had happened to you, to my mother. I wanted to live a safe life—I got a safe job, married a safe man, divorced him in a safe manner, lived in a safe neighborhood and brought up a lovely, safe child. Now she's ready to go off on her own, and what do I have? My daughter is leaving, my husband is gone, life is starting to run short and I haven't done anything significant on my own, something so people will say, 'Look at what she did, how she helped.' I want that. I want to make a difference. And if I can't do it on my own, I'll do it with you."

She stretches out her arms. "Take me, bubbe. Live with me in my skin. We'll go out and together we'll challenge the evil that still stalks our world. You'll teach me how to fight, and I'll teach you how to live." Marilyn suddenly wants to laugh, as though she's found something she didn't know she'd lost. "The bastards won't know what hit them."

There is a moment in which everything is still. And then her daughter/grandmother smiles, a lovely, joyous smile. "Come, my sweet child," she sings. "Come, my angel, my little bird, my Mirele. Let us change the world together."

The
Book of
Sophia's Family

Waiting for Jakie

A story of Gretl Held Weissbaum,
Sophia's daughter-in-law

1997

I like the blue pills best. I have others, of course—the purple ones, and the green and yellow ones. The tiny white ones? Those are just for blood pressure, and all they really do, in my opinion, is give a living to the drug companies. Not that I have anything against drug companies, God forbid; after all, they not only allow me to face each day, but gave my son Benjamin a decent living for many years until the AIDS got him, poor boy.

Anyway, the blue pills are the ones I take when I'm feeling nervous or depressed, which is most of the time. I tell the doctors this, and they try to put me on other medications, more long term, they call it, but a week goes by and I'm feeling like taking a steak knife to my wrists, so I throw away the new ones and go back to the ones that at least keep me operating on, as Willy used to say, all six cylinders.

And sometimes, if I've taken just a little bit more than I'm supposed to—not much, only a few more milligrams, nothing, an extra pill or more, who would begrudge it?—then, if I squint my eyes a little and let the living room furniture blur a bit, then sometimes, if I'm lucky, I can see Jakie. Not very clear, I admit, and usually only a little, but it's him. It's him.

And I miss him so much. Our time together was short, so short, but it was like a lifetime together. It should have been a lifetime together.

Usually he's sitting in the big stuffed chair where Willy used to sit, with his long legs stretched out in front, and a book or a newspaper in his large hands. I love when I can see Jakie. I could just sit and look at him forever. He's tall, and thin, and his hair is thick and brown. And his eyes—oy, his eyes. Those eyes are what I used to dream about after he left—large and dark and ironic. Like my father's. Which is why I first trusted him, that day when he and the other Americans came walking into the camp.

But enough of me.

He doesn't always read, Jakie. Sometimes he leans his chin on his hand and stares off to the side, his head nodding slightly, up and down. He's listening to music, I think, maybe one of the Italian operas he was so fond of. Once, one of the girls found an old scratched recording of *Rigoletto* in a bombed-out house somewhere, and I traded her a full meal for it and gave it to Jakie, and he found an old wind-up Victrola and brought it to his quarters. As soon as the music started, *La donna è mobile*, all the other soldiers started snorting through their noses like horses, as though Jakie listening to opera was the funniest thing they'd seen.

But I saw how the record helped him go away from the war, and I knew that this was the mark of a truly civilized man. I know—I grew up in a beautiful, rich home outside of Berlin, and we attended concerts, and went on holiday in Switzerland. When we went to the theatre, men and women in lovely clothing would nod respectfully at my parents and my uncle and smile at me, and I would feel so special. Jakie may have been born in America, but he too was special.

I don't think he sees me, Jakie, when he sits in Willy's chair. If I thought that, I'd die. Me with my bloated body and thin hair and god! I used to be so beautiful.

Even right after the camp, when I looked like a scarecrow, my hair still short and dry and no meat on my bones, Jakie used to tease me and tell me that I looked like Veronica Lake. And I'd laugh at him and say no, I'm too skinny. And finally he came to the barracks one day, where we were waiting to find out what would happen and where we should go, and he told me to get two girlfriends, we were "going out on the town."

And he got me a beautiful dress, and a nice pair of shoes—I never asked where he got them. And, would you believe it, lipstick—and three of us girls got together, and brushed our hair until it hurt, and scrubbed, and colored our lips and a little on our cheeks. We went to a local cafe where Jakie and two other boys whose names I don't remember, we sat and the Americans gave the proprietor, a German pig who stared at us as though he wondered why we weren't still in the camp where we belonged, they gave him money and told him they wanted wine and sausages, and we all drank, and ate, and tried to understand each other, and one of the Americans said something that made Jakie slap him on the head, and they all laughed, and when I asked Jakie in German what the boy said (because Jakie spoke Yiddish, we could understand each other after a fashion), he wouldn't say.

I was alone, and my family was dead, and we were diseased Jewish whores from the camps, but we ate, and drank, and pretended we were regular girls out on dates with three boys who would try to steal a kiss and then deliver us back to our parents. Oh, god. I was so happy that evening.

And when we went walking in the fields afterwards, I kissed him, and tried to give him of my own free will what I had been forced to give up for the last three years. He kissed me back gently as if I were a child and told me that I deserved more than a few minutes on the ground amid the dead stalks of last year's crops.

I let him take me back to the barracks. The two other girls told me I was an idiot. And they were right.

Because in the morning, Jakie and the lovely boy soldiers were gone. And although he had promised to write, I never heard from him again. (Years later, Willy said he could probably find my soldier—I had told him some of it, but not all—but I told him no. It was too late. I was married, and older, and didn't want to know.)

Eventually, I found a job as a secretary to one of the Red Cross officials. And one day Willy walked in, quiet and clean and polite, in a beautiful suit that made him look like a banker or a movie star, although he wasn't really tall enough. I thought then, what was a Jew doing in a suit like that, with so much meat on him? I thought, a collaborator, a bastard who sold Jewish lives in trade for his own. Later, I found out he had escaped and worked for the OSS, the American spies. And what did he do during the war? He never told me.

But he looked so like the boys I used to see at the skiing lodges where we spent our school holidays that my breath caught in my throat. And it was the same for Willy—he told me later that when he first saw me, for one moment he was walking into his father's office where, he said, his sister Isabeau (who later managed to escape to America, damn her) used to help with the paperwork on her summer vacation. So we found each other in a mist of dreams of the lost.

That is why I don't like admitting that it is Jakie I see, and not Willy. After all, Willy was my dear husband for nearly 50 years, and it was his chair, and he was the one who took care of me and tried to help me. When we were living in Berlin after the war, and I found out I was pregnant and told Willy that I would kill the baby and myself before I would let it be born in that damned country, didn't he tell his bosses that he had to leave Europe, and bring me to America? And when one day I started crying and couldn't stop, didn't he take me to that doctor who gave me those pills and said they'd help me? And if they didn't help me the way he'd planned, if I needed to take more of them over the years, was it his fault? He meant it for the best.

And now Willy is dead. My poor Benjamin, our lovely boy, our hope for the future, is dead. And Jakie, if he is still alive, is probably married to some smart American woman and has smart American children. And has forgotten all about me.

But I don't care.

I can still see my Jakie in my living room, thin and dark and laughing like when he took me to dinner. But he is misty, like a dream. So I limp to the bathroom, and find my pills, all the different colors and shapes, and take them back to the living room with a glass of water. I take two more pills, two more, and wait for a few minutes, then I squint my eyes and concentrate like I used to concentrate over my French lessons as a girl. And suddenly, I don't have to pretend any more—Jakie is here, sharp and clear and looking at me with that saucy American grin on his face. I stand, and so does he, and I take his hand and lead him back to the cafe.

And we are sitting at the table again, and I can hear the chatter of the other two couples. My stomach is full, and I am wearing a nice dress and real shoes, and I take Jakie's hand, and he takes one of the wine bottles off the table, and we stand and walk into the forest while his friends laugh and cheer and call out things in English that would probably have made my mother faint. But I don't care—when we are far enough away, I kiss Jakie hard on the lips. He tells me that we have the rest of our lives, but I know better this time. I will have this moment, this lovely moment.

After, Jakie strokes my hair, and touches my lips, and says he loves me, and will find out how he can get permission to marry me and take me to America. But now, he says, he's hungry, and he goes off to find some food, and I sit in the pine needles and straighten my clothes, and take out the comb he gave me to fix my hair. A large gray pigeon flutters down and stares at me. "Sorry," I tell it, "I don't have any food with me," and I think how strange it is that I can even consider giving crumbs to a wild bird.

There is still some wine in the bottle. I raise it to the strange God who killed so many but let me live, and drink it down.

And then, out of the corner of my eye, I see an old woman who is standing a little way off. She is a terrible old woman; her hair is white and thinning, her figure is thick and flabby underneath the cotton dress; she wears slippers on her nasty bare feet and only a single gold ring on her wrinkled hands. She smiles at me. "Now you are happy," she says.

Happy? Stupid old woman—how can I be happy? I am thin and used up. My family is dead, my childhood is gone, and I have spent three years screwing Nazi soldiers so that I could live.

The old woman starts to cry. "I thought this was the right time," she sobs, and I can't stand it, so I stand and walk into the forest. It is an old, beautiful forest, full of moss and thick trees. They remind me of the tall firs near our home, and the hours I spent as a girl playing there, and dreaming about my future. In the wood next to my uncle's house. Before.

My uncle Jacob's large home with the red shutters and large wooden door, and the fat cat who would not stay in the house no matter how often we tried to shut her in, and Peter the butler who frightened me because he was so tall and stern, but who would let me sit in the kitchen and watch the servants prepare dinner. This morning my father and my uncle were quieter than usual after the meal, and I knew it was because of the letter my uncle had received that morning, and that it had something to do with the political situation. They talked together until my mother came over, and touched my father on the shoulder. He smiled at her, and then we played cards because it was raining outside.

The rain stops, and although my mother tells me to put on my galoshes, it's still wet outside, I run outside and stand in the grass. It is lovely; in the sunlight, the wet grass is as bright a green as I have ever seen in my life.

There is a noise, and I look down the wide drive, and there are men in uniforms approaching, the sun bouncing off their belt buckles and buttons. I'm wearing my favorite dress, the one that my uncle just bought me for my 13th birthday party, and I'm so glad that I'm wearing it now because there is a handsome soldier behind the four men who is dressed differently than the others. His uniform is dirty and creased and he needs a shave, but he has lovely brown hair and nice eyes.

The adults have come out too, despite the wet. My mother says my name, low and with a tremor in her voice that is so strange I turn and look at her. Her face has gone still and she is standing so stiffly that for a moment she doesn't look like my mother. She is motioning me to come back to the house in quick, angry waves of her hand, as though she is afraid somebody will see her.

My father and my uncle are closer, though. They have walked down the wide front drive, and have now stopped, waiting. My father stands a little behind my uncle, his pipe in his mouth. His hands are clasped behind his back. My uncle, shorter and stouter, is shaking his head just a little, the way he does when I come to him with some complaint about my mother, his hands pushed deep into his pockets.

Just beyond them is a strange woman standing on the grass, wearing a flowered dress that is too big for her. She is very thin and has funny short hair and she is smiling at me. Nobody else seems to notice her—maybe because they are all looking at the soldiers.

"Now you are happy," she says, and that sounds strange at first. But then I realize that the sun is shining, and I am with my family, and looking forward to my birthday, and only worried about my algebra homework and whether I'll ever grow breasts.

"She can't be happy. Jakie isn't here," and it isn't the young woman talking, but an old woman who looks a bit like the beggar in town who sells eggs by the road. She is very ugly, but then she smiles at me too, so to be polite I smile back.

My mother calls my name louder but instead I run to my uncle and take him by the arm. Before I can ask, he says, quietly, not looking at me, "Darling, go to your mama. Now, please."

The child pauses, not knowing what to do. She looks back at the soldiers and squints at something—and there, down the driveway, as insubstantial as hope, is a tall young man with dark hair and eyes, and suddenly it's hard to breathe. "Jakie!" we scream. "Save me!" But he is not alone—he is holding the hand of a stranger, a woman with knowing American eyes, and he is not looking at us.

We two, the camp whore and the crazy old woman, remember running to our mother's side, watching as the world suddenly changed, but we know that this time she will not go. We watch as the young girl in her first grownup dress stands and holds her uncle's arm, her hands only trembling a little. She is young enough to be brave; to believe, to the bottom of her soul, that nothing really bad can happen.

The old woman is sniffling again—doesn't she ever stop?—and her nose is all red. "I thought he would save me from this," the old woman moans. "From the memories. I thought he would save me."

I stroke her hair, and remember the lipstick, and the cafe, and Jakie's kind eyes. "I know," I tell her. "I know. But we will have to do it ourselves."

She nods, and wipes her eyes. "You are right," she says. "Of course. It's all up to us."

My uncle has stepped forward, and one of the clean German soldiers, an officer I think, takes a gun from his pocket and points it at him just like the gangsters in the American movies. I know I should run back, but I won't leave my uncle. "You fucking Jew," the officer says, calm as if he were just saying hello, "You fucking rich Jew, you think you own the world?"

My uncle pushes me away. "Back to the house," he says, his teeth clenched, every word distinct. "Now! Do you hear?"

The soldiers are scaring me, so I look at the two women. They are crying about something, but then they hold their arms out to me. "Come, sweetheart," says the old lady. "It's a beautiful morning. Forget the handsome American soldier. He will not save you. Come to us—come and show us your lovely new dress."

I walk towards them, passing in front of my uncle. There is a loud sharp sound from far away, and it all stops.

In the Gingerbread House

A story of Isabeau Weissbaum Stein, Sophia's daughter

1928

"Here we are, darling. Look—isn't it exciting? This is where all the actors are when they're not on the stage!"

Isabeau's Papa and her big brother Willy have just taken her to what they explained is the backstage of the Berlin State Opera, and Isabeau (named, her mother told her, after a beautiful medieval Bavarian queen) doesn't like it at all. She is just four years and six months and five days old, and although she is trying to be brave, there are too many strange adults around, some wearing bright costumes, some wearing ordinary clothing, some with their faces stiff and strange under heavy makeup. "Why is that man wearing lipstick?" Willy asks, and Papa says, "So he can be seen more clearly on the stage. He'll take it off before he goes out of the theatre. Don't point, Wilhelm, it's rude."

Isabeau doesn't like it here. It's loud and frightening. She wants to go home, which has deep carpets, and the servants speak in quiet tones, and she can play with her bunny and her music box and listen to Grandmama's pet bird making comfortable noises in its sleep.

"This way, Isabeau," and her father steers her gently through the confusing mass of grownups. Her brother, who kicked her under the seat when she started to cry during the third act of *Hansel and Gretel*, now stares around wide-eyed. Perhaps, she thinks, he won't take the head off her new doll like he threatened, because he is now obviously very happy with this strange adventure.

"Look," Willy says, pointing excitedly. "That must be the gingerbread house!" Four men carry a large, flat thing that looks like the front of a house. At least, it doesn't look flat, but the men are carrying it like it's flat. It makes Isabeau's head ache.

Her father places her hand in her brother's. "Wilhelm," he says, and his voice has that slightly louder ring that means he's about to give an order, "you hold your sister's hand, and don't move. I want to find you both here when I get back. Are you listening to me, Wilhelm?"

"Yes, Papa," says Willy in that eager way that says that he's really interested in what's happening here, and he'll even mind his baby sister if it means that he can stay a little longer. Isabeau isn't happy about being left alone in this forest of adult legs with her brother, who is a big boy but sometimes can forget about her when something exciting happens.

"Willy," she asks, "where did Papa go?"

Willy is so consumed by the activity around him that he temporarily forgets how much he hates to be questioned by his little sister. "He'll be right back," he says. But when she sniffles a bit, he reasserts himself. "Issa, don't cry. Papa will take us home, and I want to see everything. Issa, if you cry, I'll hit you." But Isabeau can't help it, she's tired and frightened. In desperation, Willy looks around.

"Look Issa!" he cries, and bending quickly, picks something shiny off the floor and puts it in her hand. "I found a magic jewel. It probably fell off the dress of the witch. It will protect you, even when Papa isn't here. Look, Issa, isn't it pretty?"

Isabeau (who hates being called Issa) opens her hand and looks at a blue-green gem, glittering and reflecting the lights in the ceiling. There is a small loop on the back where it was sewn to the witch's dress. "It really is magic, isn't it?" she breathes.

"Yes. So you don't have to cry now. Here." Willy, impressed with his own ingenuity, reaches into his pocket and brings out a grimy piece of string. He puts the string through the loop and ties it around Isabeau's neck. "Now you won't lose it."

"What kind of magic does it do?" Isabeau asks excitedly, but Willy is back to filling his eyes with the activity around him. "Look," he whispers. "Look at that man with the toolbox swearing at all the actors. I want to be like that when I grow up."

Isabeau is nothing if not stubborn. "Willy, what will it do?" She knows that if she pitches her voice just high enough, her brother will be forced to pay attention. He'll either answer her question or hit her—and in a room full of grown-ups, he's less likely to resort to the latter. "Willy, what will the magic jewel do?"

"It will tell you stories," says Willy desperately. "But only if you keep quiet!"

Isabeau lifts the jewel on its string and puts it to her ear, but she doesn't hear anything, not even as much as the sea shell that her Mama gave her last summer. "Willy!" but her brother is back to staring at the actors. She clutches at his hand.

He'll long to become a stage actor but will instead act various parts as a prisoner and then as an undercover OSS operative, whispers the jewel. *He'll suffer a stroke at age 75, leaving behind a dying son and a suicidal wife with a faded number etched on the inside of her forearm.*

"Willy," Isabeau whispers. "The magic jewel is telling me stories. What's a stroke?"

"Oh, isn't she adorable!" A lady in a beautiful blue costume with sparkles around her eyes and filmy stuff in her hair crouches in front of Isabeau so that they are nearly eye to eye. "Hello. What is your name?"

Isabeau is too struck by the beautiful lady to say anything, but Willy pokes her in the side, and she says, "Isabeau."

"A little young for you, isn't she, Lena?" says a thin man passing by, and the lady says, "Shut up, idiot," in a voice totally unlike her other. She turns back to the children.

"Isabeau is such a lovely name! Just right for such a lovely little girl." She leans forward. "Will you give me a kiss, Isabeau?"

Isabeau nods, puts the jewel to one ear, and leans forward to press her lips against the lady's cheek. She tastes of perfume and a strange chalky substance, and there is a small mole just under her ear. The jewel whispers. *She will become the mistress of a reasonably successful SS officer and travel with him to Paris, where she will live well until they escape to Berlin under less-than-ideal circumstances. She will be shot trying to protect an emerald earring from two Russian soldiers.*

"Isabeau!" It's her Papa's voice, and the lady smiles at her once again and goes away. Isabeau eagerly looks around. Her Papa kneels down next to her. "Remember the witch in the opera? The one that frightened you so much?"

Isabeau nods. "She was mean. She tried to hurt the children."

"And you remember I told you that she was only acting? That it was just a story? That she was just pretending to hurt the children?"

He reaches over and strokes her hair. The voice whispers. *He will die, naked and terrified, clutching the hand of his beloved wife Sophia, flung into a hole in the ground by the force of the bullets. His last thought will be gratitude that his children have escaped.*

Isabeau starts to cry. She throws herself at her father, clutching desperately at his neck.

Her father sighs. "God in heaven. Children," he mutters, gathers her up and stands, holding her in his large, strong arms. "Darling, listen to me. You trust your Papa, don't you? Well, I'm going to prove to you that the witch you saw isn't a real witch, but just somebody play pretending to be a witch. But you have to be a nice, quiet little girl, and not get upset, or scared. Remember, nothing bad can happen as long as you're with me. All right?"

"Yes, Papa." How about you? Isabeau wants to ask, still gulping back her tears, but her father is calling for her brother, and telling him to get over here, now, Wilhelm! Her father is so big and firm and real, so in charge of everything around him, that Isabeau decides magic can be wrong sometimes. Perhaps, she thinks, if she tries to take care of her father like he takes care of her, those bad things will go away.

They pass through the crowd of strange costumed women and men to a small hallway, through a door and into a room with a lot of tables and mirrors and lights. Somebody is sitting at one of the tables, pulling the nose off his face, and Isabeau would run away but she is still being held by her Papa.

"Isabeau," her Papa says, "This is Herr Weisskopf. He is a famous actor and singer. You remember the witch that scared you so much? He was pretending to be the witch. Now, say hello politely."

He puts her down, and Isabeau makes her best curtsy. She knows she does it well; Grandmama has told her so. "Good evening, Herr Weisskopf," she says.

Herr Weisskopf spins in his chair and smiles at Isabeau. His face is a different color than his nose; he has funny drawn-on eyebrows and bright red lips, and a big black spot drawn on one cheek. He is wearing a bright green robe, and his hair is flat against his skull. Isabeau knows about that; when her Papa wears his Shabbat hat and then takes it off, his hair looks funny in the same way, pressed against his head by the weight.

"Hello, Isabeau," says Herr Weisskopf. "I'm very pleased to meet you. I hope I didn't scare you too much." He has a pleasant voice, low and musical, and his eyes look kind. Isabeau doesn't know why her

Papa thinks this man was pretending to be the witch; he doesn't look anything like the witch, who was gigantic and mean and had a high, evil scream.

Herr Weisskopf extends his hand to her, saying, "Would you like to shake hands and be friends?" Isabeau takes two of his long fingers in her fist and surreptitiously presses the jewel to her ear with her other hand. *In a sleeping compartment on a train heading south from Paris*, whispers the voice, *he will calmly lie to the guards while, in the false compartment below, a 17-year-old girl with a magic jewel around her neck listens as the jewel tells her to stay silent. She will eventually make it to the United States. He'll die in a work camp, deliriously croaking a song to an illusionary audience, "Nibble, nibble, little mouse! Who's nibbling on my little house?"*

"Nibbling on my little house!" Isabeau mimics, desperate to dispel the scary story, and the two men laugh. "That's right," says Herr Weisskopf. "Very good, young lady. We'll make an opera singer of you yet."

"So you see," says her Papa, "it's all just a story."

"Just a story," repeats Isabeau. She puts her arms around her Papa's legs and doesn't want to ever let go.

On her granddaughter Rachel's fifth birthday, Isabeau will take her to a performance of *Hansel and Gretel* at the New York City Opera. When the witch opens the oven door and little Rachel clutches at her arm, Isabeau will reach into her pocket, and put a cheap pasteboard jewel into the child's trembling hand. "It's a magic jewel," she'll whisper. "It will tell you stories and protect you. I promise."

Time and the Parakeet

A story of Eileen Stein Bowman, Sophia's granddaughter

2016

"**H**ey, Eileen," the parakeet said. "It's been a while."
Eileen jumped up from the couch, turned and stared. Perched on the curtain rod over the living room window, looking serenely down at her, was a little green and yellow parakeet. It scratched its head with a tiny claw, picked for a moment at the nubby beige curtain and then stared back at her, its black eyes calm and unblinking.

Her first thought was that somebody's pet had become lost and had found its way into her apartment. Her second was: *Wait, what did it say?*

"You have a tear in the window screen in your bedroom. You ought to fix that."

Eileen came closer. Yes, there was the slightly off-color beak and the small lump at the top of the head that she had not seen since she was, what? Twelve?

"You're . . . "

"You called me ParaClete. That wasn't really my name, of course, but there was no way at the time I could tell you what my true name was—and no way that you could pronounce it, anyway. But yeah, that's who I am."

For a moment, she couldn't breathe. She'd lost it. Finally and forever lost it.

It didn't surprise her. Eileen had been feeling like shit for the last few months, ever since she hit the dreadful age of 60. On the downward slope to retirement and death.

Six decades of living, and what did she have to show for it? An ex-husband who had lived the cliché and gone off with a younger woman. A grown daughter who remembered to call her mother perhaps once a month. A small apartment, a few casual friends . . . That was it. A life wasted.

And to cap it all off, today was the anniversary of her mother's death, a mother who, in her last years, had turned quiet, sad and distant. So Eileen knew it was going to be a bad night. She stopped off on her way home from work (as a paralegal in a stable but boring real-estate law firm) for a slice of take-out pizza and a bottle of bourbon, intending to become good and drunk.

But she hadn't even opened the bourbon yet, so she couldn't blame alcohol on this sudden visitation by an intelligent talking parakeet.

"What are you?" she demanded of the bird. "An hallucination? A brain tumor? An early sign of dementia? Oh, please don't do that!"

The parakeet, ignoring her, lifted its tail and dropped a small green-and-white package that landed on a fold of her curtain.

"You never minded when I did this to your mother's curtains," it said thoughtfully.

"I was 12," Eileen said. "You don't mind those things when you're 12."

"And now you're 60," said the bird.

Eileen took a breath, turned, and marched into her kitchen. She opened a cabinet and took out a juice glass. Then she returned to the living room, sat back down on the couch, opened the bourbon and poured a generous helping into the glass. She swallowed half of it, waited for the warmth to hit her stomach, and then finally looked back up at the curtain rod.

ParaClete was still there.

"I understand," he said, his voice soprano and whisper-light, "that you've been wondering whether your life could have been different."

Eileen sat back and stared up at him. "How can you know that?" she asked.

"Never mind that for now," he said. "What do you think you could have changed?"

She took another deep swallow of the bourbon. "Lots of things," she said, pouring more into her glass. The liquor was having its desired effect; she was feeling a bit more reckless about everything around her. *With any luck,* she thought, *I'll be totally soused in a few more minutes and a talking parakeet will seem completely normal.*

She thought for a moment. "Here's an example," she said. "When I was 13, a friend called to see if I wanted to go with them to a concert in Woodstock, NY. Yeah, *that* concert. I asked my mother, and she said no. If I had gone anyway, had the guts to disobey my mother, what would have happened? Would I have been allowed into the cool hippy crowd at school? Would I have experimented with drugs and sex and politics instead of being a good little girl? Would I have been arrested? Had a more adventurous past?"

"None of the above," said the parakeet. "You would have spent your first night in a field several miles from the main grounds crying your eyes out and the rest of the concert hiding in one of the medical tents, sorting medical supplies, until one of the nurses bought you a bus ticket home. And you still would have been ignored by the cool kids."

Eileen was starting to feel a little fuzzy. Which was good. She could carry on this conversation without thinking too much about it. "Well, then, how about how I acted with my mother? After my father died, she wanted her friend Lydia to move in with us. But I didn't want somebody else in our house, and my friends told me that if it happened, it would prove that my mother was a dyke. I threw a tantrum and she stopped asking. By the time I moved out, Lydia was dying of Alzheimer's. I'm not sure that my mother ever really forgave me."

"Yeah," the parakeet said, "that was pretty bratty of you. But you still would have married the same guy and taken the same job."

"Who the hell *are* you?" Eileen demanded "And don't try to tell me you're my old parakeet. He died when I was nine. We put him in a shoebox and buried him in a nearby park."

The bird turned its head and ran its beak through its tail feathers, admired the effect, and then cocked its head at her. "You've got me. Okay, here's the deal: I'm here as a representative of Time."

"You mean, like a time traveler?" asked Eileen, trying to remember some of the science fiction films she'd watched.

"No," said the parakeet. "More like a sales agent, if you want to look at it like that. I'm giving you a chance to change one of those what-ifs you've been brooding about."

"What?"

"We're going to allow you to change your timeline," it said patiently, as if talking to a rather slow student. "A switch in a decision you made somewhere along the way."

"This is crazy," Eileen declared. There was a light flutter and the parakeet flew down from the curtain rod to the arm of her sofa. It hopped onto her hand and wrapped its claws comfortably around one finger. Eileen lifted the bird so she could look directly at it, remembering how much she loved the feel of the fragile, trusting animal.

"It may be crazy," ParaClete said. "But it's true. Occasionally Time likes to play games with itself and chooses a few humans to play with. Turns out Time likes your family, so you've won the lottery this time around."

"Okay," Eileen said. "How does it work?"

"Here's what happens: You get to pick a single moment in your life where you made a decision and change it. Any point of decision anywhere in your life. Big or small."

It was an interesting proposition. Obviously not true, of course, but interesting to think about. Eileen thought about all the possibilities in her life she had missed. The boys she had never dated, the Master's Degree she had never gone for, all the things that she should or shouldn't have done . . .

But she wasn't excited. She was scared. Very scared. And she knew why.

"What if the change doesn't affect my life at all?" Eileen looked around the room, as if she could find a clue somewhere there. "Or what if it changes things for the worse? How do I decide something like that?"

"That's the chance you take," the parakeet said, without any sympathy in its voice.

"But what if I don't like it and want to go back to the way it was . . . I mean, is?"

"You can't," said the bird. "That's the deal. Time can occasionally tweak things but can't be constantly shifting them back and forth. Better or worse, that will be your life. You won't even know this happened."

Eileen stared back at it. "Wait," she finally said. "Give me a minute."

She lowered her hand to the armrest of the couch and let the parakeet hop off her finger. She poured herself another generous helping and thought while she sipped. She looked at the parakeet, which was patiently grooming itself. She was too nervous to change her own life, she thought. But if she could change someone else's . . . .

"Can I choose not to stop Lydia and my mom from moving in together?"

The bird cocked its head for a moment as if listening. "No," it finally said. "I'm afraid that now that you know the consequences of the action, it would no longer be a gamble. So that one—and the one where you go to Woodstock—is now off the table. Unless," it added, "it's a byproduct of a different change."

"That's not fair!" The parakeet didn't seem to care whether it was fair or not, it just shrugged—a weird effect, considering it was a bird—and waited. Marion thought again.

"How about if I don't specify? If I simply ask Time to change a single decision that would make my life better?"

The parakeet scratched its chest with its beak, considering. "That's an option," it finally admitted. "You can just spin the wheel and see what happens. But we can't promise 'better.' Just 'different.' After all, we're not doing this as a favor to you--it's to give Time something to play with."

"Then forget it," said Eileen decidedly. "I don't want to end up dead or homeless. How do I know that Time won't think watching me scrounge for quarters will be hysterically funny? How do I know," and her breath caught in her throat, "that you won't make my daughter go away?"

It picked at a loose thread in the couch for a moment. "Okay," it finally said. "How's this? We'll spin the wheel and if the results are that your daughter is never born, we'll throw you back here. But that's all I can promise."

The bird raised its head. "Decide. Now. You've been moaning about your life for the past two months. Give it a shot--take a chance. For once in your life."

Eileen took a breath for a moment. Maybe it was the booze, or maybe it was simply that she was tired and bored and unhappy. She said, quickly, "Yes. Go ahead."

"Okay, then. Hold on."

"To what?" Eileen asked, feeling a bit silly. She watched as the parakeet jumped up from the couch and began to fly around the room counterclockwise, first slowly, and then so quickly that it became a light green blur. That, combined with the alcohol, made her feel dizzy. She closed her eyes.

* * *

*E*ileen had done pretty well in her junior high Spanish classes, to the point where she could read a story or write an essay with reasonable fluency, if slowly. But she had trouble speaking--the words simply didn't come quick enough--and so when she started high school, she decided to sign up for Conversational Spanish.

When she walked into the classroom, however, she saw she had made a mistake. The classroom was full of kids chatting fluently in Spanish; the school had a large population of students whose parents had moved to New York from Puerto Rico, and many of them obviously saw this class as an easy A.

Eileen sat at an empty desk and watched uneasily as the teacher, a tall, elegant woman with dark, carefully coiffed hair, walked into the classroom. "Silencio!" she said sharply, and the class quieted.

"First," she said, in carefully enunciated Spanish, "I would like you to introduce yourself to the class. Tell us about yourself, and what you expect to get from the class. You first," and she pointed at Eileen.

Eileen froze in panic. It felt like everyone in the room was staring at her. A couple of girls whom she knew from her other classes whispered together and grinned. Eileen knew she was about to make a complete fool of herself. Her language skills weren't good; her pronunciation was probably worse. They would laugh at her. They would make fun of her.

"Comienza, por favor," the teacher said impatiently.

Eileen sat there, unable to make a sound.

The teacher looked around at the class. "This is not a class where you can just sit like a lump and expect to pass," she said in English. "This is a class where you are expected to participate. If you cannot do that, you might as well quit right now."

The rest of the class went by in a blur. Once it was over, Eileen collected her things and walked, almost without thinking, to the assignment room. She would quit Spanish Conversation and take Typing instead. Typing would be useful, and nobody would laugh at her, or make her feel small or embarrassed. She put her hand on the door to go in.

Something changed.

Eileen was angry. What right had that teacher to make fun of her like that? After all, it was a class to learn conversation, wasn't it? Not one for kids who already know conversation! If she quit now, she'd only be giving that teacher even more satisfaction. She'd show her!

Eileen took her hand off the doorknob and ran to her English Lit class where, in a sudden burst of inspiration, she introduced herself to

Camila, the shy girl who always sat next to her. Camila, it turned out, was happy to have somebody to talk to. She hadn't been brought up in a city—her father back in Salinas had sent her to live with an aunt in Brooklyn so she could get a better education, and she felt lost among the street-smart kids in the school. She was also, it turned out, as terrified of English Lit as Eileen was of Conversational Spanish. They made a pact: Each day during lunch, the two girls would sit together. (This meant that Eileen wouldn't sit with the almost-but-not-quite-popular crowd that she had been edging into, but she didn't mind that much. They weren't that nice anyway.) Eileen would help Camila get through Great Expectations *and Camila would coach Eileen in conversational Spanish.*

Eileen opened her eyes. She must have dozed off for a moment; she was more tired than she thought. The unopened bottle of bourbon she had brought home was still on the living room coffee table; she reached for it and then stopped—there was a scratching sound near the window. She got up and walked over: A small green-and-yellow parakeet was on the window sill, pushing at the screen of the open window with its head.

"How did you get in here?" she asked it. It chirped frantically and continued to batter its head against the screen. Eileen remembered the tear in her bedroom window screen and shook her head. "Gotta get that fixed."

She slowly opened the window wider and then pushed up the screen. In a moment, the parakeet had flown out the window and was gone.

"Maybe I should have kept you," she said, pulling down the screen. "You might have been somebody's pet. But," she considered, "you did look like you really wanted out."

She decided to forget it and went back to the couch. She started opening the bourbon, thinking about how nice it would be to get really drunk and wondering if she should watch something on TV in the meantime. Something meaningless and funny. She could use funny.

Almost in answer, her phone rang. Eileen picked it up and looked at the display. It was her supervisor at work. Of course—why would they expect her to have a life?

She put it to her ear. "Hi, Camila," she said, a little impatiently.

"Hola, Eileen," Camila said, sounding contrite. "I'm so sorry to bother you. I know it's after hours, and I wouldn't have called, except that it's an emergency. But if you're busy . . . "

"No, it's fine," Eileen said, immediately contrite. "Just a little sad, that's all. It's the anniversary of my mother's death."

There was a short silence. "I'm so sorry," said Camila. "Your mom was a wonderful lady. I still think about the stories she used to tell about her childhood in Paris. And her friend, who moved in with her later? She was very sweet as well."

"Yes—Lydia," Eileen said. "I probably wouldn't have made it through my teen years without her. Or, at least, not as well as I did."

"I'm sorry. I should have remembered."

"Really, it's fine." Eileen shrugged, even though she knew Camila couldn't see her. "What's up?"

"There have been three more raids," Camila said, anger leaking into her voice. "Three restaurants, and ICE has taken 17 people. Luckily, one of the restaurant owners called me; we need to get down to the station and make sure everything's kosher and that we get as many out on bond as we can. I'm on my way, and Julio from the Pottstown office said he could come as well. It would really help if you and he could handle the intake interviews while I'm dealing with the authorities."

"Oh, hell," Eileen said. "The raids are becoming more frequent, aren't they?"

"Not surprising, considering who's in charge these days," Camila said. "Can you come?"

"Of course. Just give me a minute to grab my things. I should be there within the hour."

"Gracias, querida," Camila said.

"De nada," Eileen said. "It's why they pay me the big bucks."

Camila groaned and hung up.

Resigned, Eileen picked up her coat and shrugged it on. *It's too bad*, she thought. *It would have been nice to have had a real life, with a husband who stuck around, a kid who calls more than once a month, and enough savings to retire on.*

She picked up the bag with the cold pizza in it. She could eat it while she drove to the police station. And the bourbon would still be waiting when she got back. *If only I had done something about it when I was younger. Maybe made a different decision somewhere along the way . . .*

She grabbed her car keys. "Just stop it," she told herself sternly. "You don't have time for a pity party. You have work to do."

Time grinned.

Under the Bay Court Tree

A story of Carlos Acosta, Sophia's grandson-in-law

1996

I met Mrs. Delaney the first time I saw Bay Court.

It was only weeks after we had spilled Ben's ashes into the lake in Prospect Park. In fact, I guess it all started after the ceremony and the balloons and the useless attempts to comfort Gretl, his heartbroken mother, who had lost her husband only the year before. We went back to her apartment afterwards, where we sat awkwardly in her living room, surrounded by old photos, books and memories that neither of us wanted to talk about. Finally, the few relatives who had also shown up—Ben's Aunt Isabeau and Uncle Gabe, their grown children, and a noisy little girl named Rachel—made their excuses and left us alone.

Gretl sat and stroked her arm where you could still see the ghost of her concentration camp tattoo. "When he was little, I told him the numbers were magical," she moaned. "I told him they would protect him from evil."

I gave her the fistful of pills she needed to get to sleep, put her to bed, and listened as she drifted away, murmuring about somebody named Jakie.

After leaving Gretl, I had planned to go to a bar and get completely smashed, but I realized that I was too exhausted. I stopped off at a bodega, bought a six-pack of beer, and went home. And found a note from my landlady under the door that said she needed our apartment for her daughter, so I had a month to move out. Oh, and she was sorry about Ben.

I couldn't face looking for a place just yet. I boxed up all our stuff, had it put into storage, and crashed with a bunch of friends. Luckily, they were patient with me—my savings were starting to dwindle, my very Catholic parents hadn't spoken to me since I came out to them five years earlier, and I just didn't have the energy to start looking for work.

Still, I couldn't depend on the kindness of friends—or even strangers—forever. I called in a couple of favors, got some part-time work doing layouts for some small-press magazines, and started to search for a new place to live.

It turned out to be a lot harder than I thought. Gentrification had hit the outer boroughs. Everywhere I looked, the place was either tiny, too expensive, or in the kind of neighborhood where you don't go out after dark—and the fact that I didn't have a steady job didn't help. I was too broke to buy, too old to share, and was starting to wonder if I'd end up in New Jersey or have to leave New York entirely.

Then, early one Saturday morning, one of the realtors I'd signed with called and said she had something in south Brooklyn that might suit.

"Two bedrooms, a living room, a dining area and a small kitchen," she said and quoted a rent that was nearly within my budget.

"Okay," I said. "What's the catch? Is the place falling down?"

"The place is fine," she said. "Actually, it's in excellent condition. They're just very picky about who they rent to, and a quiet, single, middle-aged man would suit them just fine. Look, Carlos, what do you care? Just go and look at it. If you like it, and they like you, I'll see if we can negotiate them down a tad."

She paused. "You'll pick up a key from one of the neighbors, a woman named Mrs. Delaney. I understand she can be a bit, well, forthright in her opinions, but if she likes you, you're in. So be polite."

The place was a few blocks from the last station on the subway line, and what with slowdowns and changing trains, it took longer than I thought. When I finally emerged from the subway, I found myself in what looked like an old-school working-class Brooklyn neighborhood. There were stores on one side of the street and a large old-fashioned Catholic church on the other; around me, retired men sat glumly outside a dark bar sucking on paper cups filled with beer; teenage girls of varying hues surreptitiously passed around a cigarette; a woman in too-tight denims chatted with another wearing a hijab while toddlers ran around their legs.

A white working-class neighborhood in the process of integrating. I wondered if I could fit in.

Following the directions the realtor had given me, I found the right street, turned and walked toward the middle of the block. About halfway down, a small green sign reading "Bay Court" pointed to a stone staircase between two red brick houses. I climbed the six stairs—and stared.

I had expected some kind of bleak apartment complex. Instead, I was standing in a small, quiet courtyard lined on either side by narrow two-story attached brick homes, each with a yard hardly larger than a bed sheet. It was quiet and nearly deserted—any sounds from the streets around seemed muted, far away.

A sudden chatter from my left: A mockingbird sitting in a nearby bush scolded me for a moment and then flew to the center of the courtyard—where there grew the biggest, strangest fir tree I'd ever seen outside of Rockefeller Center.

It looked like a cross between a tree and a huge green lollipop. For the first ten feet, the trunk was as straight as a telephone pole, although it was wreathed in so much ivy that you couldn't see the color of the wood beneath. Above that, there were a few green branches, and then a few more from which a torn web of what looked like netting dangled. Past that, the tree sprouted huge, thick branches that reached out so far they nearly touched the roofs of the houses on either side. I craned my neck up; the tree had to be about 20 feet high, at least.

"And who are you, young man?"

I quickly looked back down. A woman was sitting under the tree in a wooden folding chair, a paperback in one hand—for some reason, I hadn't noticed her before. She was wrinkled and blue-veined, with bright silver hair hanging in a page boy cut that made her look like a somewhat dried-up 1920s flapper. She put her other hand up to shade her eyes and squinted at me from under a blue cotton sun hat.

"Are you the new tenant?" she asked in a distinctly Irish accent.

"Excuse me?"

She sighed in obvious exasperation. "For number eight. Over there." She pointed to one of the houses, which had a small "For Rent" sign stuck into the tiny lawn. "I'm Mrs. Delaney."

Oh. Right. Good, Carlos, piss off the new neighbor before you even take the place. I mentally shook myself. "I'm sorry. The realty company told me that you'd let me in." I smiled, trying to look like a nice, quiet, perfect renter. "My name is Carlos Acosta."

"Yes, they told me your name." She stared at me for a very long minute while I waited, wondering if I should ask her for the key. "I see you've noticed the tree," she finally said. "What do you think of it?"

I shrugged. "It's a bit weird-looking for a tree. But then, I like weird."

Mrs. Delaney smiled and dipped into the pocket of one of the ugliest polyester jackets I've ever seen. She pulled out a key hanging from a huge paper clip, which she tossed it to me. "Take your time," she said. "I want to finish this chapter." And she opened her book and started reading as though she'd completely dismissed me from her mind.

I unlocked the door and pushed it open. My first impression was that the house was indeed small; I'd seen apartments that were larger. There was a living/dining room (with, Dios mío, a gas fireplace) and a tiny kitchen downstairs; walking up the narrow stairs, I found two small bedrooms and a bathroom.

The place needed work—the paint job was abysmal, and the bathroom had probably been designed by a refugee from 1962. And I wasn't too sure how well I'd fit into an enclave that was overseen by an obviously nosy Irish lady.

But it was a *house*. With a fireplace. And a dishwasher. And a staircase. And a lawn.

I did one more short tour, went over to the door, put my hand on the knob and then stopped. "Should I take it?" I asked and looked behind me as if Ben would suddenly manifest there, in the living room, wrinkling his nose at the color of the walls and figuring out which tchotchkes would go on the mantelpiece. I hadn't made a major decision without asking for his input for nearly a decade; it was hard to get out of the habit.

Of course, he wasn't there. He would never be there. But I knew what Ben would have said: "You like it? You can afford it? Then for god's sake don't spend time thinking about it—grab it before somebody else does."

He was right. Of course. "Okay," I said, and opened the door.

Mrs. Delaney was still sitting under the tree. "So," she asked as I approached, her bright blue eyes fastened on my face, "you've decided to take the house, have you? Ah, well, that's lovely. I'm sure you'll like it here."

I offered her the key. "I'll think about it," I said, a little miffed at being taken for granted.

She smiled and waved away the key. "Nothing to think about. Just call your real estate agent and tell her that I said to arrange for the lease. You can move in whenever you like."

I wondered later if she'd heard me talking to my dead lover—the walls of those homes didn't strike me as very thick. Still, the next morning I sent in my answer and my references; a two-year lease arrived in my email an hour later. I forwarded it to my lawyer, who told me it was a standard lease with nothing objectionable added. I signed it, sent it, and two weeks later stood outside my new home watching the movers drive away with a good chunk of my change.

It was a Friday afternoon and the courtyard was quiet; most of the other residents were probably out at work (although I did see a few curtains twitch—no doubt neighbors trying to figure out who I was).

I went inside, shut the door, and began to unpack.

After a couple of hours, I sat back and contemplated the piles of boxes on the floor and on my couch. Part of me—the part I inherited from my efficient, no-nonsense mami—said that I should keep unpacking, and that the sooner I got that done, the faster I could get on with my life. The other part wanted to take a walk and check out the local bars to see if any looked friendly.

"Nu-uh," I finally told myself. "You can check out the bars tonight. Work first." I reached out to another box.

And then I smelled it. Smoky. Strong. Very unpleasant. Coming from outside.

There were two windows in the front wall of the house, one on either side of the door. They were covered by cheap white blinds, which I had decided to keep until I got something a bit snazzier to protect my privacy. I pushed a dusty slat down and peered outside.

In front of the house next door, a man was carefully pushing small sticks into his lawn and setting the tip of each on fire with a lighter.

Okay. So I had eccentric people living next door. I was a New Yorker—I could handle eccentric. I decided to ignore the whole thing.

Fifteen minutes later, I realized I couldn't ignore it. The smell was getting intense, to the point where I had to crank open the kitchen window and dig out my fan to try to air the place out.

Time to meet the neighbors. I went for the front door.

Once outside, I wasn't sure what to do or say. The man acted like I wasn't there—just kept pushing each stick into the ground, lighting it, and going on to the next. Small plumes of evil-smelling brown smoke drifted up and dispersed throughout the area.

I cleared my throat. "Hi, there," I said, in what I hoped was a conversational tone of voice.

The man turned and stared at me. He was practically a caricature of an aging Brooklyn mook: Somewhere in his 70s, with thinning white hair and an impressive paunch. "Hello." he said, noncommittally, in the sort of gravelly, well-used voice that I always associated with construction workers and ex-cops.

I walked over to him and stretched out my hand. "Carlos Acosta. I just moved in."

"Yeah," he said. "We saw." He gave my hand a cursory shake. "Bob Halloran. Where you from, Carlos?"

"Queens. Astoria, to be precise." He scowled at me, but I plowed on, determined to be polite. "I was just wondering . . . "

And then I got a better look at the sticks he was planting, and my voice trailed off. I recognized them—they were what we used to call punks, bamboo sticks with a brown coating that were used to light fireworks. They were fun to play with when I was a kid, but they weren't usually used as lawn decorations. What the hell was it all about? Some sort of weird religious ceremony?

The man saw me staring. "We got an animal problem here. Squirrels, cats—they dig holes and crap on the lawn. I figure this will keep them away." He gave a wide wave toward his lawn, which I now saw was mowed down to about a quarter of an inch, so perfectly that the grass might have been painted on.

"Oh." I was trying to figure out what to say to this when a large woman with streaked blonde hair and wearing a bright purple track suit came storming out of the house directly across from mine. "Bob Halloran!" she yelled, heading for us like a truck out of control. "What the hell do you think you're doing?"

I took a step back—she looked like she was planning to plow right into us—but Halloran just narrowed his eyes and stood his ground. "I'm minding my own business, Vivian," he shouted back. "What is your problem?"

"You know damn well what my problem is," the woman huffed, stopping just short of the row of smoking punks. "I've got two kids coming home from school in half an hour, and all I need is for them to burn themselves on one of these . . . things." She made an abortive move to kick one over, but then thought better of it and pulled her foot back.

She looked as though she would have said more, but a thin, white-haired woman wearing curlers and a bright pink apron that read, "Grandma Cooks Great!" came running out of Halloran's house. "Vivian, what is your problem?" she demanded. "There's nothing dangerous about punks—you used to play with 'em when you were a kid, and you know it."

After that, it became a verbal free for all. The three shouted at each other so enthusiastically that I was wondering whether I should call 911. Then Mrs. Halloran's eyes widened. She closed her mouth and gave each of the other combatants a quick stab with her fore-finger. As if given a signal, the other two immediately stopped and followed her gaze.

Mrs. Delaney stood a few feet away, her arms folded. "I was try-ing to watch my programs when I heard what sounded like a flock of seagulls screaming over a piece of garbage," she said, quietly but firmly. "And then I started smelling burning garbage. Which turned out to be those foul items," and she nodded at the smoldering punks.

I glanced at the three combatants. The two Hallorans looked like sullen children being dressed down by a hated teacher. Vivian looked smug.

"That stench will pollute every living thing in the Court," Mrs. Delaney continued calmly. "Bob Halloran, I'd appreciate it if you'd remove them."

She didn't wait for an answer, but turned and strode briskly back to her house. I watched her for a moment, and then looked back at the trio. Vivian smiled and nodded at me. "Come say hello when you're ready," she said, and went back to her own place. The Hallor-ans glanced at each other, and then quietly started pulling the punks out of their lawn.

* * *

I t wasn't over, though.

A week after the incident with the punks, Halloran installed an electric fence two feet off the ground, which sparked unpleasantly every time a suicidal insect decided to pass by. That lasted until a small black poodle belonging to the elderly lady in the first house on the right ran into it and scurried away uttering a frightening whine. An hour later a police officer was banging on Halloran's door and the fence came down.

A couple of weeks after that, Halloran placed several jars of water on his lawn because, he stated categorically, "Cats are afraid of the effect." Somehow, the cats seemed to have conquered their fear; in fact, they saw it as a great place to get something to drink, as did the local squirrel population. Eventually, the jars disappeared as well.

For a while after that, things were quiet. I finished most of my unpacking and dragged the less important stuff down to the basement. I put up some of my posters and one or two of Ben's. I called Gretl once a week just to keep in touch, and occasionally chatted with Ben's cousin Eileen, who was looking after her. I stripped the bedroom of some really vile wallpaper and painted it. And then settled down to find some serious freelance work.

By this time, I was on friendly, although not intimate, terms with most of my neighbors. Vivian turned out to be a loud, friendly woman who worked part-time as a paralegal for a large Wall Street firm; she and her husband (an auto mechanic who collected old dime novels) and I would sit outside on fine evenings and gossip about the latest films, local politics, and the doings of the other neighbors. Sometimes, we'd be joined by one or two others.

It was, I had to admit, rather comfortable.

On those few occasions I did see Halloran (which wasn't often), we'd nod politely to each other, but I didn't say anything and neither did he. A sort of truce, I thought, had been established.

And then one afternoon, about three months after I'd moved in, I was working on a proposal, listening to the voices of some of my neighbors gossiping outside and wondering if I should join them when I was done when there was a sudden high-pitched squeal that made me jump. I rushed to the door and stuck my head out.

Several neighbors had formed a tight circle on Halloran's lawn, staring at something on the ground. There was another ear-shattering shriek that ran up my spine; without even thinking about it, I strode to the circle of people and looked down.

A squirrel was lying on the lawn, pawing frantically at the grass, its back leg caught in what looked like an old-fashioned mousetrap.

"What the hell happened?" I asked.

"Halloran seeded his lawn with traps," said Vivian scornfully. She was standing there, shaking her head. "He must have done it last night, or somebody would have stopped him. Now look."

The squirrel's screams were terrible, but nobody else moved. It was as though they were waiting for permission, or the cops, or something. The hell with that—I was still new there, but somebody had to do something. I stepped forward. "Someone get a pair of gloves. Heavy gloves, if you have them." I looked at Vivian; she nodded and trotted back to her place.

I squatted down next to the squirrel.

"Okay," I said, "I'm going to try to pull its leg from the trap. Does anyone know a vet around here?"

"There's an animal hospital down on Fourth Ave," said Mrs. Vincelli, the woman with the dogs.

"Call a car service, somebody," I said. "As soon as we have the squirrel, I'll take it over to the hospital. And maybe somebody has a shoebox we can put it in?"

Vivian had returned; she pressed a heavy pair of gloves into my hands. I put them on, and reached slowly toward the trap, but even with the gloves I was nervous—it was nearly impossible to avoid the teeth of the squirming animal. "Shit!" I hissed.

Then I realized that, except for the squirrel's cries, it had become very quiet.

I looked up. Mrs. Delaney was standing there, holding a small cloth bag. Without a word she sat down cross-legged in the grass next to me and, murmuring some quiet words that I couldn't quite hear, slowly moved the bag close to the frantic squirrel. She didn't seem worried about a nip from those sharp and possibly diseased little teeth; she just carefully pushed the bag over the animal's head and body, and held it gently but firmly.

Whether it was what she was saying or the darkness of the bag or the loss of blood, I don't know, but the squirrel stopped struggling. I was able to take the metal bar of the trap in one hand and the wood base in the other, slowly separate them, and pull the trap from the animal's leg.

I threw the bloodied thing toward the house and sat back. I suddenly felt very tired. "Did somebody call the car service?" I asked.

"Don't bother yourself," said Mrs. Delaney. "The little anam is dead."

I looked up. Sometime during the last minute or two, the neighbors had quietly walked back to their homes. The only people left were myself, Mrs. Delaney and Vivian. I took off the gloves and handed them to Vivian, who dropped them on Halloran's lawn. "He can get rid of them," she said roughly. "God knows what kind of vermin that poor thing had."

Mrs. Delaney had picked up the bag so that the squirrel slipped completely inside it. She looked into the bag and sighed. "Too much fright and too much blood lost," she said, as if talking to the squirrel. "Poor thing. Not to die of age or to feed a predator, but caught in a nasty human trap." She looked up. "Vivian, I'm sure I can trust you to let Mr. Halloran know that I would appreciate it if he would remove those traps immediately."

"Oh, he'll hear from me," said Vivian grimly.

"Don't yell too much at the man, dear, he is miserable enough. Carlos, walk me to my garden. I need a nice strong young man like you to help me dig a grave."

We walked slowly towards Mrs. Delaney's house at the back of the Court. "I shouldn't have allowed them to move in," she said, as much to herself as to me. "I knew they were troubled souls, but her mother came from the same county as my father's first wife, so I asked no advice but welcomed them in. And see what that has brought."

We had reached the tree. She stopped, shook her head and stared at me. "I hope you will always pay attention," she said sternly. "Listen to those who love you and want the best for you."

I shrugged. "Not too many of those," I said, perhaps a bit offhandedly.

"Of course there are," she said, and then before I could say anything else, looked up to a lower branch, where a mockingbird sat and scolded us for coming too close to her tree. "Do you like mockingbirds?" Mrs. Delaney asked.

"I guess so," I said. "They've got nerve. They're not big birds, but if you go anywhere near their nest, they'll attack, no matter how big you are. And they are wonderful mimics. My abuela—my grandmother—used to say that when my mother was young, she had the choice of being as beautiful and tuneful as the mariposa or as fierce and clever as the sinsonte—the mockingbird—and she chose the latter."

I paused, remembering. "Ben and I . . . " I paused for a moment and then plowed on. "My friend Ben and I would sometimes go birding in Central Park. He was better at it than I was, but I could always identify the mockingbirds."

I waited for the questions, or the sideways glance, but it never came. We just stood in the quiet Court, listening to the bird go through its repertoire, until Mrs. Delaney smiled. "Now, if that wasn't a car alarm," she said, "I'll eat my hat. What a very smart bird it is."

She continued to walk back toward her garden; I followed. "There's a spade against the wall, behind that bush," she told me. "You can dig a small hole there, in front of the window. Just deep enough so that cats don't find her."

The soil was soft, so it took only about 15 minutes to dig a hole, deposit the tiny corpse into it, and cover it up again. Just as I was finishing, Mrs. Delaney came out of the house with a glass. "Iced tea," she said. "Tetley, with a bit of fresh mint in it."

"Thanks," I said. I drank it gratefully and handed the glass back. Mrs. Delaney regarded the small grave thoughtfully. "Something will have to be done about that Halloran," she said, more to herself than to me, it seemed. "Dedication to your garden is a worthy thing, but he is causing trouble and pain, and that must stop."

She looked back at the mockingbird, which was now fastidiously grooming its wings. For a moment, it seemed to look back at her. One of the corners of her mouth raised just slightly. "The thought occurs to me," she said. "You said you like birds. Wouldn't you like to put up one of those bird feeders? There's a pet store over on Third Avenue, run by a friend of mine—Animal Crackers, it's called. Tell him I sent you. He'll set you up."

She turned and walked back into her house without another word.

That night, I thought about her suggestion—order, rather—to put a bird feeder in my front garden. The idea was silly, to say the least. A feeder in my tiny lawn would look absurd. And the mess it would make—not to mention the care it would take—would be a pain in the ass.

However, that Saturday, I found myself walking the seven blocks to the pet store.

The feeder didn't come with any instructions, but it didn't take a genius to figure out how to assemble it. And the next morning, when I opened my front door, three small brown birds who had decided to breakfast at the new establishment took off in a panic.

I watched them fly away, charmed. For a moment, I pictured myself spending the warm evenings in a small deck chair, a beer at my side and a guide to New York City birdlife in my lap. Then I thought about the daily outdoor gossip sessions and the constant parade of neighbors, delivery people and kids that pass through the court. There would be no quiet birdwatching here.

Still, each morning, before I even made coffee, I would go replenish the feeder. And I started to keep my living room blinds open so that, during periods of relative quiet, I could watch the birds fighting over the seed outside.

A couple of weeks later, I was on a call with a client when somebody pounded on my door as though they were trying to knock it down. It startled the hell out of me—I thought maybe there was an emergency of some sort, so I asked the client to hold, put the phone on mute, and opened the door to find Halloran standing on my threshold in an obviously foul mood. "I need to talk to you about your birds," he rasped.

The man's face was a dangerous shade of purple. He didn't seem to be armed, and he didn't make any attempt to come in, so I said, "One minute," and closed the door. I unmuted the phone, told my client I'd call him the next day with my estimates, hung up, and opened the door again.

"Yes?" I asked.

"It's your friggin' birds," Halloran said.

"*My* birds?"

"Your birds. From your goddamned feeder."

"Oh. Okay. What about the birds?"

"They're crapping on my sidewalk and on my lawn," the man growled.

"Excuse me?"

"Your birds! This morning, they started leaving their goddamn droppings all over my front walk! And my chair! And my grass! The stuff is impossible to clean up. What are you going to do about it?"

Halloran stepped aside and let me look.

It was as though the Hallorans' property had been struck overnight by some weird sort of disease. Their walk and their lawn were marked all over with ugly white blotches. A small folding chair that Halloran had put out was decorated with long white streaks.

It was pretty damned disgusting. Not to mention funny.

"You going to stop it or am I going to have to call my lawyer?"

Okay, it was Alice in Wonderland time. I lost my temper and any type of neighborly restraint. "I'm sorry, but are you insane?"

"Your birds are messing up my property!"

Maybe it was the dead squirrel, maybe it was just exasperation, but I'd had it. "You stupid bastard, what are are you talking about? You think I'm ordering the birds to shit on your stuff?"

"It's your damn feeder!"

I began to laugh—I couldn't help it. "Who the hell do you think I am?" I sputtered. "The fucking birdman of Alcatraz? I don't tell the birds where to do their thing."

But the man just wouldn't let go. "Then why aren't they doin' it in your yard?"

I looked, and damn, but he was right. The white stuff was all over his walk, his grass, his chair—but the only evidence of the birds on my side was a scattering of seed hulls.

"Huh!" was all I could say.

As though to underscore the puzzle, a grey pigeon walked serenely from my lawn, where it had been searching out any seeds that had been knocked to the ground, and over to Halloran's lawn chair. It fluttered up to the seat, serenely lifted its tail and left a gift in the center of the green plastic webbing. It then looked at us, unashamed.

At that point, I wouldn't have been surprised if the bird had started a conversation like some come-to-life Disney cartoon. Halloran and I just stood there and gaped while the pigeon coolly ran a couple of its feathers through its beak and flew away.

"So?" Halloran asked, apparently not impressed by the idea of a wild creature purposefully using his chair as an outhouse. "Are you going to take that feeder down?"

"I'm not sure I should," I said, still watching the small birds fluttering around the seed. "Mrs. Delaney said . . . "

"Robert? What'd he say?" Mrs. Halloran, her hair teased into a tall structure that looked like one of the birds had built it as a nest, banged out of their door and strode over, her eyes already narrowed and ready for battle. "Is he going to take it down?"

"It was Mrs. Delaney who put up the damned birdfeeder," said Halloran to his wife.

"No, it wasn't," I said. "I put it up. She just suggested it."

"Damned, indeed," said Mrs. Halloran, totally ignoring me. "Didn't I tell you that she had something to do with it? I swear, if we were living in my mother's time, I would have reported her to the priest years ago."

Her husband scowled at her. "I don't give two cents for what your mother would have done. What I want to know is, what are we going to do about this?"

"Well," Mrs. Halloran asked, "what does she want?"

They both turned and looked expectantly at me, like I'd know the answer to whatever it was they were asking.

I shrugged. "It was the day the squirrel got caught in your trap," I said. "I helped her bury it, and she told me to buy the feeder."

"You see?" Mrs. Halloran said to her husband, "I told you that you should be more polite to her. Now she's helping out strangers instead of us, who are practically family."

Halloran looked exasperated—I wondered if he had less faith in the value of those family connections than she had—but before he had a chance, she turned and glared at me.

I took a breath. "Look, Mrs. Halloran," I said. "I'm new here. I don't want to make trouble. I'll tell you what. If you stop laying traps and setting fires, I'll do some research, ask around, see if there's something out there that will keep animals off your lawn without either killing them, or driving the rest of us crazy. But I can't guarantee anything."

"Nothing doing!" she said firmly. "We can't wait for you to find some 'acceptable' way to keep our lawn clean. You wouldn't care if every stray animal in the neighborhood used our yard as its private toilet!"

A small flock of about 15 starlings fluttered down to the Hallorans' lawn. We all watched as they lifted their tails and flew off again, chattering gaily.

She looked back at me. I just smiled.

"Fine," she said through gritted teeth. "We'll stop. What we want doesn't matter. Just tell that witch to leave us in peace." She stamped back into her house, her hair quivering slightly on top of her head.

Her husband watched her go and then turned back to me. To my surprise, he almost looked apologetic. "Look, I don't really care if the feeder is up or not if you can just stop the birds from messing up our property."

He almost made me feel a bit guilty. "I'll go talk to Mrs. Delaney," I said. "And could you tell your wife that I didn't mean any harm by putting up the feeder?"

"Sure," said Halloran. "But she won't believe me."

A mockingbird that had been eating at the feeder chose that moment to flutter up from the perch. As we watched, the bird rose, circled Halloran's chair three times, and then flew to the tree that loomed over the center of the courtyard. It came to rest on a wide, bare branch well away from the Halloran's walk, sang for a few seconds—it sounded just like a car alarm—and daintily lifted its tail. A small white parcel hit the roots of the tree.

After a moment, I said, "It looks like I won't have to go talk to Mrs. Delaney after all. Would you like some help cleaning up?"

"Nah," said Halloran. "I'll call my son. He owes me some money anyway; this will square us."

We shook hands. I went indoors, sat at my desk, and looked out my windows at the birdfeeder, where a couple of finches were daintily picking through the remainder of the day's seed. Behind them, the sun was beginning to set. I could hear Halloran raking through his lawn, probably looking for any last traps. Across the way, Vivian was scolding one of her kids for not doing his homework. Other neighbors were, I knew, cooking dinner, or watching the news, or smiling at a joke. Mrs. Delaney was doing—whatever it was Mrs. Delaney did when she was alone. And over us all, the Bay Court tree.

I closed my eyes. "Whatever my future holds, Benjamin mi amor, I will always love you," I whispered.

There was no answering voice in my head. But for the first time in a long time, I felt something like peace.

An Awfully Big Adventure

A story of Benjamin Weissbaum, Sophia's grandson

1962

"Is there going to be a war?"

Ben was seated crossed-legged on the living room rug, staring into the gray glowing universe of the TV screen, made even brighter because the lights were turned down. Behind him, his mother and father sat on the couch. They were very quiet.

The man on the screen was President Kennedy—Ben knew that for sure. The President stared slightly to the right of the TV screen and spoke for a long time about a lot of things that Ben didn't un-derstand. The word "missile" was mentioned several times; Ben knew what missiles were. And the word "nuclear" was there as well, and that was also a dangerous word.

The President wasn't smiling, as he sometimes did when Ben saw him on television. But what was even scarier was the silence in the living room—his parents weren't arguing about what the President was saying, or talking back to the screen, like they always did. So despite the flood of unfamiliar words, Ben understood that something very bad was about to happen.

"Papa, is there going to be a war?" he asked again, needing reassurance. Ben was quite ready to keep asking—he knew how to be persistent with his questions. But he didn't have to wait long.

"I don't know," his father said. "Now be quiet, Ben. Mama and Papa need to hear this."

And with those words, the bottom dropped out of Ben's world. A simple fact of his life had been that his father knew everything, could explain everything, and could make everything better.

But not this.

* * *

That night, Ben dreamed.

He was walking in the playground that was next to his apartment house. It was usually filled with kids playing and mothers talking together (and yelling at the kids), but for some reason there was nobody there; it was deserted. He was alone. A siren screamed; a siren like the ones that were sometimes tested in his neighborhood.

And suddenly he wasn't alone anymore; the playground and the street were filled with people, but they weren't playing and chatting and arguing; instead, they were crying and moaning. Some were lying still, as though they had decided to go to sleep on the pavement; some were twitching and making low, unhappy sounds. There was snow falling from the sky, even though it wasn't cold at all, and it covered the crying people.

A woman ran up to Ben and then stopped, as though she was disappointed. "Have you seen my little girl?" she asked. "Have you seen Susan?" But she didn't wait for an answer and ran on.

It was very scary. Ben looked around, and then suddenly, right in front of their apartment house, he saw his father. He was facing away from Ben, but Ben knew, with the assurance that came in dreams, that it was him. He ran over, calling as loud as he could, "Papa! Papa, I'm scared!"

His Papa turned around, but instead of picking Ben up and comforting him, as he usually did, he just stared at him. And suddenly Ben realized that his Papa's clothes were torn and bloody. He looked at Ben with wide, blank eyes, as though he had gone somewhere inside himself and didn't know his own son. It was as if he were turning into a monster. The one that had scared Ben so much on TV.

"Papa!" he called, and put out his arms. But his father still didn't recognize him. And then the skin started to peel off his face like the skin of a banana.

Ben screamed and woke up.

He climbed out of bed and ran into the living room. His father was still watching the TV, smoking a cigarette, his long legs stretched out in front of him. His mother was sitting at the kitchen table, looking at a newspaper.

Ben jumped into his father's lap, wrapped his arms around his chest and breathed in the familiar smoky scent. "Ben, what's wrong?" his father asked. He put out his cigarette in a nearby ashtray and settled Ben more firmly on his lap. "Did you have a nightmare?"

Ben nodded, still seeing the vision of his father with cold, uncaring eyes and peeling cheeks, still needing reassurance that it was unreal, that it didn't, couldn't happen.

"What did you dream?" his father asked.

"There was a war," Ben said, suddenly realizing that this was what had been happening, why all the people had been so sad and frightened. "There was a war, and you turned into a Frankenstein monster."

"I knew that we shouldn't have let him watch the speech," his mother said nervously. She stood, walked over, took the cigarette from Ben's father and took a long pull on it, which was funny, because she hardly ever smoked. "I said so, Willy. A child his age shouldn't have to think about such things."

His father was silent for a moment as his mother sat down on the couch next to them.

"Now, listen to me, Ben," he finally said. His tone was serious, so Ben sat a little straighter and paid attention. "You know that sometimes grown-ups have disagreements, right? And sometimes those disagreements are serious."

"Like you and Uncle Harry?" asked Ben. He remembered when his father and Uncle Harry had yelled at each other about Communists and blacklists and other things until his mother pulled him out of the room. Soon after that, Uncle Harry went home, and he hadn't seen him since, although Aunt Isabeau, who was married to Uncle Harry and was Papa's sister, still came to visit sometimes.

"Yes, like that," his father said. "Well, sometimes countries have disagreements, too. And sometimes, when they can't resolve those disagreements, they start a war."

"Like the one you fought in," Ben said. He had once found, in the bottom drawer of his father's bureau, a medal in a box and a photo of a thin young woman with very short hair and wearing clothes too big for her who looked a little like his mother—and a little not. But Ben had never told either of his parents that he'd found the box and the picture. Somehow, he knew they wouldn't like it.

"Yes, like the one I fought in. Well, our country is having a disagreement with another country, and there's the possibility that it may lead to another war. But whatever happens, you know that your mother and I will always take care of you, and keep you safe."

Ben nodded.

"Now, do you have any questions?"

Ben thought a moment, and then said, "Can I see the magic numbers?"

His mama and papa looked at each other for a moment. Then his mama reached over and pulled him over to her lap. "Will that make you feel better?" she asked.

He nodded.

She smiled slightly and said. "Very well. I think this is a good time for the magic numbers."

She reached around him and pushed up the sleeve on her left arm, and then turned her forearm up in front of his face so he could see the writing, light blue against the pale brown of her skin. He reached out with his forefinger and touched each, one right after the other, reciting the one letter and each number to himself in a soft whisper as his finger moved from left to right: A15384. He did it as slowly as he could, to make sure the magic would work and the moment last as long as possible.

"Better?" asked his mama as he touched the final number. He looked up at her and smiled.

"Good," she said. "Now, you go back to bed. And don't worry— the magic numbers will protect you."

She lifted him down from her lap and gently kissed his forehead. "Good night, Benjamin."

"Good night, Mama. Good night, Papa."

"Good night," his papa said.

Ben walked out of the living room and into the hallway that connected it with the bedroom. He paused then, listening.

"We should take a vacation, Willy," said his mama. "Tomorrow. We could take money out of the bank and go somewhere. Somewhere in the center of the country, away from the cities. Find a motel and wait there until—well, until we find out what happens."

The couch creaked. "Where would we go, Gretl?" his papa asked. "Cities all over the United States are targeted."

Ben's mama spoke in a fierce whisper. "At least we should send the boy away. Somewhere he'll be safe. There must be someplace. We need to make sure he gets away in time; we cannot wait until it is too late, the way my parents did..." She began to cry quietly.

Ben peeked around the corner. His papa's arm was around his mama's shoulders. "If there's another war," he said, "there won't be anywhere that's safe. And this time it will be everybody who is in danger."

Ben turned and went back to his room, closed the door very quietly, scrambled onto his bed, stood on his pillow, and pushed aside the curtains of the window that was just behind the head of his bed.

Their apartment was three stories up. Ben loved looking down at the street after bedtime—at night, the gently glowing street lamps made it look foreign and magical. Ben would usually watch the people pass by and make up stories about who they were and where they were going. But now, all he wanted was reassurance that the street was still there, just the way it had always been: the shuttered stores, the bump in the middle of the street that made the trucks bounce loudly, the pigeons pulling pieces of uneaten bagels out of the trash cans and the deli on the corner with the neon Coca-Cola sign that was never turned off.

It was all still there. And, he reminded himself, he had touched and recited the magic numbers. They would keep him, and his family, safe.

"Can we make a deal?"

Ben turned, and stared.

There was something wrong. While the lights from outside still illuminated the walls, there was smoke in his room, so thick and dark that he couldn't see his nightlight where it was always on, next to the door. Ben's mama had been in a fire once, and she told him how she had run out of the house and closed the door so that the fire wouldn't spread. Ben wondered if there was a fire in his room and if he should run out and close the door. But that would mean running through the smoke which was now thick and rolling and reaching up to the ceiling.

"What do you want? Can we make a deal?"

The voice came from the center of the smoke. This couldn't be any normal fire—fires, as far as Ben knew, didn't talk—and so he stood on his bed and said loudly (because he wasn't sure how well smoke could hear), "My name is Ben! Who are you?"

There was a moment of silence. Then suddenly, like water going down a drain, the smoke swirled down and away, until none of it was left. Instead, a woman stood in the middle of Ben's room, among his trains and books and sneakers.

Ben squinted at her suspiciously. She was obviously a grown-up, but she wasn't dressed like his mama, or any of her friends, or even any of the ladies he had seen on TV shows. Instead, she was dressed in a white tuxedo (Ben knew it was called a tuxedo because he had seen a man wear one on TV), red high heels, and very bright red lipstick. Her hair was black and long and covered one eye.

"You really are a baby, aren't you?" she said. "Or is this just a clever disguise?"

"I'm not a baby. I'll be six in 11 weeks and three days," said Ben, hurt.

"I see." The woman smiled widely, as though she were enjoying some private joke. She put one hand on her hip and another at the back of her head, and posed like the fashion models that Ben saw in his mama's magazines.

"Do you like the outfit?" the woman asked, as though she were continuing an everyday conversation. "It's a Marlene Dietrich look, with a touch of Veronica Lake. Except for the hair color, of course. What do you think?"

"I don't know who they are," said Ben, honestly. "But I think your clothes are pretty. How can you see if your hair is in your eyes?"

"It is inconvenient," said the woman. She put her hand in the air and pulled out a bright, silvery band, which she used to fasten her hair back in a ponytail.

Ben sat down on his bed, his legs folded in front of him, and considered the situation. His mother had read to him from books in which ordinary children had magical adventures, books like *Peter Pan*, *Half Magic*, and *Mary Poppins*. Ben had secretly hoped—even expected—something of the sort would happen to him, so he was prepared. He knew, for example, that magical beings could be very tricky to deal with. You had to be polite.

"How do you do?" Ben said. "Are you a fairy?"

The woman finished fussing with her hair, stared at him for a moment, and then snorted disdainfully through her nose. "Not even close, baby doll."

She extended one leg and seemed to be examining one of the red shoes critically. It turned black.

"My name is Ben," he repeated, and waited for her to introduce herself. But the women didn't reply; she just rotated her foot for a moment and then shook her head. The shoe turned red again.

Ben wasn't going to give up. "Are you hungry? Do you want some tea and cookies?" That was what his friend Marjorie always served her dolls, so he thought that might be safe.

The woman sighed. "Either I've made a very bad mistake, or you are playing some kind of weird game with me. My name is Azazel. Do you know me?"

Ben thought for a moment, then shook his head. "Is Azazel your whole name?"

The woman grinned, rather nastily, Ben thought. "It's enough for me. Is Ben your whole name?"

"No," he said, rather proudly. "I've got two names. My American name is Benjamin Solomon Weissbaum. My Hebrew name is Binyamin Sholem ben Ze'ev."

But the woman didn't seem very interested. She raised her arms and stretched; and then put her hands in her pockets and just stood there, staring off at something in the distance. Ben turned around to see where she was looking, but all he could see was the night sky outside his window.

"What are you looking at?" he finally asked.

The woman smiled. "The ending of a civilization."

She turned slightly and looked at him. "Does that frighten you?" Ben didn't know what to say, so he just continued to look at her.

Azazel smiled slightly, reached into her pocket and brought out a cigarette and a lighter. She put the cigarette in a long silver holder, placed it in her mouth and lit it with the kind of knowing flair that Ben had seen and admired in old movies. "Ben, you seem like a nice boy," she said, and blew out some smoke. "So I'll tell you why I'm here. I was curious about your dream. Do you remember your dream?"

He nodded. "It was awful."

"It was not really a dream," Azazel said, balancing the cigarette holder between two fingers and watching the smoke curl toward the ceiling. "It was—let's call it a window on a possible reality. I came here to find out why you opened that window. I thought I'd find an interfering old mage who was going to meddle with my plans. Not a small boy who hasn't the least idea of what real power is."

"What plans?" Ben asked. He didn't completely understand what she was saying, but he knew that it was important that he find out. This Azazel reminded him of Eliot, the boy down the block who always threatened to beat Ben up when nobody else was around, and Ben had already learned that it was better to find out what a bully was up to ahead of time so you could stay out of his way, if at all possible.

"Well." Azazel grinned at him and leaned against his dresser. "They're not actually my plans. They are the plans of two of your leaders—human leaders—who are about to begin yet another war. A very short war, I might add."

She took another pull on the cigarette and blew two perfect smoke rings.

"Why will there be a war?" Ben asked. "And if you know about it, why don't you tell somebody who can stop it?"

Azazel laughed. "You stupid boy," she said, and somehow, even though she didn't grow any taller, she seemed larger and not a little menacing. "Because I'm bored out of my mind. Because my lover and I were exiled to your miserable little planet centuries ago, and we've had enough of it. If you manage to kill yourselves all off—and the chances are very good right now, as good as they've ever been—then perhaps, if you're all gone, we can leave this wretched place. At the very least, we'll have it to ourselves."

Ben reached over to his pillow and picked up the stuffed panda that his mother had given him when he was little. He was getting a bit too old for stuffed animals, but right now, he felt in need of it. "That's mean," he murmured. Azazel grinned.

"You're barely out of the shell. How could you possibly understand? Humans have been killing themselves for thousands of years, and lately, they've gotten a lot better at it. Haven't you learned anything from your mother's experience?"

"My mama?" Ben asked, puzzled.

The woman laughed. "She hasn't told you, has she? Probably thought it would warp your tender little brain. Well, ask her sometime about how she survived her adolescence. If you ever get old enough to understand."

He had been completely wrong. The woman in the tuxedo wasn't a crotchety-but-wonderful magical person, like Mary Poppins. She was a bad person, like the witch in Sleeping Beauty. Ben glared at her. "Maybe you're wrong!" he said. "Maybe there won't be a war! The President will stop it and you'll have to go away!"

The woman didn't seem at all fazed by his anger. "There are some very powerful humans who want this war," she said calmly. "They think they can conquer their enemy with only an acceptable number—what an interesting phrase that is!—of casualties on their side. They don't have the imagination to conceive of what they will start. All it will take will be a small push and your dream will be a reality."

She stretched her arms lazily over her head and smiled at him. It was a terrible smile. "It's been interesting talking to you, Binyamin Sholem ben Ze'ev. You appear to be a rather bright little boy, after all. However, it's time to nudge reality to where I want it. And you know," the smiled broadened, "I'm going to start right here. And I'll let you watch. Isn't that nice of me?"

She didn't move, but Ben could see a grayness floating around her, like a dark impenetrable fog, that was slowly obscuring his rocking chair and his books. It curled and thickened, filling his room and moving upwards and outwards, toward his windows. It was the same black smoke that he had seen when Azazel had first appeared, but it looked nastier and more dangerous. And it wasn't stopping. He looked around for a weapon, something that might halt its progress, something like a sword or a gun, but there was nothing there.

Closer. Darker. Larger. Blocking out everything around it. Wisps of the darkness expanded toward him, and Ben backed away, his bed soft under his feet, clutching his panda. His back hit the wall, and there was no place else to go.

And then Ben suddenly remembered that he did have a weapon. His mother's magic number.

He stared at the tendrils of darkness reaching for him and whispered, "A15384."

The darkness seemed to pause, just a little. He took a breath and said it again, louder, more firmly, "A15384."

And then louder, in a wild shout, "A15384!"

"Hello, Benjamin. How nice to see you."

The darkness had stopped, as though contained by invisible glass. Stranger still, the walls of his room were gone. Instead, all around him, there were people—men, women and children. Some were dressed up in suits and ties and fancy-looking dresses, others in badly-fitting old clothes, and a few in ugly striped suits and wooden shoes.

The one who had spoken was a tall, elegant lady wearing a white blouse with long sleeves and frills at the neck that came right up to her chin, and a dark skirt that went right down to her ankles. She wore a funny-looking pair of glasses that didn't have any earpieces; instead, they just sort of balanced on her nose. They had a small chain that led to a large brooch pinned to her blouse; Ben longed to see her take off the glasses so he could watch them dangle.

Azazel looked surprised and rather annoyed. She tossed her head back and regarded the tall woman contemptuously. "How dare you interrupt?"

The woman ignored her. She walked through where the wall was supposed to be and sat on Ben's bed. "Hello, Benjamin," she repeated calmly. "I am your Grandmama Sophia—your papa's mama."

She examined him through her funny glasses and smiled. "My, what a good-looking little boy you are! Every inch your grandfather. Except for your eyes—those must come from your mother's side of the family."

Ben decided that he liked her, especially because she appeared to be on his side. He pointed shakily at Azazel. "She said she was going to make a war and kill everybody!" he said.

The crowd murmured, and a thin man just behind Ben whispered something that made Azazel snarl. Ben's Grandmama Sophia turned her head. "Motl Fedke, not in front of the child!" she said sharply. The man shrugged, but said nothing more.

"Come sit by me, Benjamin," she continued. Ben stepped across the bed and sat next to her; she put an arm around his shoulders, but so lightly that he didn't feel it.

"I didn't know I had a Grandmama Sophia," he said.

"You have many relatives you don't know about, child," said the woman, rather sadly. "When you get a little older, ask your papa and mama about their families. Maybe by then, they'll be able to tell you."

"If they are still alive," Azazel sneered. The crowd murmured again, a little louder; a little girl wearing a funny long dress called, "You be quiet!" in a clear, high voice.

Grandmama Sophia stared at Azazel with an intensity that reminded Ben a little like how the President looked on the TV: serious and sad at the same time.

"You have no reason to push humanity into its own destruction," said Grandmama Sophia quietly. "Millions of people have died in the first half of this century; millions will die in the second. That's enough for the Angel of Death; why isn't it enough for you? You and your partner Shemhazhai are already disgraced in the eyes of heaven; why make things worse?"

Azazel raised her hands. "You know why. We are tired of exile; we want the world for ourselves."

"But why this boy?"

Ben tugged on his Grandmama's sleeve to get her attention; it was a strange sensation, as though he were pulling on woven ice. She bent her face down to him. "Yes, darling?" she asked.

"It's because of what happened in my dream," he told her. "There were all these people, and I thought they were asleep, but they were dead."

"The boy dreamed," Azazel said. "In that dream, he envisioned a possible future reality. There was power in that vision and I thought he could endanger our plans, were he strong enough and determined enough. But it turns out he is a mere human child."

Azazel laughed. Grandmama Sophia shook her head, took the glasses from her nose and let them drop; the thin chain they were attached to snapped into the brooch pinned to her blouse in a very satisfactory manner. She looked at Ben affectionately.

"First, let me explain exactly who Azazel is," she said. "She is nobody important, although she likes to believe she is. She is simply a minor angel who got into trouble a long time ago and has been making mischief ever since."

Ben stared at his Grandmama's face. She wasn't as pretty as Azazel—she was older, and her nose was a bit crooked, and there was a mole just above her left eyebrow. "And all these," he asked, pointing at the people gathered behind her. "Are they angels, too?"

"Definitely not," said a man, who stepped out of the crowd. He had short gray hair and a short beard, and was wearing a blue suit and dark red tie. He came over and sat on the other side of Ben, a rather strange expression on his face.

Ben looked at the man. "Are you also a relative?"

"Well, yes and no," said the man. "I'm just . . . " He paused and smiled, a bit sadly, Ben thought. "My name is Carlos. I'm a really good friend. From when—from when you're grown up."

The idea of Ben being grown up was interesting, and Ben wanted to ask the man more, but there were important things that had to be dealt with first.

"Azazel says my dream is going to come true," he said. "She tried to make everything dark. Can she do that?"

"I'm afraid she can," Grandmama Sophia said.

"Can't you stop her?" he asked.

She shook her head and exchanged glances with Carlos. "She knows there is little that I or the rest of us can do," she said. "Because we are no longer of this world—or not yet of this time—we have no power to affect events."

"That's right," Azazel grinned, fluffing her hair with one hand. "I don't have to listen to you or this crowd of has-beens and never-bes that you've got behind you. Shemhazhai and I have decided we've had it with watching humanity bumble along, making trouble for themselves and for us."

She laughed again. "Let them destroy themselves," she jeered. The darkness around began to swirl once again.

"I want her to stop!" Ben said, his lip trembling.

"Then make her stop," said his Grandmama Sophia. She looked up at Azazel. "This boy does have power," she said firmly. "Undisciplined and unconscious, but with a child's complete belief. And I, and all those who lived before him and will live after him, and those who died before him and will die after him, we all stand with him."

Azazel stared at Ben. "Yes," she said after a moment. "The power is there. But there is a price."

She walked over to Ben, wisps of black fog trailing behind her, and knelt so that her face was close to his. "Ben, darling," she said in a falsely sweet tone that made Ben shrink back, "has your dear Grandmama Sophia told you that using power has a cost? That the more power you use, the more days of your life will be pulled away, bit by bit, year by year?"

She turned her head and stared coldly at Carlos. "You know. Tell him!"

The man bit his lip, and looked down at Ben.

"Don't pay attention to her," said Ben's Grandmama sharply. "She's playing her usual games." She reached over Ben's head and touched Carlos' cheek gently. "Think. If this is not done, if there is a war, will he live any longer? Will he live any happier? And you and he will lose your time together. Would that be better for Benjamin?"

"Grandmama?" Ben asked uncertainly, not sure what they were talking about. Carlos nodded, put his hands on Ben's shoulders, and turned the boy slightly so that they faced each other.

"You are such a very good boy," he said. "And you will be a good man. Yes, what she says is right—if you stop Azazel from doing this bad thing, you may need to pay for it someday. But that won't be for a long time yet, not until you're grown up. For now, you do what you think is right, and everything will be fine."

He smiled at Ben. It was a nice smile, much nicer than Azazel's, and Ben smiled back. "Okay," he said.

Ben looked back at Azazel, who stood up and stared down at him. He climbed back to his feet, so that, standing on the bed, he was almost eye-level with her. He reached down and took the hands of Carlos and his Grandmama Sophia. Their hands were cool but comforting.

"You're a bully," he said to Azazel. "You want to hurt a lot of people just because you can."

"Remember your dream?" asked his Grandmama Sophia. "Remember all the people who were hurt and crying? This is what she wants. This is what will happen if she gets her way."

"My Daddy was hurt. I wanted him to pick me up, but he didn't see me," said Ben. His breath started to come faster; tears began to gather in his eyes.

Azazel back away and opened her arms wide. The darkness began to grow again; the tendrils of fog twisting and turning and reaching. Azazel's fingers worked, molding the oncoming darkness into something palpable and infinitely threatening.

"Look at him," she jeered. "Look at the great, powerful child. Sniveling and terrified."

"I'm not scared," Ben told her, his voice rising. "I'm mad."

And he was. Something was happening in Ben's head, something that was starting to hurt, but strangely enough, in a good way.

He took great gulps of air, watching as Azazel began to laugh, her eyes closed, her arms out to the heavens. Clouds around her blotted out his toys, the pictures on his walls, and rolled to the ceiling, toward his windows and to the door of his room. Beyond that door, Ben knew, was his apartment, and his mama and papa.

"Stop that!" Ben shouted furiously. He scrambled off the bed onto the floor. "You're mean!" he yelled. "You want to hurt people! I hate you!" His whole body felt hot and cold at the same time. "I hate you!" he said again, pointing to the angel.

Carlos and his Grandmama stood up as well. "Now you've gotten him angry," Carlos said, a new note in his voice. "That was a mistake. He can be a real pain in the butt when he's angry."

For a moment, Azazel was absolutely still. Something stirred in her eyes, and she flickered like the TV picture did when there was a storm. The woman in red shoes and wavy hair and shiny dress shifted and moved, becoming something large and bright and hard to look at.

"Don't stop," said Carlos. "Be mad. Be really mad."

"But what should I do?" Ben asked tearfully. "She's making all that smoke, and she's going to hurt my mama and papa. And everybody else! What should I do?"

"What do you do when you get really, really mad?" Carlos asked him. "What did you do when Eliot pushed you off the swing and made you skin your knee? You told me all about it. Did you just stand there and cry?"

"I yelled," Ben said.

"You yelled really, really loud."

Ben took a deep breath. "Stop!" he shrieked. "You stop! You're mean and I hate you, and they hate you, and we all hate you!"

Azazel stopped looking amused. Small flames licked her skin while the darkness seethed and rolled around her. "Idiots!" she cried out. "You who are dead and who shall soon be dead, do you think to challenge us and win?"

Ben stared at the huge, dark, awful thing that threatened his parents and his world.

"It is up to you, child," said his Grandmama. "We're all here. We're your family. We won't leave you. Ever."

Carlos leaned over, and lightly kissed Ben's forehead. "I love you," he said. "Whatever happens, I always will. Now go ahead—yell the house down." He smiled.

Ben smiled back at Carlos, and at his Grandmama. He squeezed his eyes shut, clenched his hands into fists, took a deep breath, lifted his head and screamed.

It was the high, piercing wail of a furious young child—a child who had never before experienced true injustice. His shrill cry filled the room and was amplified by the voices of the past and future souls who surrounded him, those who had and would witness the hate that would be used against them and others. His voice and theirs joined into creating a tapestry of sound that flowed over and into the dark reality that Azazel had been building—and suddenly there was a tiny crack, a thin spill of sunlight within the roiling gloom.

Azazel growled and extended her arms further. She opened her mouth and began to howl, a frightening sound like a cage full of angry dogs. For a moment, Ben hesitated. The crack began to close.

"Louder!" Grandmama Sophia urged. "Hurry, child!"

Ben squeezed his eyes tightly shut, turned his face up to the ceiling and to the sky above that, and screamed, louder and higher, until his body burned and he was aware of nothing but his own voice, filling his room and his universe.

Somewhere in his head, Ben watched as the crack widened, pushing a steadily brighter stream of light through Azazel's carefully built reality. There was a shattering crash and the darkness split apart with an intense, blinding flash.

And then, just as suddenly, everything was quiet. Ben breathed deeply, tears streaming down his face. He gulped.

"Shh, kindele," said Grandmama Sophia quietly. "Be still. All is well."

"Hush, querido," Carlos whispered, stroking his hair gently. "You did it. I knew you could. Everything will be fine now."

Ben, shaken and still a little tearful, took a slow, careful breath. "My head hurts," he complained.

The boy opened his eyes and looked around. His room was there again, the way it always was, the walls all back in place. The streetlights shone through the window. His nightlight glowed in its place next to the door.

But his Grandmama, Carlos, all the people had who been there, were gone.

"Where did you go?" Ben said, looking around.

"I'm right here."

Azazel still stood in the center of his room. She had regained her long hair, tuxedo and red shoes, and was looking at herself critically in a small mirror, arranging her hair and pouting her lips.

"Perhaps," she said, "This look is a little old-fashioned, after all. Perhaps next time, Marilyn Monroe with a touch of Tony Curtis thrown in?"

She threw the mirror away and stared coldly at Ben.

"You realize," she said, "that this doesn't change things. Not really. Humanity will continue to kill its own kind continually, stupidly and unnecessarily—just not as quickly. And as far as you're concerned, remember, there will be a price to pay. There always is."

Ben looked back at her, unafraid. "Go away," he said. "This is my room."

Azazel grinned. "No hard feelings. See you later, alligator," she said. And then, she was gone as well.

The boy sat on his bed and pulled his stuffed panda to him. He was sorry that his Grandmama Sophia and his friend Carlos had to go away. He wondered who the little girl was who had spoken up and if they could have played together if she stayed. And he felt tired and a little strange, as though he were a glass of water that somebody had drank all up.

"Benjamin Solomon, what are you doing awake at this time of night?" It was his mama's voice, the tone she used when she suspected he was thinking of doing something she didn't approve of. She had opened the door; the light from the hallway outside spilled into his room.

"Get back into bed, young man," she said sternly. Ben climbed back under his covers while she walked over, tucked him in and then sat next to him on the bed. She reached out and stroked his head.

"Are you still frightened?" his mama asked gently.

"No," he said. "You know what, mama?"

"What, mein Kind?"

Ben smiled. "The numbers really *are* magic."

For a moment, her hand on his head was still. Then she pulled him to her and rocked him gently, back and forth. "For you, yes, they are magic," she whispered. "Just for you, my baby."

Ben closed his eyes and let her carry him to dreams of an enchanted future.

Rosemary, That's
For Remembrance

A story of Lydia Jacobson, Isabeau's housemate

1981

I remember.

When I was a girl, I loved going to the beauty shop. It had light blue walls, I think, and a radio. I sat under the dryer wearing a pink smock, reading the latest issue of Vogue, and listening to . . . what was her name? . . . to one of my friends talking about her latest boyfriend. It was nice.

Kay's is nice, too. The woman in charge comes to greet us; she has bright yellow hair and thick glasses and she says hello to me, not just to the woman who brought me (should I know her?) the way a lot of people do. And she wears a nametag on her pink smock so that I always know her name; it says "KAY" with tiny purple flowers entwined around it.

Even though I've only lived in this neighborhood for . . . well, for a few years (I remember that I grew up in Williamsburg and brought up my children in Canarsie; I remember those years very well), Kay's looks like all the beauty shops I ever knew. Once, I remember, I went to a new one, and it had deafening music and strange machines and tall boys talking loud and winking at the others when they thought I didn't see. (I know I'm old. I can't help it. They'll be old one day too, and why don't they understand that?)

Kay smiles at me, takes my coat and my pocketbook, and helps me sit down in one of the chairs while the woman who brought me goes and sits in front of the salon and starts reading a magazine.

"And how are you today?" Kay says while she puts a towel around my neck and then covers me with a flowery cape to protect my clothes. I'm fine, I say, although we both know I'm not fine at all. I'm disappearing. Bit by bit.

I don't know why and neither do they. The doctors, I mean. Tests are inconclusive. (You see? I can understand these things; I've got a Masters in History, after all.) They say it past me, to the woman who lives with me, who says she's my friend Isabeau. (I remember an Isabeau, but she's young and slim and has two lovely children, not elderly and sad like this woman.) But I listen. And sometimes I remember.

Kay chats to me while she dampens my hair and takes out her scissors. I had beautiful hair (I have photos), thick and brown. Jack used to run his hands through it and beg me not to cut it, although long hair wasn't the fashion and I really looked better with short. Now, I look in the mirror and it's all dull gray and I can see parts of my scalp showing through; it makes me want to cry, more than the wrinkles and the pieces of my life that have disappeared.

I start to get up, to get away from the mirror, but the moment I start to move Kay swings the chair around so I'm looking instead at the TV set that's been set up high on the back wall. "There," she says. "You don't mind facing the wall, do you? It's so much easier for me." She chatters on, about her friend's daughter who is pregnant and miserable; about how the weather has been unseasonably icy and why do they call it global warming when things are getting colder?

Beneath the TV set, a young Asian girl with a sour expression works on the nails of an old woman with bright orange hair (am I that old? Surely I'm not that old) and nods, and says we've ruined the world and that one day we'll wake up and all the oxygen will have disappeared from the earth. She says it with satisfaction.

On the TV, a man walks around the streets of a foreign country (because nobody else is speaking English), and stops in a market-place and talks to a man who is frying foods in a little booth, and tries some of the foods, although it looks extremely unappetizing. (Let Julie eat what she wants, I told Jack when he tried to make our daughter eat her vegetables, and what does she look like again?)

"There you are!" says Pat (no, not Pat, that was the woman who cut my hair when I was a girl, this is Kay, it says so on her name tag). "Ready for the dryer?"

Kay puts a pillow on the chair so I can sit comfortably and settles me in. She puts a magazine on my lap and brings over a small can of ginger ale, placing it on a table next to the chair. "There," she says. "We like to make our ladies comfortable. Ready?"

I nod, and look up at her. She takes her glasses off and smiles, and wait, something is wrong—her eyes are striped, completely striped through the pupils and the iris and whites, all green and silver. I want to call out, to warn somebody, but I don't know who here will help me and then she pulls the dryer over my head down like a giant upside-down cup and turns it on.

Something hums and grabs my head and my brain and where am

I smell morning and hear eggs frying and there is sunlight coming through the gauze kitchen curtains Julie! it's a school day young lady do you know what time time time is on our side and her eyes are getting cold it's cold outside please stop blowing bubbles in your milk round like a hairdryer yes honey your tie is on the hanger does he still love love me do don't tease the bye baby bunting have a good day at the office, dear, and don't forget and there he goes and she goes and they go and it's quiet and oh the baby's crying but what is that sound and where did everyone go and what was I going it's all going it's all

"There now," a voice says. "That didn't hurt a bit, did it?"

There's a woman standing over me wearing a smock with flowers and a tag. I suppose it's a name tag, but I can't read it, it's just squiggles. I'm in a . . . a . . . someplace with a lot of women and it looks nice, but something is missing.

The woman smiles at me and bends down. "It's all right," she whispers, and her eyes are pretty stripes and somewhere under her voice is something, a hissing or a crackle. I can't tell what it is or what she is. "I can't," I tell her. If I could only. But. "I just can't. They're missing."

"Don't worry," she says. "We've got them. We've collected them from you and many like you, and we'll keep them safe long after you and yours are gone." She puts on a pair of glasses and raises her voice. "Now, let's go back to the chair and I'll comb you out."

She helps me up and takes me to a chair. I sit, and look at the old woman in the mirror, and wonder who she is.

Stoop Ladies

A story of Julie Jacobson, Lydia's daughter

1983

This is the way the world ends, Julie reads. *Not with a bang but a whimper.* She lifts her eyes from T.S. Eliot's poem to a puffed-up pigeon grooming itself on the windowsill. "That's me," she tells the pigeon. "They fired me, and all I could do was whimper." A typical Brooklyn bird, it doesn't seem particularly interested.

A high cackle bounces into the room from across the street. The pigeon flaps anxiously away while Julie peers outside.

The ladies have gathered.

Every summer evening, after the dishes are done and their men placed safely in front of the television set, they sit in the small yard next to the stoop: some on folding chairs and others on the concrete steps. The youngest in her 50s, the oldest past 80, they watch the passersby and talk of schools and children, of changes in the neighborhood, of the new theater on the corner and the cops who ticket double-parked cars.

On her walk home from the subway every evening, Julie usually nods at the ladies as she goes home to chicken-and-rice or a pizza from the restaurant on the corner. Although they nod back, and even wave their hands in invitation, she typically just waves back as she climbs the steps to her front door. Only once or twice has she felt comfortable joining the crowd of elderly, gossiping women. It's bad enough, she tells herself, that she has to work so hard to be accepted by the beautiful, thin executives at her office, or the well-dressed middle-aged men at the bars (who look past her without even focusing). She's not going to associate herself with a group of obvious losers, blue-haired women past their prime. That would be admitting defeat. Admitting that her life is over, after never having happened.

162

Although, Julie sometimes concedes to herself, the few times she let the voices draw her from her solitude, the ladies made her welcome. And it was pleasant, standing around with people who talked to her as if she was important, and asked for her sympathy and advice on stolen cars, misbehaving computers, children going astray . . . .

Her beeper buzzes at her; she pulls it quickly from her belt and checks the message. *No luck so far*, it reads. *Will try to talk to Sam. Stay cool. Ginnie.*

She reaches for the phone and dials Isabeau, whom her mom had always called "my extra-special friend," and who always lent a sympathetic ear when Julie had a problem. When Julie's father left, Isabeau persuaded her mom, who had no idea how to do things like hire a mechanic or write a check (never mind handle a divorce), to leave the large, lonely house and move in with her and her two kids. And when Julie's mom was diagnosed with Alzheimer's, it was Isabeau who helped make those last couple of years as easy as possible.

Isabeau's phone rings several times, and then the answering machine clicks on. The hell with it. Julie hangs up, turns on the TV, and flips through the channels for a few moments, settling for a sitcom in which a man tries to avoid an oversexed, overweight, badly dressed secretary. But the chatter from outside pushes past the canned laughter and demands her attention.

Julie sighs, leaves the bedroom and goes into her tiny kitchen. I'll make myself a snack, she tells herself, but halfway through a lettuce and tomato sandwich she changes her mind, pulls the half-full garbage bag out of its plastic can, ties the ends, and takes it out her front door and down the steps.

On the bottom landing she passes Mrs. Golini's door. Living one on top of the other, both she and her landlady have maintained a respectful distance. They smile hello and exchange holiday gifts at Christmas and ignore each other's existence the rest of the year.

Outside, a slight breeze eases the summer humidity. Julie drops her garbage in one of the cans at the side of the stairs and glances surreptitiously across the street. Six of the ladies are out tonight. Julie glances up at her windows, where the blue light of the television reflects off her shades. The loneliness of the evening is nearly overwhelming. Slowly, almost without thinking, Julie turns her back on her building and crosses the street. "Hi," she says tentatively.

The women smile at her. "We were wondering when you'd come over again," says Mrs. O'Neill, sitting back in her wheelchair. The wheelchair is more for convenience than necessity; after breaking her hip two years ago, she decided that it was more comfortable than her folding chair and told the hospital authorities it had been stolen. As usual, she wears an old, threadbare pink sweater over a long, flowered housedress; her chubby bare feet are pushed into a worn pair of slippers.

"We even took penny bets on it," grins Jackie, a part-time beautician who works in the hair salon around the corner. She rests one hip against the railing, a cigarette dangling loosely from her wide, sardonic mouth. "I won."

Julie smiles back. The night is pleasant and cool; a few cicadas vibrate in a neighboring tree.

"Come sit," says one of the women, a thin, dry lady named Norma, patting the step beside her.

Julie shakes her head. "That's okay," she says. "I prefer to stand."

Mary—a pleasant bleached blonde who can sometimes be heard yelling down the block for her teenaged son—nods at her. She is, as usual, sitting next to Mrs. O'Neill on a small cloth director's chair. "How are you, Julie?" she asks in a voice tinged with the Irish accents of her childhood.

Julie shrugs. "Fine," she says. In her loose green tee shirt, sweat pants, and old sneakers, she feels a little underdressed next to Mary's careful polyester fashion.

"I was sorry to hear about your mother," said Mary. "We said hi a few times when she was visiting. She was a nice lady."

"Thanks," Julie says, a bit tersely. She still hasn't figured out how she feels about her mother's death—sad because her mom is gone, or relieved because the woman who finally died was, in the end, no longer her mother.

"I understand you're looking for a new job. Have you found one yet?" asks Mrs. O'Neill, shooting a quick look at Mary. Surprised, Julie starts to ask how she knows, but doesn't get the chance.

"Why is she looking for a job?" demands another woman whom Julie doesn't know, a withered form in a bright pink jogging suit who sits comfortably crocheting in an old blue folding chair.

"That's my older sister Myra," explains Mrs. O'Neill, not bothering to look at her sibling. "She's staying with me for a couple of days while her house is painted." She sniffs. "Of course, if it were me, I'd want to supervise their every move. You never know what painters are up to."

Myra doesn't seem bothered by her sister's apparent contempt. "My husband Joe is perfectly capable of watching the painters," she says. "No reason why I need to put up with the mess and smell if he's willing to." She looks back at Julie, inquiring.

"They laid me off," Julie tells her.

There is a general murmur of sympathy. "That's too bad," says Mary. "You were there a long time, too, weren't you?"

"Seventeen years. They said that they had to cut back on the payroll in my division."

"I hear a 'but' in there," says Myra, a knowing tone in her voice.

Julie smiles ironically. "Sam, my boss, hired an 'assistant' for me about two months ago—young woman, right out of college—and somehow she is being kept on while I'm being let go. He said it was because they had to eliminate some of the higher salaried workers."

She pauses. This is where her listeners usually change the subject or offer vague reassurances. "But you don't think that's the whole story," Mary prompts. The others look on expectantly, their faces friendly, sympathetic. Julie feels something rise to her throat.

"No," she finally says. "The company is one of the major PR organizations around for technical corporations. When we started out, we were small, taking whatever clients we could get, but now we've got offices on both coasts, and handle a lot of the biggest companies around. We had a meeting last month and Sam told us that we were going on to the next 'plateau of success'—he talks that way—and that we were going to have to refine our image in order to pick up more Fortune 500 firms." She takes a breath. "I think that a size 16 PR representative doesn't quite fit into that image."

There is a moment of silence.

Mrs. O'Neill snorts, something between a laugh and a sneeze. "Well, never mind," she says, and launches into a long explanation of how the oldest son of a distant relative was fired, found another job through some kind of vaguely illegal connection, and was eventually rehired into a higher level of his former company. Julie soon loses the gist of it, but the sound of the narrative, and the murmurs of the listeners, is strangely soothing in the fading light. It's as if all of them are caught in some old-time photograph that will never change— just the ladies, and the street, and the summer evening.

Mrs. O'Neill finishes her story. "You don't think that something like that could happen to you?" she asks. Julie, startled into awareness by the question, shrugs.

"No. A friend of mine said that she's going to ask around, see if there's anything she can find out that might get me back in, but we both know that it's pretty useless. And in today's market, not too many other firms will have openings either. I'll probably have to look into relocating."

"You know," calls out Bev, whose considerable girth is comfortably ensconced in a loud muumuu, and who has been concentrating on filing her nails, "It's too bad that companies like yours consider a few pounds to be some kind of crime against humanity. When I worked for that Greek travel agency, they were grateful to have somebody as good as I was."

"I remember that agency," Jackie says. "Went out of business, didn't they? Something about the Department of Immigration?"

Bev scowls, and returns her attention to her nails. Mrs. O'Neill cackles, and turns to Norma. "What do you think?" she asks. "Is this a wine occasion?"

For a moment, the ladies are quiet. Julie looks at each, but they all seem otherwise occupied, pulling at stray threads or lighting cigarettes. Norma finally shrugs. "Why not?" she says. "It's been too long since we treated ourselves."

Jackie clears her throat. "I have a box of wine that I picked up today," she says. "I'll just go and get it." There is a general murmur of approval. Jackie stretches and ambles down the block to her house.

Rusting metal squeaks as Mrs. O'Neill pulls herself awkwardly from her wheelchair. "These bugs are driving me crazy," she announces. "I'm going to get that bad-smelling candle that my son sent me. He said that it would keep the mosquitoes away." She shuffles back to the door that leads to her ground-floor apartment.

A car bounces along the street, its suspension badly in need of repair. "I hope he breaks an axle," Bev says, irritated. "That's what he gets for going so fast. On a block with children, too."

"Do you have any children, Julie?" asks Myra. Julie shakes her head. "But she still could," says Mary. "Couldn't you?"

Julie hates conversations like this. "I could, I guess. It's not very likely though. I mean, I'm nearly 48. It's not as though I've got much longer to go."

"No." The listening women nod noncommittally.

"Don't worry," Mary tells her. "The menopause isn't so bad. At worst, it's a pain in the butt for a few years. Then you don't have to worry about it again. And there are other things you can do then. New things."

Julie nods again but looks away. It's fine for her, middle-class woman with a house and a 13-year-old son. I've got nothing. Nobody. Unless you count my mother's elderly ex-housemate, her grown kids who have their own lives to live, and friends who constantly try to set me up with jerks.

Just cut the crap, she reminds herself sternly. Your friends mean well. And what does Mary have that you want so much? A divorce, a mortgage, and an adolescent? So stop pitying yourself and get on with it.

"Here we go, ladies." Jackie ambles back up with a large cardboard box labeled Chablis. She places it on one of the steps, while Mary gets up and goes into the house, returning a couple of minutes later with a package of paper cups in one hand, and a large bag of popcorn in the other.

Jackie takes the paper cups, and starts filling them and handing them around, while Mary offers Julie the popcorn bag. "Open this, would you?"

"So," asks Myra, "what was the name of that company of yours?"

"Caesar Communications," says Julie through her teeth, trying to pull the stubborn plastic apart.

"Interesting name," says Mrs. O'Neill, lowering herself back into her wheelchair. She is holding a small candle in a jelly jar, which she balances on the armrest. "In the city?"

"Yes," Julie mutters. The bag finally splits open. "Midtown." She takes a handful of popcorn and gives the bag to Mrs. O'Neill.

"It's too bad that you might need to move. But you should find something."

Julie accepts a cup and sips cautiously. Not as bad as she expected.

A small gray cat ambles out from under one of the parked cars on the street and stops, regarding the group of people with a surprising lack of fear. Julie, who is still standing outside the area railing—and who likes cats—kneels down, trying not to alarm the animal, and holds out the hand with the popcorn. Above her, the conversation goes on.

The cat stops, and stares at her for a few moments. It then cautiously ventures forward, bright green eyes flickering warily from her face to the food.

"Do cats eat popcorn?" Jackie asks above her.

"My sister had a cat once, would eat lettuce," Bev says. There is the quiet flick of a lighter and a faint acrid smell—the candle?—tickles her nose slightly.

"You had a cat once, didn't you?" asks Mary. Julie nods carefully, trying not to alarm the animal. "Yes," she says. The cat doesn't seem to mind her voice; it continues to edge closer. "Darwin. He died about four years ago."

"Why didn't you get another?" Norma asks.

"Mrs. Golini doesn't like cats. She told me once that she couldn't ask me to get rid of the one I had, but after Darwin died, she didn't want any more in the house."

"Pity," Mary comments.

Julie nods. "Come on, cat," she whispers as the animal edges up to her hand. "Come on. I won't hurt you."

It stares up at her, down at the popcorn.

"It would be a pity if you left the neighborhood," says Mary. "Just when we were starting to get acquainted. We would miss you at our little gatherings. We'd like you to sit with us regularly."

"We would, indeed," says Jackie.

"We would," echoes Myra.

"It would be a blessing if your company decided to keep you on," says Norma.

"A real blessing," Bev agrees.

"A blessing," Mrs. O'Neill whispers, and then hums, a strange, singsong murmur that Julie can't quite catch. Her attention turns back to the animal.

It stretches out its neck, sniffs at her fingertips. "That's it, cat," says Julie as, having decided that her offering is acceptable, it begins nibbling at the popcorn. Julie, charmed, places her cup on the ground, reaches over, and gently scratches the animal's soft head. For a few seconds, there is nothing in Julie's world but the quiet purring of the cat trembling against her fingers.

A sudden hiss from behind her. Startled, Julie looks up. A small gray wisp of smoke curls up from the extinguished flame. "Oh, dear," said Mrs. O'Neill. "Now look what I've done. Spilled my wine. And right on the candle, too."

"Don't worry about it," Jackie says. "Plenty more where that came from."

The cat quickly turns and scoots off. Julie reaches for her cup and stands with some difficulty, feeling unexercised muscles protest. She takes another sip of wine.

"I'll bet you miss having a cat," Mary says.

Julie smiles. "Yes, a bit. Things are a lot cleaner now without the cat litter and fur balls, but I do miss having a pet around. They seem to know exactly when you need somebody to caress."

"I'm allergic to animals," Bev complains. "Cats make me break out in hives."

"I've told you that you should get a bird," Mrs. O'Neill tells her.

"Birds are dirty," Bev grouses.

"Only if you don't clean their cages," Julie tells her. "I had a parakeet when I was a kid. It was nice. I trained it to ride on my shoulder."

Suddenly, her beeper chimes at her. "Better check that," Mrs. O'Neill says.

Julie pulls it off her belt and checks the screen. *Clients in revolt. Expect a call. Demand a hefty raise. You owe me dinner. Ginnie.*

Julie looks up wordlessly. "Good news?" Mrs. O'Neill asks, accepting another cup of wine from Jackie. "Maybe that Sam found he needs you after all?"

Julie stares at her. But the woman just brushes some popcorn crumbs off her housedress and smiles.

"Good," Mary says. "It would be a pity for Julie to have to leave just when we were getting to know her."

"You know," says Jackie, "That cat really took to you. Maybe you should adopt it."

"If you do, get it fixed," Norma says. "Too many wild cats around here."

Julie looks at her neighbors. "Mrs. Golini won't let me have any pets," she says slowly.

"Maybe," Mrs. O'Neill says. "We can change her mind."

Escape Route

Julie Jacobson's story continues

2016

Escape had become necessary. But Julie wasn't sure it was still possible.

Time had not slowed, even for her. For several years, especially after she retired, she sat with and learned from the ladies who gathered on the stoops of her Brooklyn neighborhood. But then, one by one, they disappeared into nursing homes or the care of their children. Their houses were sold and occupied by prosperous, polite but distant young families who were too busy finding private schools for their children to be interested in sitting and gossiping on stoops.

The stoop ladies weren't the only people Julie lost. Her mother and her mother's friend Isabeau were both long gone. Other relatives moved away and forgot her—or died. Friends, displaced by rising rents or simple restlessness, also left, to become online ghosts, untouchable and far away.

She even lost touch with Isabeau's children, Mark and Eileen, who still lived in the city. Every spring, they sent her a newsy letter along with an invitation to their Passover seder. But Julie had never been close to them—she was over 15 years older than they were, and even when her mother was alive, she had only seen them occasionally. So each year, when the letter came, she assumed that the invitation was made out of politeness and would, with equal politeness, decline.

And then one day the second-floor apartment that she had rented for 30 years was claimed by her landlady's daughter, now grown and visibly pregnant, who gave her a month to vacate. Unable to find anything nearby that she could afford, Julie gave her cat to a willing neighbor and moved to a small apartment on a noisy street in a neighborhood where she was completely unknown.

Her life crashed. Circumstances and her own body had finally betrayed her. The expenses and tensions of the move—exacerbated by a nasty case of arthritis, for which she had to visit several doctors—drained her retirement savings. She was old, and slow, and lame—and alone.

Even her former energy and power—the power that had been taught her by the small community of stoop ladies—had ebbed away, stolen by time and isolation. All she had left was a locket that Mrs. O'Neill had given her. And that wasn't something she wanted to use. Yet.

Each night, Julie would sit and stare out the window at the people passing, feeling as though she were watching life from a distance. "I understand now, mom," she told the framed photo that sat on a side table. "It all goes away in the end, doesn't it? Everything just fades away. Maybe you were luckier than I am. You forgot what you once were."

Existence narrowed to the daily grind of surviving one more week, one more day. Her main avenue of escape became the worlds of fiction, and she was starting to lose even those. The local movie theatre went out of business and became a large and unneeded drug store. Her old TV stopped working, and she couldn't afford a new set (never mind a cable subscription or Internet feed). Finally, the only place she had left was the public library.

Unfortunately, the nearest branch was several miles away, and the way to get there was neither short nor simple. So she had to limit her trips to once a week; the rest of her days were spent in anticipation and hope.

Each week, when the day came, Julie planned carefully. The night before, she laid out her clothes, the books she had to return, a sandwich for lunch and everything else she would need. In the morning, she got up early so she could shower, dress and breakfast—none of which could be done quickly—and still be able to leave in plenty of time.

When she was ready to go, Julie first had to navigate her way down from her tiny apartment to the street—assuming the elevator was working. Then there were the three blocks to the bus stop, which could take anywhere from 15 minutes to half an hour, depending on the weather.

Luckily, today was easier than usual; it was a cool, sunny autumn day—"sweater weather," as Julie's mother used to call it—and that would make things a little more pleasant.

Once she got outside her apartment building, Julie made sure her pocketbook—large enough to carry her keys, wallet, medications, a small bottle of water and two library books—was slung around her shoulders, and that her locket was securely fastened around her neck. She then began to make her way down the sidewalk, her walker tapping a slow, steady rhythm against the cement.

She usually timed herself so that there was no chance she would miss the bus. Today, however, she must have left late, or taken longer to walk, because the bus pulled up only about five minutes after she arrived.

As soon as the bus driver spotted Julie, she hit the switch that would sink the front of the vehicle down so there would be less need to step up. "Do you need help?" the driver asked, and Julie shook her head.

She folded her walker and clutched it in one hand as she pulled herself up into the bus using the handrail. She dipped her senior citizen card into the slot, smiled at the driver, and made her way down the aisle to the first available seat, ignoring the irritated glances she was getting from the riders who obviously resented the time she was taking (and the fact that driver was waiting until Julie was seated to resume the trip).

The bus ride itself was about 20 minutes. When she reached her stop, Julie began to climb down from the bus; the driver squeezed out of her seat, took Julie's walker, carried it easily out of the bus and then unfolded it for her.

"Have a good day," the driver said to her, smiling, and then yelled, "Okay, just a minute, for chrissakes!" at somebody in the bus as she went back in. The door shut with a pneumatic whine and the bus continued down the street.

Julie took a breath, made sure all her belongings were where they should be, and started the four blocks to the library.

Pedestrians strode around her quickly, trying not to look, impatient with her sluggish pace and terrified of what she implied about their own mortality. A group of teens knocked into her and ran on, laughing, as she stopped to collect herself, clutching desperately at her last treasure: The locket at her throat.

It had been given to her by old Mrs. O'Neill as she lay dying, shrunken and immobile, in a hospital bed. "When this was given to me," Mrs. O'Neill whispered to Julie all these years ago, "I thought

I would use it at a time like this, when I was old and bedridden and with not much time left in my body. I thought that I would be prepared to be part of two selves in a newer, more healthy body. But I can't."

"Use it with me," Julie begged, terrified that she was about to lose a woman who had become one of her closest friends. Mrs. O'Neill smiled.

"That's sweet of you, darlin'. But I'm too used to being on my own. And I'm tired. I'm ready to leave. You take it. Use it if you ever need to or want to. But if you do use it," she said, so quietly that Julie could hardly hear her, "choose someone who might not mind sharing."

The locket was still there. Julie took a deep breath and held on to it for an extra few seconds, watching the youngsters and considering. But then she let her hand drop and began walking again, anxious to get to her destination. She couldn't blame the kids—she remembered her own contempt for the aged when she was young. Because she had known, as all children know, that she'd never get old.

By the time she got to her destination, she was winded and already tired. She paused just before the steps to the building to catch her breath for a moment. But only for a moment. She wanted to get inside.

The library was typical of the type of building built in the mid-20th century: A low, one-story construction that had had seen better days. Julie made her way up the three steps, pushed through the front door, and then stood at the return desk for a moment to get her bearings.

To her right was the long, curved desk behind which the librarians had, for over half a century, stamped books in and out. While there were still librarians behind the desk, they no longer stamped books; instead, there was a separate table with a machine on it. You put your book on the machine to be scanned and then collected a little paper ticket that told you when you needed to return it. Julie had tried using the scanner once, but she just couldn't get the hang of it; it made her feel stupid and lost in a future that she couldn't understand. After that, she would just hand her books to a librarian to be checked in and out. They didn't seem to mind.

Today, the young woman behind the main desk—her name was Maria, Julie remembered, and she had just been working there for about nine months or so—waited patiently until Julie pulled out the books that she had brought and placed them on the desk.

"Do you need the computer today?" Maria asked, and when Julie nodded, said, "Steven will help you. He's got a couple of things to do, and then he'll be right with you. Since we knew today was your usual day, we've already reserved a system for you."

Julie smiled at her and went to sit near the "Recent Arrivals" shelf. She examined the books on it, finally choosing one and placing it in her bag to check out later. She then watched the after-school children and unemployed adults wander in and out of the building for about 15 minutes or so until Steven, a stout, cheerful young man with a shining bald head, came over to conduct her to one of the computers.

"Hey, beautiful," he said. "How's it going?"

Today, besides checking her email, Julie also had to order more checks from her bank. According to the rules, the librarians weren't supposed to help her with financial matters, but they did it anyway. "After all," said Steven, as they finished up, "I might need help myself someday, if I'm lucky enough to get old."

"Lucky," Julie told him, "isn't the word I'd use." He smiled at her the same way they all smiled at her, as if she were five years old and anything she said didn't really matter.

"You want to browse some more?" he asked. "Or are you just going to go straight to the auditorium?"

At 3 p.m. on Wednesdays, the library showed films in the back room—one of the main reasons she now tried to come every week.

Recently, the choice of films that the library had been showing had been, to Julie's mind, unfortunate. The movies were fast moving and confusing, with little or no plot as far as she could tell. Just a lot of pretty people running around and shooting amid a lot of explosions—worlds in which Julie had no desire to spend much time, if any. But, she told herself, there was always hope.

This week, she took her seat in the first row as usual (because her Medicare-issued hearing aids weren't worth shit). A large, flat-screen monitor waited up front, connected to a small laptop computer on which they ran the videos (they had replaced the old film projector about five years earlier).

She opened the book she had chosen—a biography of Alan Turing that was apparently a best seller these days—but couldn't make herself concentrate on the words. Instead, she found herself remembering her mother, and the long years of caring for her. The men whom she occasionally dated but who never seemed to want to stay. The children she never bore, and the adoptions that never happened.

Of a life that seemed over before it ever began.

Thankfully, she was interrupted by Steven's voice. She put the book back in her bag, folded her hands in her lap, and waited.

The young man stood in the front of the small meeting room, looked out at her and the six other people there (two in wheelchairs) and said, "Before I introduce this week's film, I have an announcement to make—a rather sad one, I'm afraid. Most of you may be already aware of this, but the city has decided to cut down on funding for the library system, and this branch has been slated for closure. We are trying to change their minds, but if we can't, we will be closing permanently at the end of the month."

Oh, hell, Julie thought. She took several long breaths to try to quiet the panic that was hitting her throat and stomach.

"Meanwhile," Steven said in a fake-enthusiastic voice, "on with the show. This week, we're going to do something a little different. Instead of a current movie, we're going to show a film that was produced in another era of financial difficulties, and which was recently restored: Gold Diggers of 1933."

Julie bit her lip and thought hard. 1933. Breadlines, poverty and desperation. Jazz, sound films, Roosevelt and the end of Prohibition. And the possibility of pushing your way up if you were young and healthy and smart enough.

Not a bad deal, actually—especially if you considered the alternative.

Steven started out of the room. On the way, he stopped at Julie's seat. "I'm so sorry, beautiful," he said. "I know you love coming here. If you want, I'll see if there's another branch that you can get to."

"Thank you," Julie said. "I'd appreciate that. This is, you see, the only chance I have to escape."

The young man smiled sadly at her and left. Julie watched him go and then turned to the screen as the film started.

Ginger Rogers, pert, sexy and impossibly young, sang "We're in the Money" while a line of young women dressed as coins swayed beside her. Julie knew these types of musicals; there would be a lot of big numbers with lots of pretty girls in elaborate costumes—and careful close-ups of smooth faces, bright eyes and darkly lipsticked mouths. She watched as the camera panned away from Ginger and across the anonymous faces of several chorines—young, cheerful, and completely unaware of what the future held.

There, she thought. That one. Fourth from Ginger, as pretty as the others but with a distinct look of intelligence in the knowing smile. Somebody, Julie mused, who would do whatever it took to earn a few spoken lines, or an extra 30 precious seconds on the screen. Who might welcome a bit of advice from someone who knew what was coming.

The camera moved on and the girl was gone.

Julie reached up with her left hand and clutched her locket—and just kept watching. Jazzy music and energetic dance routines. Sharp dialogue and wonderfully overt sexuality. It was the kind of film that Julie used to love—but now she just waited with barely concealed impatience.

The plot, such as it was, continued to unfold until it was time for the big musical numbers. Ginger and Dick Powell sang "Pettin' in the Park." The chorus chimed in, gamboling and singing in an obviously fake landscape of winter and ski chalets.

The camera focused in close on the faces of girls lying in the "snow" and beaming at the unseen audience, their faces surrounded by furred hoods, their eyes open and vulnerable.

And there she was again, the dark-haired girl with the knowing, lopsided grin.

It was a chance. Possibly Julie's last chance.

She took a deep, careful breath, put the locket to her lips and blew gently. Her breath misted the amulet.

The film stopped, frozen at a single moment. There was a dissatisfied murmur from the audience; Steven ran into the room and to the computer. He poked at the keyboard, confused, trying to see what the problem was.

Julie, however, ignored him. She stared firmly into the unmoving celluloid eyes of the dark-haired chorine. The girl was still smiling, but something seemed to stir in those monochrome eyes.

Something like surprise. Or fear.

I'm sorry, little girl, whispered the old woman. I've no time left to wait. You may not deserve this. But for the first time in my life,

I'm going to be selfish. So whether you want to or not, you're going to have to learn to share.

She hissed a phrase, quick and powerful and effective.

And escaped.

Sophia's Legacy

A story of Rachel Bowman, Sophia's great-granddaughter

1998

"**D**o you remember what we told you about your great-grand-mother's earrings?" asks Rachel's Aunt Susan.

Rachel just shrugs. She's irritable because she's been pulled away from her weekly chess club match. But when Rachel's mother came to the school that afternoon, she didn't accept any excuses—she waited until Rachel had exhausted her arsenal of arguments and then just said, "This is important," with that note in her voice that meant no more talking, get your stuff, we're going home.

Now Aunt Susan opens her right hand and shows Rachel a pair of earrings with long, teardrop-shaped green jewels dangling from small gold wires. Rachel puts out a finger and touches them gingerly.

"We're going on a small expedition," Aunt Susan says. "To the park. And you get to wear the earrings."

She hands them to Rachel, who has forgotten her pique in the wonder of owning such a lovely (and grown-up) pair of earrings. "But they're screw-ons," she says, a bit dismayed.

"We can have them converted to pierced later," her mother says. "Meanwhile, just put them on the way they are."

"Here, let me help," says Aunt Susan. She carefully removes Rachel's small gold hoops and screws the earrings on. "There."

Rachel moves her head slightly; the earrings feel heavy and elegant as they swing against her cheeks. "Why am I wearing these to the park?" she asks. "And why are we going there, anyway?"

And then she stops, struck by a sudden, breathtaking thought. She asks in an excited whisper, "Are we going to do a Seeing? Am I old enough? Will we . . . "

"Never mind," says her mother, but she smiles as she says it. "We'll tell you when we get there. Put a sweater on; it's getting chilly."

The park is just across the street. Once they get there, Aunt Susan leads the way past the large lake where a few children feed the ducks and geese, into a grove of trees off the main road and down a darkened path. Rachel pauses as she sees a tall, old oak tree with a large, lower branch that is so large and weighted down by its foliage that it touches the ground. She walks slowly forward, looking past the green and gold leaves. "There's another path there," she whispers.

"Don't dawdle, Rachel," says Aunt Susan. "You can explore another time." Rachel makes a mental note to remember the location of the hidden path and rushes to catch up. She could, she thought, persuade her best friend Annie to come with her and investigate the trail. It would be a shared adventure, like in a book.

They finally reach a small pond, dense with moss and surrounded by tall reeds. "We're here," her mother announces.

Several blackbirds squawk and flap away as they approach. Aunt Susan pulls a thin cloth from her backpack and spreads it out at the edge of the pond, and they all sit. They eat chicken salad sandwiches and drink flavored ice tea; Rachel's mother gives her a brownie for desert while she and Aunt Susan share a small thermos of strong coffee. They put all the garbage into a plastic bag and stuff it into the backpack.

Then they just sit, the adults chatting casually about work and salaries and the rising cost of theater seats while a reddening sun slowly edges toward the horizon and a harvest moon pushes up against the darkening sky. Rachel's a little nervous; although she's pretty sure her mother and aunt know what they're doing, she has never been in the park after dark, and her friends have told her all sorts of stories about the drug dealers, thieves, rapists and other human monsters that prowl there after everyone has gone home.

And then Aunt Susan looks at the sky and announces, "I count three stars." She immediately pulls a thick candle in a large white glass out of her bag and places it in the damp earth by the pond, twisting it slightly to make sure it is secure.

"Rachel," she says, and hands her a book of matches.

It takes three tries, but Rachel finally gets one lit and touches it to the wick. "We light this candle," murmurs Aunt Susan, so quietly that Rachel can hardly hear her, "to bring peace to the soul of Sophia,

daughter of Rokhl and mother of Isabeau." The flame flutters in the
night breeze like a tiny, incandescent banner.

Meanwhile, Rachel's mother drags her right hand through the
grass until she comes up with a long, slim twig. She begins to pull
long strips of bark from it, revealing the smooth blonde heart of the
wood.

"Listen, Rachel," Aunt Susan begins, in the way that she began
stories when Rachel was a little girl. "Every evening, after dinner was
over and the children were put to bed, your great-grandmother Sophia would have the servants light the fire in her sitting room, pour
two glasses of sherry, and set up the chess board."

Aunt Susan's eyes drift from Rachel's face to the surface of the
water, so Rachel stares into the pond as well, letting its small eddies
and currents pull at the corner of her vision.

"Your great-grandfather Meyer would have gone into his study
after dinner, presumably to read the evening paper, but actually to
take a short nap. When Sophia was ready, she would send a servant
to the study in order to bank the fire, and Meyer would wake up, put
the paper away, and join Sophia. He loved to play chess with her in
the quiet hours just before bed, and on their first anniversary, he gave
her a carved chess set with pieces in the style of French and English
Napoleonic soldiers."

Rachel's mother bends forward and dips the end of the twig into
the water, clearing away the moss. When she sits back up, the water
still ripples slightly; Rachel watches as they resolve into the wavy
lines of her great-grandmother's dark blue dress, heavy and rich with
embroidery and tiny pearl buttons.

*Sophia sat at a small mahogany table, carefully placing small,
brightly painted figures in their places on the chessboard. Her dark auburn hair was neatly braided on top of her head. Her earrings glinted
in the firelight. On the painted squares, the kings, queens and bishops
were dressed in elaborate court costumes; all the other pieces were wearing blue or red uniforms and carried long, black rifles. It was a beautiful chess set.*

She looked up from the board and smiled. "I'm ready," she said.

From the other side of the table came a puff of gray smoke.

"My great-grandfather smoked cigars?" Rachel asks, shuddering
slightly. "Ugh! How could she sit in the same room with those great
smelly cigars?"

"Women put up with a lot of things in those days," says Aunt Susan. "Cigar smoke was the least of it. And according to family stories, your great-grandmother liked the scent of cigar smoke. She said that it made her feel that she was at home, and that everybody was safe."

Rachel privately doubts it. She looks at the woman playing chess, and watches how her nose wrinkles slightly when the smoke drifts her way.

"The interesting thing is," says Rachel's mother, "that however much your great-grandmother played chess, she only won against her husband once. And it happened exactly 100 years ago tonight."

"Only once?" asks Rachel, annoyed, although she isn't sure why. "Was he that good at it?"

"Yes," says Aunt Susan. "He was. He also liked winning. And his wife knew it. Oh, hell!"

A pigeon has miscalculated and has landed at the edge of the pond, close enough so that his wings flap at the water, disbursing the image. Recovering quickly, he turns and stares at the three visitors, hopeful that they'll toss some food.

"Shoo!" says Aunt Susan. "Go away!"

Rachel's mother tosses a small rock in the bird's direction, careful to miss it by several inches. The pigeon skitters back, but then returns and examines the rock to make sure it isn't a particularly heavy piece of bread; disappointed, he pokes through his back feathers a few times to prove he is master of his own fate and wanders away into the grass.

The ripples caused by his passing gradually subside. While they wait, Rachel says wistfully, "I wish Annie were here to see this."

Disturbed, Sophia looked up, a slight frown making her forehead wrinkle.

"Something the matter?" asked a male voice, deep and a little impatient.

"Not at all," said Sophia. "I was just remembering a girl I knew before the war. A Russian girl named Chana. I was wondering what happened to her. It's not important."

She held out two hands, both closed into fists. Her husband lightly tapped the left fist; it opened to reveal a small red-coated soldier. "Your move," said Sophia, putting the two soldiers in their places and moving the board so that the British soldiers were on her husband's side.

"Can't I see my great-grandfather as well?" asks Rachel.

"Not this way," says her mother. "But you can get a glimpse."

She dips the twig in the water and revolves it as though she's mixing cake batter. "Close your eyes," she says, and touches her daughter's eyelids with the twig, one after the other, so that a drop of water creeps through the closed eyelids and into her eyes.

She (Sophia/Rachel) set the scene very carefully. A well-stocked fire created shadows that danced around the room (although they had a modern coal-fire furnace, she knew that firelight set her looks off well), the bottle of sherry was well within reach in case a refill was called for, and the servants were warned not to interrupt unless for an emergency.

She looked across the table at her husband. Meyer was pulling slightly at his beard, staring at the board. The beard was just starting to gray slightly, but his hair, about which he was rather vain, was still a deep brown. He wore the same dark gray suit that he had changed into for dinner; his only concession to informality was his unbuttoned jacket and slightly loosened tie. Rachel finds him a bit frightening, but Sophia looked at him with fondness and understanding. He reached out and moved a pawn two spaces.

Rachel opens her eyes and looks at her mother and aunt. There is a slight mist in the night air; it has begun to bead in her aunt's hair, moistening her forehead.

"This is how they spent their evenings?" asks Rachel doubtfully. "It seems boring. And unromantic."

"Your idea of romance is a bit different than theirs," says Aunt Susan, smiling. "But listen—here comes the important part." They all bend over the pond.

Sophia moved a bishop. "I had tea with the Mitburgs yesterday. They are sending their oldest daughter to a rather nice school in Paris. She's learning French and English, and making some excellent connections." Her tone was casual, her eyes were on the chessboard, but there was a tension in the hand that smoothed the silk folds of her skirt.

"And," says Rachel's mother, "she was learning to think. Because that school in Paris was a real school, run by people who wanted educated daughters, and not just a finishing school for fashionable nitwits."

Rachel giggles.

Meyer's hand reached over and placed the lit cigar on a small silver humidor next to the chess table. His hand rested loosely on the side of the chessboard. "Yes," he said. "So?"

"Isabeau is getting to be of school age. I would like her to go away to school as well," said Sophia.

A pause. "You told me," Meyer said, "that you loved this town. Why can't our daughter simply go to the local Volksschule like all her friends?" There was a bit of irritation in his voice.

Sophia reached across the table and put her hand gently on his. "Of course," she said. "I love it here. But Isabeau is a very bright little girl. In the Volksschule, she will learn just enough to keep the household accounts and read a recipe. In Paris, she will learn both scholarship and refinement."

Meyer pushed a pawn forward. "It is too expensive," he said decisively.

As Sophia reached toward a knight, he added, "Besides, Wilhelm is doing well in school and will attend the Gymnasium eventually, which will take money. Isabeau will do fine right here."

Aunt Susan takes Rachel's hand.

"Listen carefully," she says. "Your grandmother loved going to school in Paris. She especially loved the arts, and as she got older— about your age, in fact—she began to associate with painters and actors. So later, when the Nazis came into power and things became dangerous for Jews and others, her friends smuggled her out of the country, at great risk to themselves."

"In fact," Rachel's mother adds, "One of those friends got arrested helping her get away. An opera singer, I think."

"What happened to him?" Rachel asked.

Her mother shrugged. "He disappeared, like so many others."

There was a pause. Aunt Susan then continued, "Eventually, your grandmother found her way to Canada and then to America."

"So why are we here?" asks Rachel.

"Watch," says her mother.

Sophia's husband finally made his move; the cigar was now gone from the humidor and there was smoke drifting over the board. Sophia studied the board. One hand drifted over her ear; she tucked a stray lock of hair back into place.

"I will make you a wager," she said.

Her husband laughed. "A wager? Our games have become so boring to you that you feel you need to add the excitement of gambling?"

She laughed as well. "Not at all," she said. "But I thought you might enjoy it. Just to add a bit of interest to the game."

He took a sip of sherry. "And what is the wager?"

"If I win," she said, "I would like Isabeau to attend the Paris school."
She stretched out a hand and moved a piece.

"Things could have been very different," says her mother, "if your great-grandmother lost this chess game. Your grandmother would have gone to the local elementary school, married a neighbor's son, and lived in the same town as her parents. Until the Nazis came to power and rounded up all the Jews for deportation. Including your grandmother."

There is dampness against Rachel's cheek. The mist has become thick, swirling about them in heavy white tendrils. The three women seem to be alone in a world made up of clouds and candlelight.

Rachel looks at her aunt. "Aunt Susan?" she says hesitantly. "That wasn't a good move she made just now."

"That is why you are here," her aunt tells her. "To complete the story that your great-grandmother Sophia told your grandmother Isabeau, who in turn told it to your mother. To make sure that she wins this game. Because she can't do it alone. She needs somebody who can play chess well and who has the knowledge and the ability to help. Somebody like you."

For a moment, Rachel can't breathe, terrified at the responsibility. What if she makes a mistake? What if she can't figure out the right move?

Aunt Susan presses her lips gently against Rachel's forehead. "Don't worry," she says. "You'll do fine. Just watch."

"And if I win the game?" asked Meyer, sitting back in his chair. "What do I get out of this wager?"

Sophia smiled knowingly and raised an eyebrow. Meyer laughed.

"Well," he said. He moved a knight and stared at his wife with fond confidence. "Your move."

Rachel looks down into the lake. She can see the board without effort—it is so plain, so real, that she almost reaches down to move a piece.

"He's not really a good chess player," she says out loud, almost crying with relief. "He's just following a classic pattern. I know this one—we did it in class! And it only takes one move to turn it around."

"Tell her," says her mother.

Rachel bites her lip. "How?" she asks.

"You are wearing her earrings," says Aunt Susan. "Look at her closely. Concentrate. Whisper to her. She will hear you."

Rachel bends down until her lips almost touch the water. "Queen to Queen's Rook 5," she whispers. "Mate in three moves." Her breath creates ripples that dance outward, downward and backward.

Sophia smiled, reached out and moved her queen. "Check," she said. "Mate in three moves."

A pause. A chair scraped back. "Where did you learn to play like that?" asked Meyer, a bit annoyed.

"By watching you," said Sophia. "How else could I learn it?"

He shook his head doubtfully and stood.

Sophia stood too, and as her husband passed, she put out a hand and stopped him. "If Isabeau goes to a good school in Paris," said Sophia, "she will not only get a good education, but she will make friends with other girls whose families have influence. Influence you can use. That alone will be worth the tuition."

"True," said her husband, after a thoughtful pause. "That is an aspect of the case I hadn't contemplated. But won't you miss her?"

"Yes," his wife said quietly, "I will miss her very much."

He reached out and took her hand. "This is important to you," said Meyer.

"It is important to Isabeau," said Sophia. She waited.

Rachel and her aunt and her mother wait.

"Very well," said Meyer. "Far be it from me to renege on a wager. I will contact the school and find out whether there are any openings."

The night is clear; overhead, a half moon burns gently over the park. Rachel straightens, and looks at her aunt. "So everything turned out the way it needed to," she says. "Grandmother Isabeau went to school in Paris and then came here. But what happened to great-grandmother Sophia and great-grandfather Meyer?"

"After the war, your granduncle William spent years looking for them, but never found them," Rachel's aunt says. "Your grandmother Isabeau said that she knew they hadn't survived, but never explained how. Even to me."

Rachel's mother bends forward, but Rachel puts out her hand. "Let me," she says, and takes the twig.

Rachel carefully stirs the pond until her great-grandmother disappears.

Husband and wife walked sedately up the stairs toward the bedroom. On the way, Sophia pulled off her earrings and cupped them in one hand. "I think I will give Isabeau these to take with her to Paris," she said with satisfaction.

"And perhaps," her husband said, as he slipped his arm around her waist, "they will teach her chess."

Completing
the Circle

The Clearing in the Spring

A story of Chana and Sophia's great-grandaughters

1999

On a cloudy spring afternoon, two nine-year-old girls sat on the stoop of a Brooklyn building, throwing breadcrumbs at the pigeons that, attracted by the prospect of food, had flown over from the park across the street.

The first girl had a long auburn braid and a thin, intense face; she was trying to get at least one bird to eat out of her hand by tossing the crumbs closer and closer and then holding some out in her open palm. Unfortunately, the pigeons, while obviously greedy for the food, didn't seem interested in interacting with any humans.

Her friend, shorter and stouter with cropped, tousled brown hair, threw her last handful of crumbs at the birds so suddenly that several flapped away. She took a deep breath, pulled something out of her pocket and held it tightly within her two closed hands.

"Rachel," she said, without any kind of preamble, "I've got a secret. But you can't tell anyone, especially not your mother, because she'll tell my mom, and I'll get in trouble."

Rachel gave up on her efforts to tame a pigeon and turned to her friend. "What kind of secret, Annie?" she asked, excited. "I love secrets."

"Well, I took something from my mom's drawer that I'm not supposed to touch, but I'll show you, if you promise not to tell."

"I promise!" whispered Rachel. "What is it?"

Annie opened her hands to reveal a wooden box; the top decorated by fading red houses with green roofs on a wintry landscape. She pulled the cover off with one hand and held the open box toward Rachel with the other.

There, on a piece of cotton batting, laid a short length of ribbon, worn and threadbare, a faded blue-gray with a bit of darker blue on the edges.

"It's just an old raggedy piece of ribbon," said Rachel, disappointed. "It isn't at all pretty. When I was really little, my grandma Isabeau gave me a shiny jewel once that she said was magic. It was gorgeous, but I dropped it on the subway tracks on the way home and my mom wouldn't let me go on the tracks to get it back."

"It's only faded because it's really old," said Annie, not at all fazed at her friend's reaction. "It's so old that my great-grandmother Chana brought it to America with her when she came here years and years ago. Mom keeps it in the back of her closet, behind a bunch of old albums. She said when great-grandmother was a girl, she got it from her best friend and kept it as a token for when she'd see her friend again one day, but she never did. See her, I mean."

"That's really awesome," Rachel said, her eyes wide. "The two friends separated forever, but always hoping that one day they'd meet."

Annie shrugged. She didn't have quite as romantic a nature as Rachel. "All I know is what my mom told me. She told me a few days ago, because we're going to your family's seder tonight and she said I should know something about my own family's stories so that I can tell one if I want to. And she showed me the ribbon and told me not to handle it too much, because it might fall apart. But I wanted to show it to you, so yesterday when she was running errands I took it out of the drawer."

"Can I touch it?" Rachel asked. "Just for a second? I never touched anything that old."

Annie looked doubtful. "Okay, but be careful. If anything happened to it, my mom would kill me."

She picked the ribbon out of the box and handed it to Rachel, who took it and stroked it slowly. "It feels nice," she said. "Weird to think that it's that old."

"You know," Annie said in an almost whisper, "My grandma told me once that if I ever went to a wedding and took home a piece of the wedding cake and put it under my pillow, I'd dream about the man I was going to marry. Well, I thought maybe if I put the ribbon under my pillow, I might dream about great-grandmother Chana."

"And did it work?" Rachel asked fascinated. She paused as a small brown pigeon, possibly wondering if there was any more food to be had, came almost to her foot and stared at her for a moment. Its curiosity satisfied, it settled down and began to preen.

"No," Annie said. "I mean, I don't believe that about wedding cakes, because they'd get all squooshed anyway and you're much better off eating them. But this ribbon is really, really old, and I thought it might work. But I didn't dream anything."

Rachel pursed her lips, thinking. "Maybe," she said, "it's gotten weak because it's so old."

She thought for a moment and then leaned forward, her voice lowering dramatically. "What we have to do," she said, trying to sound as mysterious as possible, "is to touch the ribbon at the same time, close our eyes and concentrate. That will double the power of the magic, even if it is so old."

Annie regarded her friend with admiration. "But what if it doesn't work?" she asked.

Rachel had become caught up in her role. "No, you have to truly believe it will work!" she said. She took one end of the ribbon and held the other out to Annie. "You take the other end. Then we'll close our eyes and wish as hard as we can that we can find your great-grandmother's friend."

Annie shook her head doubtfully. "That doesn't make sense," she said. "Even when my mom was a kid, my great-grandmother's friend would have been so old. Like over 100 or something."

Rachel just continued to hold out the piece of ribbon. Annie sighed, and gingerly took the other end.

"Now close your eyes and concentrate," Rachel instructed. "Concentrate on your great-grandmother Chana and her best friend and wish as hard as you can."

The two girls squeezed their eyes shut. After a moment, the pigeon, encouraged by the lack of movement and attracted to the small piece of material, edged closer. It cocked its head for a moment, examining the pale little piece of material, and then reached out and snatched it out of their hands.

The two girls jumped up. Annie ran forward and tried to grab the pigeon, but all she succeeded in doing was to frighten it into flight—it took off, wings batting at the warm Brooklyn air, and soared across the street and into the park. Annie, dismayed, watched it go.

"My mom's going to kill me!" she moaned.

"Then we've got to go catch it!" Rachel said decidedly and ran to the curb. "Come on, we'll lose it!"

"We're not supposed to cross the street without permission," Annie said, hesitating on the stoop. She looked up. "And it looks like it's going to rain."

"This is an emergency, so it doesn't count. And if it rains, we'll run back. Come on!"

Annie paused for another moment, and then grabbed the box off the stoop, pushed it back into her pocket, and went to the curb. Rachel seized her hand, waited for another moment while several cars passed, and then dashed across the street, pulling Annie behind her.

Once safely on the other side, the two ran into the park, dodging mothers with strollers, dog-walkers, and other passersby. They followed the main path past a playground, filled with children battling for precedence on the slides and swings; past the park's inner road, filled with bike riders, joggers, and the occasional car; and down a short slope to the lake, where geese and swans paddled frantically around, snapping up the bits of bread and bagels that were thrown at them by picnicking families.

"We'll never find it," Annie muttered, nearly in tears. A few pigeons strutted nearby, but none of them resembled the one that had grabbed the ribbon—and the ribbon itself was nowhere to be seen.

"I bet I know where it went!" Rachel said suddenly, pointing over to the left. "I saw it fly into those trees. There's a path there; we can follow it and maybe find the pigeon."

The two girls ran past the lake and into the small wooded area. They immediately slowed to a walk, examining the ground and trees to see if they could catch sight of a pigeon with a faded ribbon in its beak.

As they walked, the concrete beneath their feet became a packed dirt path, and the city noises quickly faded away behind them. Instead, all they heard was the rustle of the freshly leafed trees above, until a mockingbird sang out a warning to its mate. On the ground, new weeds pushed up from the dirt on either side of the path, while bees and flies and spiders around them went about their business of hunting, eating and mating.

Rachel led the way confidently, remembering the walk her mother and Aunt Susan had taken her on only a few months before.

Annie followed, almost forgetting her anxiety in the growing feeling that she was having a real adventure.

Suddenly, Rachel stopped.

"I remember that tree!" she said excitedly. It was the old oak tree that had caused her to pause last time; there was still that one large, lower branch, now decorated with bright green leaves, stretching parallel to and nearly touching the ground. She put her hands on the rough wood and leaned over to look beyond it. "There's a path there!" she cried out. "A hidden path!"

"Like in *The Secret Garden*?" Annie asked. Annie was a dedicated reader of Victorian and other old-fashioned children's literature, and had always wondered whether something exciting like in one of those books might happen to her.

"Maybe," said Rachel who, unlike her best friend, preferred movies to books. "We need to see where it goes."

"But what about my great-grandmother's ribbon?" Annie asked dutifully, although she was as curious about where the path led as Rachel was.

"Maybe the pigeon went this way," Rachel said, now completely dedicated to exploring the new path. "Maybe we'll find it here. Come on!" And without waiting for a reply, she hoisted herself onto the fallen branch and slipped down onto the other side. Seeing herself without any kind of alternative—and now equally as eager to explore what she now saw as a storybook quest—Annie followed.

The path beyond the fallen tree was narrower than the other; in places, patches of grass and leaves left from last year's autumn nearly obscured it, and they had to step carefully past bushes full of sharp twigs and brambles. Annie, who had been taught never to go on a hike without clear, painted blazes to show the way, asked, "Shouldn't we mark the trail so we can find the way back?"

"This is Prospect Park," said Rachel confidently. "How large can this forest be? If we get lost, we just have to keep walking in the same direction and we'll find our way out eventually."

Despite that, the path went on for a bit longer than either girl expected. Annie stopped once to pick some wildflowers that, despite the earliness of the season, were full grown; she thought she'd perhaps take them back and put them in a vase for the seder. "Have you ever seen anything so pretty?" she asked, holding them out and admiring them. Rachel grinned at her. "They are nice," she admitted.

They kept walking—and then abruptly the path opened up into a clearing.

The two girls looked around, astonished. "I didn't know there was anything like this in Prospect Park!" Annie exclaimed.

"Neither did I," Rachel admitted, "and I live right across the street."

The circular clearing was filled with grass and a few early flowers; the trunk of a long-dead tree lay along one side. The surrounding trees were large enough so that only a little sunlight filtered through their branches. "This is so cool!" Rachel said enthusiastically. "I bet we could have plays here. This can be the stage and that," she pointed to the log, "can be the orchestra seats!"

She immediately placed herself opposite the log and struck a pose. Annie, who was used to Rachel's attacks of dramatic enthusiasm, obediently sat on the log, put down her flowers, and tried to look like an audience.

"The wind was a torrent of darkness among the gusty trees," Rachel declaimed, waving her arms to indicate the wind. "The moon was a ghostly galleon tossed upon cloudy seas. The road was a ribbon of moonlight over the purple moor, And the highwayman came riding, riding, riding . . . "

"Ribbon!" Annie suddenly squealed.

"That's what I said," Rachel said, annoyed at the interruption, but then stopped as she saw her friend run to the edge of the clearing and pick something up with an air of triumph.

"You were right!" Annie called, waving the small piece of faded ribbon in one hand. "You were right! Here it is!"

"And there's another!" Rachel had seen a flash of red just beyond where Annie stood. She ran over to it; Annie turned around and stared.

A piece of bright red cloth, larger than the ribbon, was tied to a stick that had been stuck in the ground. Annie fingered the cloth curiously. "What do you think it is?" she asked. "A flag?"

"Maybe it's decorating a grave," said Rachel. "Look, there's a stone right next to it. Maybe someone's buried there. A pet mouse or something."

"People don't put flags next to graves," Annie said doubtfully. "Unless they're veterans or something, and then it's an American flag."

"Well, let's see," Rachel said. "Help me."

Annie put the ribbon carefully in her pocket, and joined her friend in pulling at the rather heavy stone. After a few minutes, the girls managed to pull it up and over, exposing the dirt underneath.

"There's something buried here!" Rachel said happily. "I'm going to pull it up."

"Be careful," whispered Annie, concerned that they might indeed be disturbing the interment of a pet or some other creature.

"It's a jar or a bottle or something like that," said Rachel, and scraped at the dirt until she could pull the jar out. She examined it carefully. "It's got a note inside! I'll bet we've discovered the meeting place of two lovers, whose parents won't let them marry, so they have to leave notes arranging trysts in this romantic glade!"

She twisted the lid of the jar open, removed the paper, and carefully unfolded it. "It's got writing on both sides. But it's in Hebrew," she said, disappointed. "I can't read it."

Annie looked over her shoulder. "That isn't Hebrew," she said. "That's Yiddish. It's got vowels, and Hebrew doesn't use vowels." She added defensively, "I only know about it because my mom taught me the letters and a few words, and said she'd send me to Yiddish school if I wanted."

"Can you read it?" Rachel handed the note over, and Annie examined it for a moment. "Not really," she finally admitted. "It's in handwriting, and I can only read print, and only a little." She looked at it more closely. "I think this is a name," she said, pointing to the top of the page. "I've seen it in one of the readers my mom showed me. It says Chana."

Rachel sat back on her heels. "Chana?" she asked breathlessly. "Like your great-grandmother Chana?"

Annie stared at her for a moment and then shook her head. "That doesn't mean anything," she said. "It can't. In Borough Park where all the really religious Jews live I'll bet there are lots and lots of Chanas."

"How about the other side?" Rachel asked. When Annie hesitated, she said, "Oh, come on. Please? I found your ribbon for you."

Annie put her finger to the top line of the paper and sounded out the letters silently, her lips moving as she tried to read the unfamiliar lettering. "The first word is something like "Tierer," she said. "The second is . . . S . . . So . . . Sophie. I think."

"Or Sophia?" Rachel said and took back the paper as though it would tell her something she missed. "My great-grandmother's name was Sophia."

The two girls stared at each other for a moment. Finally, Annie shook her head. "Don't be silly," Annie said. "My great-grandmother lived in Russia until she was a teenager and then came to America. Where did yours live?"

"Germany," said Rachel, remembering a chess game and a pair of antique earrings. "And she never came to America."

"So there. They lived way far apart and probably didn't even have telephones, so they couldn't have been friends. And look," she pointed at the red cloth, "that's not nearly as old as the ribbon. It's practically new."

"Maybe," Rachel said, undeterred, "we've time traveled. Like in Doctor Who."

"Or maybe it's just a coincidence and we should put the note back where it belongs so that the person who is supposed to get it won't miss it," said Annie firmly. She folded the note and returned it to the jar. "Come on. It's getting late."

Reluctantly, Rachel closed the lid, put the jar back in its hole and covered it up. The two girls patted down the earth and then, together, pushed the stone back to its former place. They sat back and regarded their handiwork.

"Annie?" Rachel whispered. She thought again of the pond not far from the path to this clearing, where not too long ago she had helped her great-grandmother—whose name was written on this note. Who had said that she once knew a Russian girl named Chana. Was this clearing—and Annie's ribbon—part of the same story?

"Yes?" Annie asked.

"What if this is really a magic place? What if that really is a note that your great-grandmother left for her best friend?"

Annie shook her head, but she bit her lip as she considered the possibility. "Even if it is," she finally said. "we did the right thing. We put everything back where it's supposed to be."

"But that's not enough," said Rachel. "We should let them know that we've been here. That we know it's them." She looked at Annie. "We need to give them back the ribbon."

Annie reached into her pocket and pulled out the ribbon. She stroked it lightly with her thumb. "I told you—my mother will kill me," she said reluctantly.

"This is more important." Rachel reached over and took Annie's other hand in her own. "Don't you see, this will show that we know."

"But we don't know. Not really!" Annie looked down at the ribbon and then at the red cloth. Then she took a deep breath and tied the ribbon to the stick, just above the cloth.

"I guess I can think of something to tell my mom if she finds out," she said. "And you're right. This is more important."

Rachel nodded, and then looked down at her wristwatch. "Hey, we gotta go," she said, suddenly alarmed. "My mom is going to be looking for us. We need to get dressed for the seder. Come on!" She jumped to her feet and dashed out of the clearing and down the path.

Annie stood as well, but just as she was going to run after Rachel, she stopped and paused for a moment. The first drops of rain began to patter on the grass; a cool breeze blew through the clearing. Annie watched as the two pieces of cloth, bright red and faded blue, danced together in its wake and then tangled together.

"Shalom, Chana," she whispered. "Shalom, Sophia."

And then she turned and ran after her friend.

The History of Soul 2065

Annie and Rachel's story continues

1999

It all started at Rachel's first real seder.

Until then, the only Passover seders she had attended had been at her Grandma Isabeau's house, where she and several of her cousins—most of whom were older than she, and not very nice—sat at the end of the table while a relative of her grandfather (who died before Rachel was born) droned through incomprehensible Hebrew verses. The children were then conducted to their own table in the living room, where they threw pieces of matzoh at each other until one of the grownups came in and yelled at them.

This year, however, Rachel was also going to the second-night seder that Aunt Susan—who lived with Uncle Mark, Rachel's mother's brother—held every year.

She was a little frightened. Since, at age nine, she was going to be youngest person there—her best friend Annie, who came with them so Rachel wouldn't be the only child, was four months older—Rachel was going to have to ask the ceremonial four questions.

"She's a little nervous," her mother told her Aunt Susan as they took off their coats. "I told her that she didn't have to say them if she doesn't want to."

"Of course she'll say them, Eileen," Aunt Susan said, and she grinned at Rachel as though they were sharing a secret. "I've heard her recite. She has the makings of a damned good actress. She'll do a fantastic job."

Despite her nervousness, Rachel grinned back. Rachel liked her aunt and uncle, especially because they never talked down to her.

It was hard to move around in the living room, which was largely taken up with a long, rather unsteady metal folding table decorated with a bright blue paper tablecloth and white paper plates and cups. There were real knives and forks, and wine glasses, and two white-and-blue ceramic candle holders with tall blue candles in them.

A bright purple paperback book sat at each place setting; Rachel picked one up and paged through it. It was a Hagaddah, the book that was used for the ceremonies before and after the meal. But unlike the one at her grandparents' house, which was only in Hebrew and had nothing of interest in it, this one had a lot of English in it, and had lots of pictures and photographs of foreign looking people celebrating the holiday.

Because the living room was so crowded, everyone had to sidle around the table in order to get to the dining room, which, because it was actually used as a sort of library, was nearly empty of furniture, and so had space for people to stand and chat. Rachel took the Hagaddah and she and Annie made their way to a corner.

"You won't tell about the ribbon?" Annie hissed as soon as they were away from the adults. "You promise?"

"Of course! Don't be silly. I'd get in trouble too," Rachel said impatiently. "Here, let's look at the pictures." The two girls started to page through the book. But they lost interest quickly, and Rachel started describing the adults in the room to Annie in a careful whisper.

"The man over there, the one with the beard? That's Abram, an old friend of Uncle Mark's. They were both in high school together."

"He's bossy," Annie observed. "And he interrupts all the time."

Rachel shrugged. "I don't like him," she said. "But Mom says it's not polite to say so."

She pointed surreptitiously at a stout, smiling young woman who was talking to Abram. "That's Yolanda, Aunt Susan's best friend. She brought a pineapple for dessert. She's studying to be a minister and used to live in Namibia."

Uncle Mark came into the kitchen with a quick stride, holding a thin brown bottle, and thrust it at Abram. "Here," he said irritably. "Kosher enough for you? Oh, hi, Eileen. Glad you brought Rachel and—Annie, is it?—with you this year." He kissed his sister on the cheek and ruffled Rachel's hair.

"Hi, Uncle Mark," said Rachel. "It's raining."

"Really hard," Annie added, unwilling to be left out of the conversation.

"Of course, it is," said Uncle Mark. "God forbid we should have good weather on a holiday."

Abram, who appeared not to mind Uncle Mark's tone, was examining the bottle carefully. "I don't see anything problematic," he said. "The reason I had a problem with the glaze you used last year was the corn syrup. Things need to be kosher for Passover."

"This from a man who has milk in his coffee with his hamburger," said Uncle Mark, addressing the room at large. He grabbed the bottle back and returned to the kitchen.

"Time to start," Aunt Susan said loudly, and everyone wandered slowly into the living room and began to sit at the table.

"So I was looking for something to watch the other day," Abram said, as he started opening a bottle of wine, "and I stopped at a channel where a writer, a rabbi I think, was talking about a legend that there were originally only 600,000 souls in the universe. At some point after the creation, each soul broke into many pieces. Which means we are all actually made up of a piece of a soul, and when all the pieces of that soul find each other, part of the universe is healed and made whole."

Yolanda looked thoughtful. "How many pieces were in each soul, originally?"

Abram shrugged. "I missed that part of it," he said, handing her the bottle. "Some say that each soul was made up of two parts, and when a man and a woman find each other and marry, that is the entire soul. There is also some argument as to whether the souls truly blend during life or after death. But as with everything, it's all a matter of interpretation."

Yolanda handed the bottle to Aunt Susan, who poured some for herself and Uncle Mark, and then passed it to Rachel's mother. "Here," she said, reaching across the table to another bottle, "we bought some grape juice for the girls." She poured generous helpings into their wine cups.

"Suppose that we're all part of an original soul," Yolanda said, leaning across the table, "is it possible that by coming together tonight, we're helping to heal the universe? Would that include all of us?"

"I don't see why not," Susan said. "After all, in this presumably enlightened age, we can assume that whatever fractured soul is involved, all the pieces aren't necessarily Jewish. Here, it's going to be a while before we eat," and she broke a large flat matzoh into two pieces and handed them to the girls.

Abram's finger came up, a sure indication that he was going into lecture mode. "Actually," he said. "Most rabbis would probably argue that the legends only refer to Jewish souls—not that they are saying that other souls aren't valuable," with a nod toward Yolanda, "but they aren't part of the Jewish mythos."

"My father's not Jewish," said Annie, distressed. "Can't I be part?"

"Of course you can, Annie," said Yolanda, frowning at Abram. "There is enough room for everyone."

"How many?" asked Rachel, carefully biting her matzoh into a circular pattern.

"How many what?" Yolanda asked, puzzled.

"Rooms in heaven?" said Rachel, and the two girls giggled.

"Exactly 652 and a half," said Uncle Mark, sitting down. "The half is a bathroom. Which everyone has to line up for each morning."

The girls broke up and Susan blew a kiss at her husband.

"You know, maybe it's more like a union," Uncle Mark continued. "That would make us all official members of, say, Soul 2065."

"Does our union have a good health plan?" asked Yolanda.

Rachel's mom smiled. "Maybe we should have tee shirts. 'Member of Soul 2065.' Or hats."

"Can I have one?" asked Rachel, immediately perking up at the idea of a present. Then she suddenly remembered. "Even if I get the four questions wrong?"

"Of course," Aunt Susan said. "And you won't get them wrong. I promise. Even if you make a mistake, just pretend you did it on purpose, and everybody will believe you did it right. That's what actresses do."

"Really?" Rachel brightened.

"Really." Aunt Susan grinned. She stood and tapped her wineglass with her knife. "I hereby declare that this meeting of Soul 2065 is called to order." She sat down. "Now, let's start the seder."

Ten years later.
Passover had come practically at the same time as Easter this year, which meant that Yolanda, who had pastoral duties in Minneapolis,

wouldn't be present. To make up for the loss, Rachel's mom invited her friend Edward, who was getting a name for himself writing horror novels.

"You wrote *Bite Me, Darling?*" asked Annie, awestruck, as they took their places at the table. "That is just so incredible!" At age 19, both Rachel and Annie were heavily into vampires, and Edward's latest, in which a Jamaican lesbian vampire works the late-night shift at a NYC cable station, was right up their alley.

"That's me!" Edward beamed, delighted to have found a cheering section.

Rachel's mom leaned over and whispered, "I'm sure he has a couple of copies of the book with him. If you want, I'll ask if he'll sign one for you."

Annie grinned and hugged Rachel's mom. "Oh, thank you so much!"

"Hey, I'm the famous author with the book and the autograph," Edward objected. "Don't I get hugged?"

"She's 19," said Aunt Susan, staring at him with mock sternness. "So you get bupkis."

Uncle Mark came back from the kitchen, having taken the turkey out of the oven. "That's what we're having with the turkey," he said. "Baked bupkis. With an olive sauce."

"Should we start?" asked Abram. "It's getting late."

"You're right." Aunt Susan tapped her fork against her wineglass to get everyone's attention. "This meeting of Soul 2065 is hereby called to order."

Edward leaned over to Rachel. "Okay, what's going on?" he whispered.

"It started ten years ago," Rachel whispered back. "We decided we were all part of a single soul, and so every year, everybody tells everyone else about the most significant thing that happened to them the past year, because it affects us all."

"Cool," said Edward. He looked intrigued.

Aunt Susan continued. "One of our members couldn't be here in body, but is here in spirit—and email," and she waved a tablet. "Okay, Mark, you start."

"I had a bit of a scare when I woke with chest pains a couple of months ago," said Uncle Mark. "I went to the emergency room, but it turned out to be a bad case of acid reflux. Which isn't good, but is a lot better than a heart attack."

"Damn right," said Rachel's mother. "You gave us all a hell of a scare, you know that?"

"No comments allowed," Mark reminded his sister.

"I reconnected with my sister after five years," said Abram. "She called me out of the blue right after Yom Kippur. We talked for about a half hour, and I got her email address, so maybe we'll stay in touch."

"I tried out for a part in a Broadway show," Rachel said. "They wanted a bunch of teenagers who could sing and move, and I tried out for that. I was so nervous that I went into the bathroom and threw up and had to make my face up all over again, and then I got eliminated in the first round. I was really upset at first, but then I thought about how much fun it was just to be there. Which was important."

"You were wonderful," said Annie. "She showed me what she was going to sing before she went. She was great."

"Isn't she a bit young to be running around to auditions?" asked Abram, looking as if he disapproved of the whole idea.

"It's fine," said Aunt Susan. "She's over 18 and very responsible. Annie, it's your turn now."

Annie brightened. "I've been looking into my family's history," she said enthusiastically. "My mom has become a real activist lately."

"Yeah, I understand Marilyn is now a second Emma Goldman," Mark grinned.

"You were the one who said no comments," his wife reminded him. "Don't interrupt."

"Anyway," Annie continued, unfazed, "my mom's been telling me about her grandparents, who were very radical, politically. I'm going to interview my grandmother so I can find out more about them, and the rest of my ancestors."

Rachel's mom looked down at the table. "There's somebody I, well, sort of like," she said. "I haven't had the chance to ask him out yet. I need to do that." She bit her lip as though she was going to say something more, but had decided not to.

"Yolanda writes," Aunt Susan said, reading from the tablet, "I am slowly learning about how difficult and wonderful it is to be a minister, although I have to deal with red tape and bureaucratic idiocy, and some of these people test my patience. But it's all worthwhile."

Aunt Susan put down the paper and sighed. "Okay," she said. "My turn. As most of you know, I lost my job, which isn't something we need right now. But I'm getting some freelance gigs, and this gives me a chance to work on some of my knitting techniques."

"You knit?" asked Annie. "Hey, I just started learning."

"You know," Edward said, "this one soul thing doesn't sound bad. Can I join as well?"

"Don't know," Aunt Susan said, grinning. "Rachel, what do you think?"

Rachel propped her chin on her fist and looked at Edward thoughtfully. "You have to do something to qualify."

"Like what?" Edward said, amused.

"Rachel . . . " said her mother, a warning note in her voice.

Rachel ignored her mother and continued to study Edward carefully. "I know," she finally decided. "You have to write me and Annie into your next book."

"Done!" Edward said.

"Cool!" said Annie.

Twenty years later.

The new apartment was in a rather inconvenient part of Brooklyn, but they were all there—all except, of course, Abram.

Even though Mark insisted on cooking the meal, Susan had asked several of the guests to bring side dishes to make things a bit easier. "I don't want him to overexert himself," she told Rachel's mom.

"Of course," Eileen said, and then smiled as Rachel, who had appointed herself and Annie the unofficial serving staffers, brought in some of the silverware. "And just think," she added. "You have a famous actress shlepping for you."

"So I understand," said Yolanda, who was sitting at the table. "Congratulations."

Rachel wrinkled her nose at Susan. "It's so Off-Broadway that even a GPS could hardly find it," she said.

"What Rachel isn't telling you," Annie said, "is that live theater is what everyone is into these days. They don't want fake 3D—they want real 3D."

"And they want 20-year-olds," said Rachel. "I'm already too old for a lot of producers."

"Modesty isn't a virtue in an actress. I saw your notices," Edward said. "Good ones, from major sites."

"And she got interviewed," said Eileen proudly. "It's on at least 16 different streams."

Rachel smiled tolerantly at her mother and leaned over to Susan. "It really doesn't mean anything. You have to be on at least 30 to be noticed."

"Give it time," said Annie. "I think you're starting to create a splash."

"Could it go viral?" asked Yolanda. "Is that still a used term?"

"Occasionally," said Edward. "And even if it isn't, the general idea is the same. It's what happened to my latest book. Especially after I did this," and he waved his hand at the top of his head—he had shaved most of his hair except a small white round patch at top.

"It looks like a monk's tonsure, reversed," Yolanda said.

"Makes good video, though," Edward said. "Especially the 3D version. It looks like a weird sort of halo."

Susan tapped her glass. "This meeting of Soul 2065 is hereby called to order," she said. Everyone quieted.

"I . . . I was thinking how to handle . . . " She paused, and cleared her throat. "We greet Abram and ask him to remember us," she said. Mark looked down at the table. Nobody said anything for a minute.

Susan looked at Yolanda. "Things are going well with my new assignment," Yolanda said, "although I still think that Minneapolis is too cold for humans. As you know, there has been a new movement among some of the more radical members of my faith to disallow female ministers; sometimes it feels as if we're running backwards at a fast clip. But with any luck, this too shall pass."

"I'm thinking of moving to Los Angeles," said Edward. "My new series is doing well, but I can't afford to be a one-shot wonder. Out west, I can diversify more. And—well, I think it's better for me and for others." He glanced at Eileen, who stared back coldly. There was a moment of silence.

"With Rachel no longer around, and my job being only part time, I find myself sitting in my apartment watching too many movies," Eileen finally said in a careful tone. "I don't think that's healthy. I'm going to have to find something else to do. Somebody else to be with." She looked away.

"I'm having a great time doing live theater," said Rachel, quickly, "but it isn't enough, even with the feeds. The pressures are just too great—if we charge as much as we need to in order to keep it going, nobody comes, and if we charge less, we won't be able to keep it open. And only the big studios can afford to do a big PR push. So I was also thinking of going out to the West Coast—maybe even next month."

"And I'm coming with her," said Annie. "Oops—sorry, did I interrupt?"

Rachel smiled, and touched Annie's cheek. "It's okay. I was done."

"Well, actually," Annie said cheerfully, "so was I. Except that if Edward is going west, I think we should wait a few months, so he can get settled and then help Rachel out a bit." She grinned at him.

Edward reached over and tugged a lock of her hair gently. "Honey, I'm too old to move quickly," he said. "You go when you want to, and as soon as I get there, I'll make sure Rachel gets in to see the right people. Promise."

Annie smiled. "Okay," she said.

"I'm tired of doctors," said Mark. "I go, and I go, and they give me tests, and feed me pills, and nothing changes. I'm just . . . I've had it with doctors."

"I want Mark to take better care of himself," said Susan. "That's all."

"Oh, for Christ's sake," said Mark. "Can't you give it a rest?"

He stood and limped back to the kitchen.

"He'll be fine in two minutes," Susan said. "He just gets angry at not being healthy. He doesn't think it's fair, because he stopped smoking and has been taking good care of himself, and now this."

Rachel reached over and took her hand. "He'll be fine, Aunt Susan," she said.

Susan smiled, and kissed her gently on the cheek. "Of course, he will," she said, and then looked around the table. "Well, as soon as Mark gets back, we'll start."

Thirty years later.

There was no seder, because there was no longer a New York City.

* * *

Forty years later.

Susan kept saying that she would find someplace else to live. After all, she wasn't all that badly off. She rather liked California, and Congress had finally come through with at least a small amount of compensation for former residents of NYC. She was sure she had enough to invest in a condo somewhere.

Rachel, who knew exactly how much income her aunt really had, and who also knew how much medication Susan needed to sleep at night, told her that she wasn't going anywhere. Rachel and Annie had more than enough room in their house, and anyway, Edward depended on Susan to help him with his latest series.

"Don't be ridiculous," Susan said, while she watched Rachel put the spinach kugel in a warmer. "You girls don't need to have an old lady tottering around in your way, and Edward doesn't need my help. He's just trying to make me feel useful. Which is very sweet of him, but there is no way in hell . . . "

"Oh, for the sweet love of Shiva," Annie cried, throwing down the towel she was using as a potholder. Annie had put on quite a bit of weight over the last few years; she insisted on blaming genetics, since, she said, she and Rachel ate the same foods and Rachel was still absurdly svelte. "Do you have any idea how ridiculous you sound? Edward has a writer's block so big that you could run a truck into him and he wouldn't feel it. He is driving us completely insane. You are the only one who can save us."

"Besides," Rachel added, "he said that once you and he come up with a new series, he could sell it as a dramatic stream, and I could star in it. So please, don't do the oh-poor-me thing. Please, Aunt Susan."

Susan sighed. "Well . . . "

"Edward is asking for admittance," the house said. It had an Italian accent this week, which Annie said was in honor of her father's family.

"House, yes," said Annie loudly, and then turned back to Susan. "We're agreed?"

"So," Edward said, having just come through the security door, "have you told her that resistance is futile?"

Susan didn't laugh, but one side of her mouth quirked. "Edward, stop quoting old TV series that Rachel won't recognize," she said. "It's a symptom of senility."

"Hey," Rachel protested. "I'm an actress. I've studied the classics."

Edward kissed Susan loudly on the cheek and gave both Annie and Rachel a hug. "Hey, baby doll," he said to Rachel. "Were you able to get Yolanda to come?"

"She wanted to," Rachel said, "but there was another transportation lock-down yesterday, and her tickets were cancelled. So she'll just have to vid in."

The house was sparsely furnished—simplicity was the fashion these days—and much of the furniture was foldaway, so it took only a few minutes to put away the couch and replace it with a dining room table and chairs. Annie fiddled with the display while the others set the table.

"I wasn't able to find the Haggadah that we used to use," said Rachel, putting a sheet of e-paper next to each place. "It was probably never digitized. But I did find a 'roll your own' Haggadah, and put together something as close as I could get it."

"I'm sure you did a great job," Edward said, settling himself into one of the chairs.

"Okay, we're all ready," said Annie. "Going to external visuals." The display, which she had set up at one end of the table, brightened to show Yolanda sitting in an old-fashioned armchair in what looked like a living room. She grinned.

"Hi, there," she said. "Sorry about missing the seder, but I've only got a third-tier priority in the airline's lists, and got bumped at the last minute."

"Of course," Susan said. "Don't even think about it."

"Should we begin?" asked Rachel. "Susan, you start."

Susan shook her head. "It's your house," she said. "You or Annie head the seder."

Rachel was going to protest but Edward put a hand on her arm. "Go ahead," he said.

Rachel took a breath. "This meeting of Soul 2065 is hereby called to order," she said, a little huskily. "We greet Abram, my mother Eileen and Uncle Mark, and ask them to remember us." She glanced over at Susan, but the woman was dry-eyed. "Yolanda?"

On the display, Yolanda nodded. "I'm doing well, although I still have moments where I become very sad at the loss of our friends, and of all those who died, even ten years later. As you know, I've been part of an organization that represents many of those who were forgotten in the compensation agreements. I'm also concerned at reports that the environmental damage may be worse than we were led to believe." She stopped, and shook her head. "Sorry. I'm so involved in this stuff that I can get boringly didactic. Forgive me."

Edward drew on the tablecloth with the tip of his finger. "On a more selfish level," he said, "I haven't been able to produce a lot that was worth anything for the last year or so. It could be just a temporary setback, but I'm a little nervous about it. I'm hoping that certain people will help," and here he paused, and directed a long look at Susan, "and that next year I'll be able to report several well-paid sales."

Annie sat back in her chair. "I don't have much to say about myself," she said. "I've been helping Yolanda with fundraising. And I want to add that we're doing well enough that certain members of this household should shut up about money and just remember how devastated we'd be if they left." She took a deep breath and stopped.

Rachel reached out and smoothed Annie's hair. "What Annie said. Especially the last."

Susan looked down for a moment, and then said, "Thank you. I'm not going to talk about how much I miss Mark, and your mother," looking at Rachel, "and everyone else who is gone now. I'm trying not to feel guilty that I happened to be visiting here when . . . when it happened. I'm trying not to feel that I should have been with Mark."

She paused. The rest waited. "I remember my mother talking about how hard it was to outlive all the people she grew up with, and now I know what she meant." Susan looked around. "But still, I'm luckier than many—I have you all now, and perhaps the rest of Soul 2065 to take care of me later. Who knows? Stranger things have happened."

Fifty years later.

Although the seder had to be cancelled when Susan had a sudden crisis, after three days she had recovered enough that Annie and Rachel decided to hold what Annie dubbed a Late Seder. They called Yolanda and Edward, and two evenings later they all sat together in the bedroom and nibbled on matzoh.

"We greet Abram, my mother Eileen and Uncle Mark, and ask them to remember us," said Rachel a bit too brightly; despite the help of the mechanized bed and the nursing aide who came once a day, she insisted on tending to Susan herself, and hadn't been sleeping well at night.

She looked at the others and said, "I called my agent and told him that I was taking a vacation. I just don't have the personal bandwidth to handle any jobs right now."

"I disagree. I think Rachel needs to go back to work," Annie said. "I'm perfectly capable of looking after things here, and the knitting shop practically looks after itself."

"No," said Rachel. "Just . . . no."

"If somebody is offering you a part," said Susan, "I don't see why . . . " She started to cough.

"It's not up for discussion," Rachel said. She put a hand behind Susan's back and supported her until the coughing fit subsided, and then settled her again.

"Actually, it is," said Edward, and put up a finger when Rachel started to speak. "It's my turn. I'm tired of the rat race. I've decided that I'm going to hang out here instead and visit one of the few people around who still remembers when I was young and good-looking."

He smiled gently at Susan, who smiled back. "Thank you," she mouthed.

Rachel stared at him. "Edward!" she said. "I can't ask you to . . . "

"It's okay," he said. "It's a purely selfish act. I'm expecting you to mention my name to your public at least twice a week until somebody re-options one of my series."

He grinned, and Rachel threw a pillow at him. "Ouch!" he protested.

Yolanda smiled slightly and simply said, "Susan's asleep."

They quietly stood and left the room.

S ixty years later.
Yolanda called Rachel and said that one of the members of her congregation—a former child survivor from New York—was giving a seder and would be delighted if she and Annie came. Rachel said she'd think about it. Annie glared at Rachel, then said that of course, they'd be happy to come.

"I can't do that to your friend," Rachel said impatiently. "Ever since I mentioned I attend an annual seder in that interview a couple of years ago, our systems are deluged every year by cards and gifts from fans. It's a pain in the ass. We have to farm out part of our feed to avoid bringing the whole thing crashing down."

"His wife works in communications," said Yolanda calmly. "We've got it covered. Reserve your flight."

Yolanda and her congregants lived a few miles outside of Minneapolis in a suburban community that was protected from airborne toxins by a large bubble of forced air and chemicals that surrounded several miles of territory. By the time Rachel and Annie had arrived, preparations were well under way. While the adults bustled around in the kitchen and dining room, the family's children put on a play for their guests, who laughed and applauded.

"Kids," came the cry, "Come set the table!" The children dashed away, leaving a sudden silence, broken only occasionally by the voices at the other end of the house.

"They're great kids," said Rachel. "But isn't it strange for them, growing up in such an artificial environment? I mean, they never get outside. Really outside."

"It's healthier for them," Yolanda said. "Better that than having to reach for an airsock every time the particle levels get too high. And we take them on trips in the cooler weather, when things are safer."

They sat quietly for a moment. Suddenly, without speaking, Yolanda reached out to Annie and Rachel, and took their hands. Rachel took Annie's other hand, completing the small circle.

"Go ahead," Yolanda said to Rachel.

"We greet Abram and Edward and . . . " Rachel started, and then pressed her lips together. "I can't," she whispered. They just sat, heads bowed, remembering, while an errant breeze stirred the window curtains.

S eventy years later.
Rachel sat and stared at the ocean. These days, she liked to come to the shore as often as possible to watch the birds dip and soar, scuttle along the shore hunting for small shellfish and insects, or dig through the sand for leftover food from human visitors.

It was getting harder, though. Oh, Rachel could get herself to the boardwalk easily enough; her chair moved her around with only the twitch of a finger. But the discomfort—hell with that, the pain—was getting worse. At some point, even these days, medications could only do so much.

A few days ago, she had filled out all the necessary forms and had all the required interviews. They then fitted the small ampule in a special section of the chair.

Now, Rachel sat for a few more minutes, watching the birds and listening to their distant calls. A brown pigeon fluttered down in front of her chair and pecked at an interesting piece of shell.

After about half an hour, Rachel lifted her head and said, as clearly and loudly as she could, "Annie."

The small holographic portrait appeared on the tray that extended from the left arm of her chair. Annie, gray-haired but still mischievous, blew a kiss and grinned at her.

"I'll just be a few more minutes," Rachel told her wife, dead these three years now. She tried to smile at the holo, failed, and shut it down.

It was a nice sunset. A few passersby walked along the boardwalk, and from a small building just behind her, there was a sudden spurt of sound: The raucous but pleasant noise of people singing badly but enthusiastically. Rachel had chosen this day and this spot purposefully—the building was a shared religious center, and tonight was the second night of Passover.

She listened for a moment. Had it really been that long since . . . ? A sharp twinge bit at her stomach like a small arrow.

"Okay," Rachel said out loud. "Enough of this shit."

She reached down into the bag that hung from one arm of the chair and pulled out a pre-filled glass of wine. She peeled a layer of protective film from the top of the wineglass. She then tapped the glass lightly with the ring that she still wore on her left ring finger. It rang faintly but satisfactorily.

"This meeting of Soul 2065 is hereby called to order," she told the pigeon. "I greet Abram, Yolanda, Edward, my mother Eileen, Uncle Mark and Aunt Susan, and my dear Annie, and ask them to remember me." She paused. "No. I am the last living member, and so I ask them not simply to remember me, but to allow me to join them." She paused and smiled slightly. "Along with any of our forebears who may want to join as well."

Rachel placed her hand flat on her chair's arm, and carefully recited the series of numbers and letters she had memorized. She felt an almost imperceptible vibration against her palm. Then she smiled and raised her face to the ocean. A breeze caressed her cheek.

"You were right, Aunt Susan," she said. "If you just pretend you got it right, nobody will notice the mistakes."

She sighed.

And part of the universe was made whole.

Acknowledgments

All families have their stories. Over the years, as they are passed from generation to generation, these stories can become ornately embroidered—so much so that those who actually experienced the events would probably not recognize themselves in the telling. It doesn't mean that the tales should not be told.

Many of the stories in this book were inspired by accounts passed down from my family and the family of my partner. A few are partly true, none are absolutely true, and one or two I only wish were true. I simply took those seeds that had been planted in my imagination and went on from there.

I've been helped by many people along the way.

First, all the family members whose stories I listened to, remembered and misremembered, stretched and remade, in order to create these histories: the Krasnoffs, the Novicks and Novacks (don't ask!), the Schwartzes, the Gritz's, the Freunds, and all the other aunts, uncles, and cousins of varying degrees whose legacy I hope I have honored here in some small measure.

My friend Catherine Guido, who has patiently listened to my various stories over the years.

Carolyn Fireside, who first helped to give this book shape, and who I wish were still here to see the results. She is truly missed.

Bill Contardi, who read my proposal for the book, listened to my ideas, and freely shared his advice and experience.

The members of the Eighth of February and Tabula Rasa writing groups, whose critiques improved many of my stories over the years, with a special shout-out to Rick Bowes, whose insights I could not have done without.

Mercurio D. Rivera and Kay Holt, who were kind enough to do beta reads of the manuscript.

Jane Yolen, Samuel R. Delany, Carlos Hernandez, James Morrow, Jeffrey Ford, Rick Bowes and C.S.E. Cooney for writing such lovely sentiments about these stories.

Mike and Anita Allen, without whom this book would not exist.

And all the other friends, colleagues, talented writers and independent publishers who have encouraged me over the years. You know who you are. Thank you so much.

About the Author

Barbara Krasnoff was born and bred in Brooklyn, and has the accent to prove it. She has sold over 35 short stories to a variety of publications; "Sabbath Wine," which appeared in *Clockwork Phoenix 5*, was a finalist for the 2016 Nebula Award. When not producing weird fiction, she works as Reviews Editor for *The Verge* and investigates what animals and objects are really thinking in her *Backstories* series on Facebook, Twitter and Instagram (#theirbackstories). You can find her at BrooklynWriter.com or on Twitter as @BarbK.

Copyright Information

CPSIA information can be obtained
at www.ICGtesting.com
Printed in the USA
LVHW092137160619
621419LV00001B/194/P

9 781732 644014